MAN OF STEEL™
THE OFFICIAL MOVIE NOVELIZATION

MAN OF STEEL™

THE OFFICIAL MOVIE NOVELIZATION

A NOVEL BY **GREG COX**

BASED ON THE SCREENPLAY BY **DAVID S. GOYER**
STORY BY **DAVID S. GOYER** & **CHRISTOPHER NOLAN**
BASED UPON SUPERMAN CHARACTERS CREATED BY
JERRY SIEGEL AND **JOE SHUSTER**
AND PUBLISHED BY **DC ENTERTAINMENT**
BY SPECIAL ARRANGEMENT WITH THE JERRY SIEGEL FAMILY

TITAN BOOKS

For the gang at Captain Blue Hen Comics in Newark, Delaware,
my primary source for superhero adventure for the last twelve years.
Up, up, and away!

MAN OF STEEL: The Official Movie Novelization
Print edition ISBN: 9781781165997
E-book edition ISBN: 9781781166000

Published by Titan Books
A division of Titan Publishing Group Ltd
144 Southwark Street, London SE1 0UP

First edition: June 2013
10 9 8 7 6 5 4 3 2 1

MAN OF STEEL™

CHAPTER ONE

"Push, Lara!"

Jor-El crouched beside his wife, holding her hand. The medical suite in his ancestral Citadel now served as a delivery room, the first on Krypton in untold memory. Lara Lor-Van strained upon an antique birthing couch, laboring to deliver their child. Her long black hair was spread out across the cushion beneath her head. A crimson sheet was draped over her trembling form. Sweat bathed her pale skin. Despite the sophisticated medical technology filling the spacious chamber, much of which had been designed or customized by Jor-El himself, the scene could not have been more primal, more elemental…

He prayed they had not made a terrible mistake.

Worry showed upon his features. A short brown beard framed his face. The sinuous crest of the House of El was emblazoned on an everyday blue skinsuit which clung tightly to his fit, athletic frame. Alert brown eyes watched anxiously as his wife attempted to do something no Kryptonian woman had accomplished in ages. Computerized monitors pulsed and beeped in the background. A pair of household robots hovered in attendance.

"Sir!" Kelor addressed Jor-El. A feminine voice emanated from the levitating robot who had served the House of El for longer than he could remember. A three-dimensional display screen occupied the center of its thorax, which resembled a floating steel teardrop roughly the size of an adult Kryptonian's torso. Versatile steel tentacles extruded from the 'bot's base. "The child's vital signs are plummeting—"

"We don't have a choice," Jor-El said. For better or for worse, they were committed to this perilous course. "We have to keep going." He squeezed his wife's hand. "Lara, my love, please push. *Please.*"

Pain and exhaustion contorted her exquisite face. She writhed atop the birthing couch. Tears leaked from her eyes.

"I *can't!*"

Jor-El could not let her falter, not when they were so close to achieving what they had hoped and planned for. Awed by her bravery, he sought to lend her whatever strength and encouragement he could.

"*Push!*" he repeated.

For a moment, he feared that they had dared too much, that their reckless endeavor would end in tragedy. But then, just as he was on the verge of abandoning hope, Lara gritted her teeth, managed another heroic effort…

…And gave birth to a baby boy. A shock of black hair, as dark as his mother's, crowned the infant's tiny cranium.

Our son, Jor-El thought. *Kal-El.*

Kelor gently lifted the baby with her metallic tentacles, cradling it as securely as any flesh-and-blood midwife could have managed. Kelex, her male counterpart, hovered nearby. He resembled Kelor, but his contours were sharper and less rounded, as befitted his masculine programming.

Jor-El was deeply moved by the sight of the child, even more than he had anticipated, but relief and elation swiftly gave way to concern as he observed that Kal-El was silent and unresponsive. A sickening possibility filled him with dread.

What if the child was stillborn?

He held his breath, unable to inhale until his son did. Kal-El seemed so small and fragile. An endless moment elapsed, stretching out as interminably as a sentence to the Phantom Zone—until the baby finally breathed in and, for the first time in generations, the cries of a newborn infant echoed off the venerable walls of the House of El.

The bawling, lusty and full-bodied, escaped the Citadel to ring out over the vast estate below. Rondor beasts, grazing in fields of genetically-engineered grass, lifted their bovine heads in surprise. They gazed up at the huge domed structure, which was anchored to the peak of a looming basalt cliff. Tiny birds, nesting in the Rondors' armored hide, took flight in alarm.

We did it, Jor-El thought in triumph. *We truly did it.*

He beamed at Lara, sharing with her a moment of undiluted joy.

If only it could last...

"He's beautiful," Lara said. "He's perfect."

She reclined upon the couch, holding Kal-El in her arms. She gazed down at him warmly, smiling despite her exhaustion. Sitting beside her, Jor-El thought she had never looked so lovely, so radiant. He wished he could stay here, enjoying this tender scene, forever.

But forever was not to be.

"I knew he would be," Jor-El said. He rose reluctantly to his feet. "I have to go."

Her azure eyes implored him. "Please don't."

It tore his heart out to deny her. The last thing he wanted at this instant was to leave his family's side for what was probably an exercise in futility, but a sense of duty compelled him. He owed it to Krypton—and his newborn son—to fight for the future. The sigil on his chest reminded him that hope was eternal.

"I have to give it one last try," he said. "Make them listen—"

Lara refused to let go of his hand.

"What if they don't?"

A determined look came over his face. He glanced over at the Citadel's observatory, which was located on the other side of a wide curved archway. His preparations were almost complete. The vessel awaited only its precious cargo.

"Then I'll do whatever I have to."

The Council chamber sat atop a towering black pinnacle overlooking the capital city of Kandor. Most of the population had retreated underground, seeking the warmth and energy of the planet's core instead of the ruddy light of Rao, their aging red sun, but ancient towers still jutted from the surface.

Curved walls, buttresses, and ramparts flowed organically into one another, shunning right angles and emulating the nature that the people of Krypton had conquered in ages past. The sprawling cityscape was like the spiny shell of some enormous living organism—one that had perhaps grown too old and calcified to survive. The immense red sun was beginning to set, slowly surrendering the dusky sky to Krypton's four small moons, as Jor-El made his final plea to the Council of Five.

"You don't understand!" he protested.

He stood upon the polished circular floor of the vast chamber, facing the Council members who peered down at him from their elevated thrones. Jor-El had donned his most formal attire for this audience, and was wearing a layered blue robe over his skinsuit. His family crest was embossed upon a gleaming gold breastplate. A golden belt girded his waist. A long red cape hung from his broad shoulders.

"Krypton's core is collapsing," he said again. We may only have a few weeks left!"

Eminence Ro-Zar, the leader of the Council, appeared unimpressed. Like his fellow solons, he wore an elaborate robe of muted purple and gold over his skinsuit. An ornate crown towered above his furrowed brow. Honor guards, armed with lances of burnished steel and bone, stood at attention around the perimeter of the chamber. Ribs of bioengineered carbon-silica supported the high vaulted ceiling.

Ro-Zar scowled at Jor-El from his lofty perch.

"The Council has already submitted your findings for peer review—" he began.

"There isn't time for review," Jor-El said. "Harvesting the core was suicide!"

Council Member Lor-Em, seated to the right of Ro-Zar, waved away Jor-El's impassioned declarations.

"Our energy reserves were exhausted," he replied. "What would you have us do?"

"Reach out to the stars… like our ancestors did." Jor-El tried to get through to the Council members, all of whom had inherited their positions by virtue of genetic heritage. Like too many Kryptonians, they seemed more concerned with preserving the status quo—and their comfortable lifestyles—than worrying about the future. "There are other habitable worlds within reach. We can use the old outposts—"

"Are you seriously suggesting we evacuate the entire planet?" Ro-Zar scoffed at the notion.

"No," Jor-El conceded sadly. The best they could hope for, he knew, was a plan that would save a sustainable fraction of Krypton's endangered population. "It's too late for that. But with your help I could—"

Before he could continue, noises from outside the chamber interrupted the debate. Frantic shouts, screams, and the sizzling report of plasma weapons heralded the sudden arrival of a band of armed intruders who burst through the doors into the chamber. Jor-El spun around, staring in shock at the newcomers, whom he knew only too well.

Zod and his dissidents, he thought. *The so-called "Sword of Rao."*

The intruders were led by a stern-faced soldier whose rigid expression and bearing betrayed his military roots and training as surely as his severe black uniform and cape. His dark brown hair was cropped short, as befitting a soldier. Roughly the same age as Jor-El, General Zod carried a handcrafted plasma carbine that had been passed down through the warrior caste for generations. A fusion of steel and petrified bone, the weapon was still capable of dealing death and destruction despite its age. Glyphs carved into the carbine's bony stock told its bloody history, to which Zod was clearly ready to add.

The terrorist leader, whom he had once considered a friend, was accompanied by his top lieutenants. Jor-El knew them, as well—if only by reputation.

Lithe and pitiless, Faora-Ul was known and feared throughout Krypton as the "Tigress of Zod." She stalked beside her general, wearing a predatory smile on her face. Cropped black hair matched her dark uniform and cape. Although attractive in her own fierce way, she struck Jor-El as being as vicious and violent as Lara was warm and gentle. She was in her element here, waging war and spilling blood.

Flanking them was Tor-An, a muscular, dark-haired insurgent who was known to be a cold-blooded killer without a drop of mercy or compassion in his veins. He was Zod's favorite hatchet man, quick to get his hands dirty when the cause required it. His eyes were as cold and hard as polished obsidian. A sadistic smirk lifted the corner of his lips.

Nam-Ek, taking up the rear, was more than nine feet tall. The hulking brute was believed to be mute. His origins were unknown, but Jor-El had heard rumors of illegal transgenic experiments, possibly involving Rondor DNA. It was hard to believe that such a behemoth could be the result of random mutation, especially since births on Krypton were so strictly regulated. In any event, the giant stomped after Zod, watching his back.

More rebels poured in after him.

Caught by surprise, the Council's guards were no match for Zod and his forces, and their ceremonial lances were little defense against the rebels' firearms. Bursts of white-hot plasma sprayed from the carbines, incinerating the protectors and reducing their weapons to slag. The "Sword of Rao" cut them down within moments, before turning their attention to the Council members, seated upon their thrones.

Taken aback by the assault, Jor-El could hardly blame the overwhelmed guards for failing to mount an effective defense. Who could have imagined that even Zod would be so bold as to attempt to overthrow the government of Krypton? His issues with the Council were well known—but to attempt a coup?

I should have seen this coming, Jor-El thought. *I knew him better than most.* He backed away warily.

If Zod even noticed his presence, he chose to ignore it for the moment. As his troops secured the chamber, their general marched toward the Council of Five and leveled his rifle at Ro-Zar.

"This Council has been disbanded," he announced.

The High Eminence reacted with indignation. "On whose authority?"

"*Mine,*" came the answer.

His rifle fired and fiery plasma splashed against Ro-Zar, killing him instantly. His charred body tumbled from the throne, while the other Council members looked on, terror etched into their features.

Zod swept his icy gaze over them.

"The rest of you will be tried and punished accordingly," he declared.

Shaken by the High Eminence's abrupt execution, the remaining Council members put up little resistance as Zod's troops dragged them down from their thrones. Trembling in fear, they cowered together as they were rounded up and placed under Faora's supervision. Satisfied that the Council was under control, Zod turned at last toward Jor-El.

He seemed pleased.

Jor-El stepped forward to challenge his one-time ally. "What are you doing, Zod?" he demanded. "This is madness."

"What I should have done *years* ago." Zod sneered at the dethroned Council members. "These lawmakers, with their endless debates, have led Krypton to ruin."

Silently Jor-El sympathized with Zod's attitude. In truth, the Council's intractable conservatism had often frustrated him as well, but he could not condone Zod's brutal actions—or his short-sighted strategy. Time was running out for all of them, and this misguided insurrection wasn't going to save anyone.

"Zod, think!" he said. "Even if your forces win, you'll be the ruler of nothing!"

"Then join me." Zod lowered his weapon and held out his hand. "Unlike the Council of Fools, I *believe* in your science. Help me save our race." His voice rang with the fervor of a true patriot—or perhaps a fanatic. "We can start anew. We can sever the degenerative bloodlines that led us to this state."

There it is, Jor-El thought. *The line of division that ultimately drove us apart.* In their youth, they had shared a common goal of revitalizing Krypton, of turning their complacent, aging society from its self-destructive path, and igniting a new era of innovation and exploration. But in time, they had arrived at radically different visions of the future. Jor-El put his faith in science and reason, while Zod had embraced force—as well as dubious theories of eugenics.

"And who gets to choose which bloodlines survive?" Jor-El asked. "You?" He scowled pointedly at the other rebels, who were still roughing up the terrified Council members. The insurgents laughed cruelly as they stripped the prisoners of their formal vestments, leaving them standing only in their skinsuits, and knocked their elaborate headdresses from their skulls. Politics aside, the rebels clearly took perverse pleasure in terrorizing their former rulers, even as the scorched bodies of the guards still smoldered throughout the chamber.

Jor-El made no effort to conceal his distaste for the ugly scene.

"I'm not sure that's a future worth saving," he said.

Zod's face flushed with emotion. He took his friend's scorn personally.

"Don't do this, El," he said. "The last thing I want is for us to be enemies."

Jor-El left Zod's outstretched hand hanging. His voice held more sorrow than anger.

"If you really believed that, you wouldn't have abandoned the principles that bound us together in the first place, and taken up the sword against your own people." He looked Zod squarely in the eye, remembering the youthful idealism that had once burned brightly there. "I honor the man you *used* to be, Zod. Not the monster you've become."

Zod's expression darkened and he withdrew his hand. He turned to Tor-An and gestured dismissively at Jor-El.

"Take him away."

CHAPTER TWO

Tor-An carried out Zod's orders.

He and two other soldiers grabbed Jor-El. They stripped away the scientist's robes and cape before escorting him from the Council chamber.

Glancing back over his shoulder, Jor-El saw Zod at the center of the throne room, surveying the carnage he had wrought. Rather than rejoicing in his victory, the rebel leader appeared oddly dispirited, as if even he was wondering how things had come to this. Or perhaps he, too, knew that ultimately he was fighting to win a planet that was already lost.

Such a terrible waste, Jor-El thought ruefully. *And all the more so if Zod's insanity keeps me from doing what I must.*

Tor-An led the way as his men roughly herded Jor-El down a winding corridor. The muzzle of rifle prodded him, poking him in the back. The unmistakable clamor of war penetrated the outer shell of the tower—from the sound of it, a major battle was unfolding outside.

Jor-El guessed that government forces were attempting to reclaim the structure from the rebels, and to shatter the

Sword of Rao. Not that it mattered. All he cared about now was getting away from this pointless conflict and returning to his family, while there was still time to carry out his plan.

My son, he thought. *Everything depends on Kal-El.*

Then deafening explosions rattled the walls. Shock waves shook the ancient tower, causing the interior lights to flicker erratically. The floor rocked beneath Jor-El's feet, making it hard for him to keep his balance. Flakes of powdered bone, shell, and nacre rained down from the ceiling.

Glancing about uncertainly, Tor-An quickened his pace—whether to join the conflict or escape it, Jor-El couldn't be sure. A major artery curved ahead of them and the party rounded the turn.

Only to find Kelex hovering in the middle of the hallway.

"Out of the way!" Tor-An snarled.

Jor-El was suddenly very glad that the 'bot had accompanied him to the Council tower. He squeezed his eyes shut in anticipation of what was certain to occur next.

Activated by preprogrammed defensive protocols, Kelex's central display panel emitted an intense flash of light, blinding Tor-An and his men. The rebels staggered backward, rubbing their eyes. Tor-An swore profanely, tears streaming.

Jor-El took advantage of the men's disorientation. Acting swiftly, he drove his elbow into one rebel's face and wrenched the rifle from his hands. At the same time, he delivered a vigorous side kick to the other man's chest. The stunned soldier tumbled to the floor, his weapon flying from his grip.

That left only Tor-An to block Jor-El's escape. Blinking tears from his eyes, Zod's henchman drew his sidearm. Murder was written on his face, as clearly as the glyphs engraved on his pistol. He was about to fire when Kelex slammed into his skull. Burnished steel smacked loudly against flesh and blood, and Tor-An dropped to the floor, unconscious.

Jor-El was grateful for the robot's solid construction. He broke into a run, clutching the captured rifle, as he dashed away from the dazed rebels. Kelex zipped through the air after him, accelerating to keep up. The 'bot had been designed for household service and assistance, not fleeing enemy soldiers.

Jor-El shouted out a command.

"Get me Lara!"

Kelex complied at once. The three-dimensional display at the robot's core reconfigured itself, sculpting a real-time rendering of Lara's face. Concern showed on her graceful features, while the walls of the medical suite could be glimpsed in the background. Her voice issued from the image's moving lips.

"Jor, what's going on? They're shelling the capital."

Kelex hovered before Jor-El, who called out as he ran. He knew that his own face was displayed on Kelor, as well.

"It's Zod," he said breathlessly. "He's finally done it."

Understanding dawned on Lara's projected image. She was well aware of Zod's bitter disputes with the Council—and of his capacity for violence. Jor-El cursed the man for choosing today of all days to stage his senseless coup. Lara had deserved at least one blissful day with the baby—they both had—but Zod had stained this sacred occasion with blood.

That alone was a crime beyond forgiveness.

On Kelex's chest, Lara's eyes widened in alarm. *"Behind you!"* she shouted.

He spun around to see more of Zod's troops rounding the corner behind him. As they entered the corridor, he fired on the rebels, momentarily driving them back, and then continued running for cover. Kelex kept pace with him, and Jor-El spoke urgently to his wife.

"Listen to me, Lara. You have to ready the launch." He gulped air. "I'll be there as soon as I can."

Flawlessly rendered lips opened to protest, but before she could speak, he signaled Kelex to terminate the transmission. He hated cutting her off like that, but they couldn't waste precious time discussing the issue. Plus, he was going to need all his wits about him if he was to make it safely back to her and Kal.

Forgive me, my love, he thought. *And be ready when I return.*

The hallway ahead was littered with the lifeless bodies of guards and functionaries the Sword of Rao had cut down on their way to the Council chamber. Scorch marks scarred the walls. Glimpsing daylight ahead, Jor-El raced out of the curving corridor onto a wide terrace overlooking the embattled city below. Kelex was close beside him.

The sun had not yet set, and was casting crimson shadows over a sprawling expanse of ancient temples, palaces, arenas, and towers. Opalescent domes and spires gleamed in the twilight—biology itself had been harnessed to create Kandor, which was now under attack by men and women who literally had been born to defend it.

Civil war raged beneath the dimming red sky. The Sapphire Guard, Krypton's elite defense force, had responded to Zod's provocation in full force. Guards firing from the maws of flying gunships directed particle beam rifles at the insurgents, who fired back with their own weapons. The bio-engineered aircraft resembled huge mutant invertebrates whose segmented exoskeletons were dense enough to withstand heavy punishment. Globular thrusters, sprouting from the underside of the ships, propelled them through the twilight sky.

Blazing gouts of plasma and charged neutrons streaked through the air, spreading death and destruction. A concentrated barrage of plasma from the rebels holding the tower got past the Guard's defenses, splattering gelatinous fire over an unlucky scarab-class cruiser. Screaming soldiers, their bodies engulfed in flame, leapt to their deaths even as the crippled scarab spiraled downward toward the very terrace upon which Jor-El now stood.

No! he thought. *I can't die yet. There's too much to be done...*

His muscles tensed beneath his skinsuit. He braced himself to jump out of the way of the falling aircraft, but at the last minute an explosion blew out one side of the scarab, sending it veering off to the right. It plummeted past the terrace, narrowly missing Jor-El and Kelex, then slammed into a domed temple several stories below.

Flames and smoke erupted from the crash site, adding to the chaos. The ill-fated temple became nothing but a gaping crater, surrounded by rubble. Jor-El counted his blessings. A short distance closer, and he might have been crushed beneath that debris.

It's not safe here, he thought to himself. Now that he had a child—a son—he was more determined than ever to live until he had accomplished what was necessary. *The sooner we are gone, the better our chances.*

Looking out over the edge of the terrace, he peered many stories down to the streets and plazas below. No mortal being could survive such a jump, at least not on Krypton, so the only way out was up. Jor-El turned his face toward the sky and shouted at the top of his lungs.

"H'Raka!"

He briefly feared that the furious fighting had chased the war-kite away, but then H'Raka descended onto the terrace, her gossamer wings buzzing. Like all domesticated lifeforms—which were the only sort left on Krypton—the hybrid creature was both genetically engineered and cybernetically enhanced. Large enough to carry one or more adult Kryptonians, H'Raka set down in front of her master.

Wide gray eyes gazed out from above her rounded muzzle. Two pairs of veined, membranous wings sprouted from her sleek grey form, which she owed to chromosomes extracted from an extinct aquatic mammal. Computerized implants, melded to her nervous systems, augmented her natural reflexes and navigational abilities. A saddle, equipped with a rear robotic docking cradle, was strapped to the war-kite's back.

H'Raka yipped in greeting.

Good girl, Jor-El thought. *Thanks for waiting.*

He hastily climbed into the saddle, even as Kelex secured himself to the docking cradle. As soon as the robot clicked into place, Jor-El urged H'Raka to take flight.

Wings buzzing, the war-kite soared into the sky, carrying her passengers away from the Council tower. They glided over the besieged city, zig-zagging through a firestorm of flying plasma bursts. Repeated salvoes sprayed across the sky like torrents of liquid fire. H'Raka took evasive action, hoping to avoid being caught in a crossfire, but there was little safety to be found anywhere.

Panicked civilians ran for cover in the avenues and arteries below even as crashing aircraft and falling debris rained havoc on the capital. Emergency sirens keened loudly, competing with the gunfire, explosions, and screams. The air reeked of smoke and burning organics.

It was as though the barbaric wars of ages past had returned with a vengeance.

Despite his own desperate situation, Jor-El couldn't help viewing the widespread carnage with dismay. This was no way for Krypton to end her days...

A salvo of blazing plasma burned through the acrid fumes directly ahead, close enough that he could feel the scorching heat against his face. H'Raka banked sharply to one side to avoid the blast, and only a safety strap kept Jor-El from being spilled from the saddle. He held onto the gilded pommel with both hands, trusting in the creature's speed and agility to get them through intact. A hot wind blew against his face, assaulting him with the stink of war. The smoke stung his eyes.

The screams of the dying assailed his ears.

Damn you, Zod! This wasn't necessary!

The tumultuous ride seemed likely to end abruptly at any moment, but at last they left behind the administrative district—and the bulk of the fighting. Jor-El let out a sigh of relief as the heart-rending tumult receded into the distance. He could still hear it, like the thunder of a nearby storm, but, for the moment at least, Krypton was tearing itself apart without him.

Perhaps all was not yet lost.

He longed to fly straight back to Lara and their newborn, but he had one vital errand to which he had to attend. So he steered H'Raka toward the outskirts of the city—where the Genesis Chambers awaited.

The immense complex, which had birthed every living Kryptonian for countless generations, rose up from the earth like the gnarled trunk of a colossal tree, hundreds of lengths in diameter. Sturdy black branches, each one the size of a palace watchtower, extended out from the central hub. Pools of rippling iridescent fluid glistened atop each hollow spire, reflecting the fading sunlight.

H'Raka circled above the Genesis Chambers while Jor-El cautiously scanned the awesome vista from above. To his relief, the automated complex appeared unguarded. He guessed that all of the government's defense forces were currently engaged in combat with the insurgents.

He smiled wryly.

Maybe Zod's deranged insurrection was well-timed after all.

Not that any sane Kryptonian ever would have dreamed of trespassing here—at least not before today. The Genesis Chambers provided life and continuity to their entire civilization. Every single Kryptonian, whether rebel or loyalist, owed their very existence to this place. Who but a madman would dare to tamper with it?

Who indeed?

He took one last aerial survey of the scene before guiding H'Raka down to the nearest spire. The war-kite alighted on the basin's outer lip, which was wide enough to support her. Dismounting, Jor-El peered down into the bottomless depths of the pool. Kelex detached himself from the saddle and joined Jor-El at the water's edge. The robot probed the shimmering liquid with his sensors.

"Can you see the Codex?" Jor-El asked.

Hours earlier he had attempted to access the schematics of the Genesis Chambers, but that information had been restricted. There was a time when his status as Krypton's leading scientist might have opened doors, but that was before he staked his reputation on a "controversial" theory that few on Krypton were willing to accept. Nowadays he was regarded as far too radical to be trusted.

"It's just below the central hub, sir," the 'bot replied.

"But I am compelled to warn you. Breaching the Genesis Chambers is a Class-B crime, punishable by—"

"No one cares any more, Kelex," Jor-El said. "The world is ending." He turned toward his mount and gently stroked the beast's muzzle. "Stay, H'Raka."

The war-kite purred her assent.

Jor-El approached the edge of the pool. He took a deep breath, as much to steady his nerves as to fill his lungs, and dived headfirst into the hollow shaft at the center of the spire. Amniotic fluid, heated to body temperature, enveloped him as he swam down the length of the spire into a sprawling, liquid-filled complex. An eerie phosphorescence lit the shaft, suffusing the briny fluid with a faint green glow. He kept his eyes open as he swam, taking in sights few Kryptonians had ever been privileged to see.

Gestating embryos grew inside transparent globular sacs that sprouted like buds along branching stems that combined elements of both plant and animal life. Pink and translucent, their tiny hearts already pulsing with life, the infants slept within a clear protective gel. The drifting stems, bearing their fetal fruit, extended for as far as the eye could see, growing an entire generation of future Kryptonians according to the precise and exacting specifications of the Codex.

Krypton had long ago abandoned the unpredictability of sexual reproduction—with its reckless pairings and random mixing of chromosomes—in favor of a more orderly and scientific system that allowed for complete control over each child's genetic makeup and destiny. Nothing was left to chance. Each developing embryo was expressly designed to fulfill his or her preordained role in society—as a worker, warrior, thinker, administrator, or whatever best served the greater good.

The Genesis Chambers were the ultimate expression of Krypton's rigid caste system, applying advanced genetic engineering to an inviolate tradition that stretched back to antiquity. Jor-El had sprouted from one such stem, many cycles ago, as had Lara, and Zod, and every Kryptonian who currently breathed upon the planet.

Save for one.

Crab-like robotic gardeners, equipped with sharp metallic pincers, tended to the growing stems and buds, trimming away excess shoots, nodes, and even the occasional defective fetus. Designed to function in a liquid environment, the 'bots were smaller and less sturdily built than Kelex.

Other robots scoured the inner walls of the spire, keeping them free of unwanted mosses and fungal growths. Jor-El eyed the busy mechanisms apprehensively, but they appeared programmed to ignore him as long as he did not disturb the babies growing on the vines. It pained his heart to realize that none of the gestating embryos would live long enough to be harvested.

He kicked his way downward, trying to stay clear of the endless stems and sacs, yet the shaft grew more densely fertile as he descended, slowing his progress. Despite his efforts, he swam too close to a cluster of fetuses, which retracted back into their stems like the polyps on an undersea anemone. A nearby 'bot, busy pruning a stray branch, turned its sensors toward him, but did not take action.

Jor-El hurried away before it changed its cybernetic mind.

He was running out of breath. His cheeks bulged and tiny bubbles escaped his lips. Despite his clenched jaws, briny fluid invaded his mouth and nostrils. His lungs cried out for air. Self-preservation urged him to turn back, but he kept on swimming, hoping that he was nearing the end of the shaft—and that the central hub was not much farther.

The shaft slowly widened. Swaying stems obscured his view, but he spotted an opening ahead. Holding on tightly to his last breath, he kicked toward the large circular portal which led to an immense spherical chamber at the center of the complex. Artificial light filtered down from above.

Jor-El prayed it wasn't just a mirage caused by a lack of air.

Light-headed, lungs aching, he swam up toward the light. His head broke the surface of the water and he gasped, then sucked in air hungrily. Amniotic fluid dripping from his hair and beard, he found himself bobbing in the center of a wide reservoir surrounded by pulsing organic walls. Taking a moment to recover, he glanced around at the cavernous hub of the Genesis Chambers, from which the entire gargantuan complex was controlled.

Soon his questing eyes located what he was looking for.

The Codex.

An ancient Kryptonian skull, inscribed with glowing green glyphs, hung just above the basin, suspended by numerous neural fibers. The glyphs pulsed continuously while the Codex dictated the genetic code of millions of Kryptonians as yet unborn. In the past, such directions would have determined their futures as well—but that was when Krypton had a future.

Reaching upward, Jor-El hastily disconnected the skull from the fibers that held it in place. The pulsing glyphs dimmed and went dark. A high-pitched alarm echoed off the walls around him—like the screeching of a frightened jewel-bird.

The alarms sent a jolt of adrenaline through him, spurring him on. War or no war, his unthinkable violation was bound to trigger defensive measures—and attract the

Sapphire Guard. He needed to be away from here, with his prize, before it was too late.

He unhooked the last of the ganglia and seized the Codex. Clutching it to his chest, he dived back beneath the water. Numerous openings led to the complex's myriad spires. Unable to determine which passage he'd used before, he chose an opening at random and swam into the waiting shaft, which was identical to all the others.

Kicking upward, he rose past drifting stems laden with doomed fetuses and embryos. His lungs were tested once more, but this time he knew where he was going.

If he could just reach the open pool at the top of shaft…

But the robots had other ideas. Abandoning their gardening, they chased after Jor-El, converging on him from all directions. Metal pincers, designed for pruning, tugged on his legs and ankles. The layered fabric of his skinsuit shielded him from immediate injury, but the 'bots kept coming, determined to retrieve the stolen Codex.

Sharpened pincers dove at his face, but he batted the 'bot away with his free hand, while kicking and shaking more 'bots off his legs and torso. Shattered bits of metal and circuitry sank out of sight, yet the aquatic robots were not deterred. Whoever had programmed them had clearly impressed upon them the paramount importance of the Codex.

They were not going to surrender it without a fight.

Crimson sunlight, seeping down from above, called out to him. Breaking free from the clinging 'bots, he breached the surface of a pool at the top of a towering spire. H'Raka and Kelex were nowhere to be seen, which implied that this was a different shaft than the one into which he'd dived before.

Still holding on to the Codex, he started to haul himself out of the pool onto the sturdy, solid lip of the spire. He was halfway out when unseen pincers bit down on his ankle, squeezing hard enough to bruise him beneath his skinsuit, and yanked him back down into the fluid. Startled, he lost his grip on the skull, which rolled across the top of the spire toward the outer edge of the lip.

No! Jor-El thought.

Nightmarish visions—of the Codex tumbling over the edge and plunging to certain destruction—flashed through his brain, giving him the strength to shake loose the relentless 'bot and lunge from the water. He dove for the skull, his hands stretched out before him. His fingers closed on the runaway Codex only a heartbeat before it rolled over the brink.

Rao be praised!

Gasping in relief, he scrambled to feet, only to hear a metallic scraping behind him. He turned to see a pair of 'bots clambering out of the shaft after him. He backed away from the pool, toward the edge of the precipice. Glancing back over his shoulder, he spied a vertiginous drop. Again, no Kryptonian could survive such a fall— not unless he knew how to fly.

The robots, clumsy once they were out of the water, advanced toward him. Their pincers clacked viciously. Given a chance, they would surely snip his fingers off to rescue the skull from his grasp.

He couldn't let them do that. The Codex had to survive.

And it must be kept away from Zod and his renegades, he resolved.

Suddenly a familiar buzzing reached his ears, drawing nearer by the instant. Jor-El smiled. Trusting fate, he turned and leapt from the spire.

He plummeted toward the ground below, accelerating according to a mathematical constant he had memorized as a child. For a few heart-stopping seconds he found himself wishing that Krypton's natural gravity wasn't quite so formidable. Terminal velocity approached at an alarming pace.

He prayed that Lara would be able to carry out their work without him.

You must save the child, Lara. No matter what!

Then H'Raka swooped in beneath him, with Kelor docked at her rear. Working together, they timed the catch perfectly so that Jor-El landed heavily in the saddle rather than crashing to his death many lengths below.

He settled into the seat, checking to make sure the Codex had not been damaged by the fall. To his relief, the sacred skull was still intact, which meant there was still hope for the future.

"Home," he instructed H'Raka.

CHAPTER THREE

The war-kite soared upward, leaving the Genesis Chambers and mechanical sentries behind. It seemed as if the worst was over, but then a burst of plasma shot past them.

Pivoting in his seat, Jor-El saw that the ongoing battle had spread, and was moving toward them. Deadly sprays of energy streaked the sky as the Sword of Rao fought the Sapphire Guard for control of Kandor.

Fearing that they were about to become collateral damage, Jor-El urged H'Raka to greater speed and the war-kite responded by executing an evasive course that tested any enemy's ability to pin her in their sights. Jor-El bent low, cradling the Codex, as they sped toward the Citadel.

Almost there, Jor-El thought. *Only a little farther...*

But the agile war-kite could not dodge every blast. A stray shot shredded her left hindwing, sending her spinning out of control. H'Raka yelped in pain, but managed to level out and pick up speed. With only three wings remaining, she glided away from the besieged city. Jor-El felt her valiant heart pounding beneath him. Her breathing was ragged.

"Sir," Kelex reported. *"Your mount is exhibiting signs of grave distress."* The robot could access H'Raka's vitals from the docking port.

Jor-El was deeply moved by the animal's bravery and endurance. He leaned to stroke her muzzle. His throat tightened.

"Easy, girl," he said. "We're almost home."

They flew above the bioengineered nature preserve on the outskirts of the estate. The House of El had long employed the wilderness as a buffer zone between the Citadel and the city, granting Jor-El and his illustrious forebears a welcome degree of privacy.

Herds of horned Rondor beasts grazed in the grasslands, lowing at the wounded war-kite as it passed above them. Carnivorous blood morels sprouted amidst the foliage. Spiked morningstar seeds floated on air currents, tempting unwitting predators.

Fiery Rao, still sinking in the east, bestowed its scarlet radiance upon the savage veldt. Brilliant ribbons of crimson and carmine retreated toward the horizon, creating a breathtaking view.

How many sunsets does Krypton have left?

At last the Citadel came into view. Rooted organically to the austere black cliffs overlooking the veldt, the great domed edifice had been Jor-El's home since the morning he was first harvested. He still remembered the glorious day he had brought Lara home to live with him, after an arranged marriage that eventually yielded a long and loving union.

They had been truly blessed in their time together. If that happiness was now drawing to a close, he still considered himself a fortunate man.

H'Raka dipped sharply, then recovered. Pained whimpers escaped her jaws. The injured war-kite was also clearly at the end of her days, but found strength enough to stay on course. An outdoor terrace, at the entrance to the landing bay, served as their final destination. Her wings vibrated one last time, bringing them over the terrace, before gliding in for a crash landing.

She slammed into the hard, unyielding floor of the terrace and skidded to a stop only a few lengths away from the high arched entranceway. A low moan testified to her ordeal.

The rough landing jarred Jor-El, but failed to break any bones. He sprang from the saddle, holding onto the Codex, while Kelex detached himself from the docking cradle. Desperate as he was to rejoin his family, Jor-El paused to comfort the dying beast who had given her all for Krypton's future. He gently scratched her muzzle, just where she liked it.

"Rest now," he whispered.

H'Raka's large round eyes rolled upward until only the whites were visible. Her labored breathing stilled. The three remaining wings collapsed against her lifeless body. The pulsing lights on her cybernetic implants flickered and died.

Bruised and bloodied from his struggles with the robots, Jor-El turned away from the carcass and dashed inside. Kelex jetted after him.

"Lara!"

He ran straight to the observatory, where he found all in readiness. The starcraft, equipped with a state-of-the-art phantom drive unit, was suspended over an empty cradle module. The craft resembled the calcified heart of a giant, its inner chamber protected by dense bio-engineered plating. The rounded contours of its outer carapace had been crafted to withstand the rigors of deep space, shielding its passenger from everything from solar flares to asteroid strikes.

Biomechanical hardware surrounded the craft. He placed the Codex in a stasis beam above the cradle.

An archway on the opposite side of the domed chamber led to the medical suite, where he spied Lara nursing Kal-El, with Kelor hovering attentively nearby. The newborn nestled contentedly in his mother's arms. Lara looked up as her husband approached. Her face brightened.

"Jor-El!" she said. "I was so worried—"

He wished he brought happier tidings, but there was no time to soften the news. She needed to know the truth.

"Zod's forces are on their way," he said. "Did you find the world?"

"We did, sir," Kelor reported. *"Orbiting a main sequence yellow star, just as you said it would."*

The display screen on her chest presented an image of a distant solar system, dominated by a vibrant yellow star. Only one-fifth the size of Krypton's swollen red giant, the golden sun still had billions of cycles ahead of it before exhausting the hydrogen at its core—as Rao had already done—and entering its dotage.

It burned hotter than Krypton's sun, and would for eons to come.

"A *young* star," he declared. "His cells will drink in its radiation."

The display zeroed in on the third planet in the system, which appeared to be in the grip of an ice age. Vast glaciers covered the surface. Hairless bipedal primates, garbed in furs, struggled to survive amidst the icy wilderness. Jor-El instinctively admired their determination, vigor, and ingenuity. They spread out across the planet, thriving despite the harsh, primitive conditions.

"There's an intelligent population there," he pointed out. "They're primitive, but... they look like us, Lara."

34

She eyed the images uncertainly, clutching Kal-El to her breast. He could tell she was having second thoughts.

"What if the natives won't accept him?" she asked. "He'll be an outcast, a freak. They'll kill him."

"How?" Jor-El asked, trying to reassure her. "He'll be like a god to them."

Her eyes said that she still wasn't sure.

"What if the ship doesn't make it?" Shaking her head, she gazed down at the newborn in her arms. "I can't do it. I thought I could, but now that's he's here—"

Jor-El shared her feelings. The very sight of their child stirred him even more powerfully than he had expected. He couldn't blame Lara for wanting to hold onto her baby—*their* baby. He too felt an almost overpowering desire to shelter the boy, and watch him grow to manhood. But fate had determined otherwise.

"Lara, we've been through this," he said gently. "Krypton is doomed. It's his only chance now. Our *people's* only chance."

A strident alarm blared throughout the Citadel, interrupting the poignant moment. Jor-El looked up in dismay.

"Kelex!" he called. "What is it?"

The robot manservant had followed Jor-El into the observatory. He accessed the Citadel's perimeter sensors. A holographic display, projected from the 'bot's chest, showed five blinking triangles converging on a symbolic representation of their home.

"*Five attack ships converging from the east,*" Kelex confirmed. "*Citadel defenses are being scanned and evaluated—*"

Jor-El's heart sank.

"Gods, we're out of time." He looked urgently at Lara. "Get him ready. I'll transfer the Codex. "

He stepped forward to take Kal-El, but Lara refused to let him go. She hugged the baby close.

"Wait! Wait!" she protested. "Just a moment more!"

He wished desperately he could grant her this, but they had to complete the preparations while there was still time. Events were progressing far too swiftly.

"We *have* to say good-bye, Lara!" he replied firmly.

"No! Let me look at him!" A primal maternal instinct warred with the cruel reality of their situation as she caressed Kal-El's cherubic face. Her eyes glistened. Her voice was hoarse with emotion. "We'll never get to see him walk. Never hear him say our names—"

Her naked anguish broke his heart.

"I know. I know, my love. But somewhere out there, amongst the stars... he will *live*."

With that he gently pried Kal-El from her grip. An agonizing sob escaped her as she surrendered to necessity. Jor-El handed his son over to Kelex, who placed the baby in the womb-like cradle beneath the starcraft. Kal-El cooed happily, trusting that all was well. Jor-El was grateful for the infant's good nature. Tears and tantrums would only make their separation all the harder.

As Kelex tucked his charge securely into place, Jor-El climbed into a looming nano-surgery robot waiting silently in the wings. The sophisticated exoskeleton closed around him. A multi-spectrum visor clicked into place before his eyes. Encased in the robot, he approached the cradle and gazed down at his son. The visor allowed him to see through Kal-El's epidermis to gaze directly on the baby's tiny heart.

The sight of his son's essence, pulsing before his eyes, left Jor-El awash in emotion. That was his own Kryptonian flesh and blood, throbbing with new life.

He nodded at Kelex, who prepared the skull for the procedure.

"Uploading the Codex, sir."

A holographic readout confirmed the data link. Jor-El activated the carrier beam and a shimmering blue ray passed through the Codex on its way to Kal-El's heart. The process disintegrated the Codex, breaking it down into digitized information which was then transmitted directly into the baby's bloodstream. Kal-El gazed wide-eyed at the pretty lights, unharmed by the painless procedure.

It was over in a matter of moments. No trace of the Codex remained, save for the data infused into the unknowing Kryptonian child.

Almost done, Jor-El thought. He cut off the beam and climbed out of the surgical gear. Crossing the floor of the observatory, he retrieved a customized command key from a magnetic field. The key was a short black spike small enough to be held in the palm of his hand. The crest of the House of El was inscribed on its triangular head. He plugged the key into a matching slot in the cradle, so that it would accompany Kal-El on his voyage across the cosmos.

"Sir," Kelex said. *"Hostile forces are nearly upon us—"*

The perimeter alarms grew ever louder and more strident. On the robot's dimensional display, the blinking triangles were practically on top of the Citadel.

Zod's forces, Jor-El wondered, *or the Sapphire Guard?* Both factions would stop at nothing to retrieve the Codex.

"Put up the defenses!" he ordered, silently chastising himself for not doing so earlier. If he had not been so preoccupied with Lara and the imminent departure of their child...

On the display, a protective force field enveloped the Citadel. Jor-El had little expectation that the field would be able to repel the invaders for long, but he intended to make good use of the time remaining to them.

He watched intently as a biostasis gel—similar in composition to that used in the embryonic sacs back at the Genesis Chambers—filled the cradle, flooding over little Kal-El. A transparent enclosure formed over the module, sealing the baby inside an artificial womb.

He would never touch his son again.

Then the Citadel came under attack. Muted explosions shook the curved walls of the observatory. A punishing barrage tested the defenses, which appeared unequal to the task.

Small wonder, Jor-El mused. It had been generations since any household on Krypton had faced such an assault. The defenses were old and outdated, like the rest of Krypton.

Lara gasped in alarm as shock waves rattled the chamber. The surgical robot framework toppled over, smashing onto the floor. Jor-El glanced anxiously at the starcraft, suspended over the cradle module, but its supports proved sturdy enough to hold it safely in place above the womb.

Cracks spread across the vaulted ceiling, showering the observatory with sediment and debris. A buttress rib buckled alarmingly, while the floor vibrated beneath their feet. If he didn't know better, he'd swear that Krypton was already coming apart.

"Outer defenses are falling!" Kelex said. The force field flickered erratically on his display. Jor-El knew that the enemy would soon breach the Citadel. Time was running out. All they had left was minutes.

He peered again through the transparent enclosure at his son, slumbering now within the gel-filled womb. Kal-El was blissfully oblivious to the chaos raining down upon them.

"Sleep well, my son," Jor-El whispered. "Our hopes and dreams travel with you."

Lara joined him in front of the module. She wrapped her arms around him.

"Finish the launch, Lara," he instructed. "I'll hold them off for as long as I can."

The Citadel shuddered beneath another assault. Jor-El doubted the force-field could withstand any more strikes. He embraced his wife, sharing one last precious kiss. Her lips forgave him for taking her baby from her.

"I love you," she said.

"And I, you." Together, they gazed at their only child. "He'll make it, Lara. He'll build a better world than ours."

Blaring sirens made it impossible to forget the danger at their door. Tearing himself away from her, he exited the observatory and sprinted through the Citadel to the armory, where his battle armor awaited. The gleaming gold shell fitted over his durable blue skinsuit. His sacred crest was emblazoned on the chest plate. A bulky plasma cannon was attached to his right arm.

Kelex prepared himself for combat, as well. The floating robot lowered himself into the docking cradle atop a large armored war-bot. Humanoid in design, the robotic chassis stood at least a head taller than Jor-El, once Kelex had settled into the larger mechanism's neckpiece.

His mainframe now served as the war-bot's "head." The gilded metal chassis mimicked Kryptonian anatomy, right down to sculpted steel muscles. Servomotors whirred as Kelex tested his powerful new limbs. Plasma blasters powered up in his mechanical arms.

Fully equipped, they raced toward the Citadel's upper entrance, where even now they could hear the enemy advancing toward the gates. Concussive blasts slammed into the landing bay doors from the outside. Solid grapheme plates began to buckle under the assault.

Jor-El and Kelex took up defensive positions before the door. He wished they had drilled for this more often, but the Citadel of the House of El had never come under siege in Jor-El's lifetime. He had always counted on Krypton's security forces to keep him safe from riots, insurrections, or invasions. Indeed, Zod had been brutally effective at keeping the peace for years—before he turned against the Council.

A titanic blast blew open the doors, filling the landing bay with smoke and debris. Jor-El and Kelex didn't wait for the invaders to enter, but opened fire immediately, driving the attackers back with a blistering salvo of plasma fire. They rushed forward to defend the breached archway, even as the intruders regrouped on the open terrace beyond. Black uniforms and armor identified them as Zod's partisans. Jor-El nodded grimly. It seemed that his old friend had come calling.

Taking cover beneath the archway, he assessed the scene. Rebel gunships, encrusted with armor, flared in overhead. There was Zod, leaning from the open bay of the lead ship, directing the assault. His harsh voice carried across the distance between them.

"Concentrate fire on the main doors!"

CHAPTER FOUR

Jor-El and Kelex fought to repel the invaders. An overeager gunship came too close and Jor-El brought it down with a well-aimed blast to its propulsion unit. The sky-boat crashed into the rocky cliff beneath the terrace. Flaming wreckage cascaded down onto the grasslands hundreds of lengths below.

Frightened wildlife fled in panic. A herd of Rondors stampeded away from the fighting.

The rebels retaliated by unleashing a devastating series of blasts at Jor-El's position. Despite his heavy armor, he rolled out of the way of the bursts, but their combined force was enough to bring down the entire archway, which collapsed on top of him. An avalanche of pulverized carbon and silica smashed him to the floor, burying him beneath heaps of rubble.

His armor shielded him from serious injury, but he found himself trapped, unable to move. Grunting with exertion, he tried to free himself, but the piled debris was too heavy. No Kryptonian could lift such a load.

"Hold on, sir!" Kelex called out. *"I'm coming."*

The robot rushed to his aid. Mechanical limbs cleared

away the heavy rubble. A steel hand took hold of Jor-El's, pulling the trapped scientist free. Powdered silica clung to his face and armor as he regained his footing behind the fallen remains of the archway. This was at least twice that Kelex had saved him from Zod's soldiers, he mused.

If only I'd had flesh-and-blood allies who were so reliable…

They were fighting a losing battle, however. An armored gunship touched down on the terrace, disgorging dozens of enemy soldiers. Jor-El knew that he and Kelex couldn't possibly repel them all. Within minutes, the Citadel would be overrun by Zod's forces. The Sword of Rao was at his throat.

No, he thought. *Lara needs more time. Our child is not yet safe.*

Kelex's "head" pivoted in his direction. His servomotors whirred into readiness.

"*It's been an honor, sir,*" the robot said, and Jor-El knew what he intended to do.

"Kelex, no!"

"*I'm not important,*" came the response. "*None of us are. The only thing that matters is saving the child.*"

The robot reached back with both mechanical hands and unlatched the outer casings on the obliques of his artificial musculature, exposing a pair of plasma grenades mounted to his inner chassis. He activated the grenades, which beeped and blinked ominously. Then he swiveled away from Jor-El.

"*He is our future!*"

Dashing out from behind the heaps of rubble, Kelex ran straight at the gunship and its crew. His robotic limbs carried him across the terrace at astonishing speed. Panicked soldiers, recognizing a suicide run, fired frantically at the charging war-bot. A plasma burst blew off Kelex's right arm, but he kept on coming.

He sprang over the heads of the rebels and into very gullet of the ship, landing amidst the assault team. Doomed men scrambled away from him.

Abruptly the grenades went off, blowing apart the robot, the ship, and the surrounding soldiers. Jor-El watched wide-eyed as the scene transformed into an explosion of flying plasma and shrapnel. He ducked his head to avoid being tagged by the molten metal.

As the debris settled, smoke rose from the gutted remains of the gunship.

Ever loyal, Kelex had destroyed himself for the House of El.

Jor-El resolved not to let that sacrifice go to waste. He retreated back into the Citadel, hoping that the rubble and burning gunships would slow Zod and his renegades long enough for Lara to complete the launch.

Hurry, my love, he thought. *Zod is coming.*

The cradle module ascended into the waiting starcraft. An open hatchway sealed behind it, putting another layer of separation between Lara and her son. She stood at the launch controls, accompanied by Kelor.

"Phantom drives are coming online, mistress," the 'bot announced.

Lara nodded and initiated the launch sequence. Despite the Citadel-shaking combat raging outside, and fears for her husband's safety, she forced herself to focus on the task at hand.

She and Jor-El had been partners in this endeavor since the beginning, ever since his research revealed the truth of Krypton's impending doom. An accomplished scholar and historian in her own right, she had gladly volunteered to give birth to Kal-El as their ancestors had done. Yet the entire time, she had known that they would not raise him as their own.

She had just never expected it would be so hard.

The starcraft, now bearing little Kal-El, rotated into position. Vapors vented from the engines as the vessel powered up its thrusters. Biomechanical umbilical cords detached themselves from the craft.

The realization that she was sending her child away from her, forever, was like a dagger to the heart. Chances were she would never even know if he arrived safely at the primitive world so many light-years away. Nor could she guess what lonely fate awaited him there.

I have to do this, she reminded herself. *We have no choice.*

So she keyed in the penultimate sequence. High above her, the vast dome of the observatory began to open...

Zod's personal transport touched down on the terrace, not far from the flaming remains of the advance ship. Exiting his craft, he scowled at the wreckage. He had watched as the events unfolded. That suicidal robot had cost him many loyal soldiers.

Damn you, Jor-El, he thought angrily. *This is unnecessary. Why couldn't you work with me to save our people... and restore Krypton's greatness?*

Flanked by Faora and Nam-Ek, he marched briskly toward the collapsed archway. His dark eyes scanned the battleground, and he remained on guard for traps. As far as he knew, Jor-El had few allies these days, but a smart soldier never underestimated the opposition. *Even when the enemy is your oldest friend.*

Monitoring the comms, Faora lifted a hand to her ear. Her brow furrowed pensively.

"General, we've identified an engine ignition within the Citadel—"

An engine? Zod tried to make sense of this new development. *What in Rao's name is Jor-El up to now?* His forces had intercepted the alarms from the Genesis Chamber. Could it be that Jor-El was attempting to escape with the stolen Codex?

That could not be permitted. Zod had his own plans for the Codex—and for the future of the Kryptonian race.

"Hold this platform, commander!" he ordered, leaving Faora behind as he quickened his pace toward the entrance. Avid soldiers were already clearing away the rubble that blocked the way. Zod led a contingent into the building, which he knew well in happier days.

The unmistakable thrum of engines drew him to Jor-El's well-equipped observatory, where he found his old friend standing alongside a compact vessel that appeared designed for interstellar travel. Its thrusters pulsed with pure light.

Lara stood nearby, at a post in front of a pulsing control panel.

The glow from the starcraft cast Jor-El in stark shadow. With his back to the newcomers, he resembled some mythic hero from Krypton's illustrious past. If he knew they were there, he gave no sign, A plasma carbine rested in his grip. Powdered silica dusted his hair.

Zod drew his sidearm.

"I know you stole the Codex, Jor-El. Surrender it, and I'll let you live."

"Why?" came the response. "So you can pervert our lineage, to your own ends?" Jor-El shook his head.

"This is a second chance for *all* of Krypton. Not just the bloodlines you deem worthy."

What second chance? Zod wondered. Ignoring his prisoner's sanctimonious lecture, he searched the scene for clues to whatever audacity Jor-El was attempting. His gaze darted from the adjacent medical suite—where an antique birthing couch had been dragged out of obsolescence—to Lara herself. Her lovely figure was less slender than he recalled, almost as though...

Suddenly an unspeakable possibility forced its way into his mind. It dragged up foggy memories, of certain radical notions Jor-El had once shared with him in private, back when they were young and chafing at the Council's growing calcification.

Zod's gaze shifted from the medical suite to the birthing couch, and then to the miniature starcraft, which seemed scarcely large enough to transport anything larger than a child.

A chill ran down his spine. He stared at his former friend in horror.

"What have you done?" he demanded.

"We had a *son*, Zod," Jor-El said, without even having the decency to deny it. "Krypton's first live birth in centuries. Free to forge his *own* destiny."

"Heresy!" Zod felt sick to stomach, but his disgust quickly ignited into rage. He turned to the soldiers, and pointed emphatically at the hovering starcraft and its obscene cargo.

"Destroy it!" he commanded.

That propelled Jor-El into motion. He spun and fired on the soldiers, attempting to provide cover for the craft. The escort fell back, taking up defensive positions, but Zod knew more than they what was at stake.

Heedless of his own safety, he charged into the

observatory, desperate to halt the launch. He knew without being told that Jor-El had entrusted the Codex to the abomination he and Lara had conceived. Rao only knew where Jor-El intended to send his son.

Perhaps one of the old outposts?

A plasma burst sizzled past his ear, close enough to singe his hair—a warning shot, perhaps. Zod gambled that Jor-El, for all his mad schemes, wasn't prepared to murder a friend. So he dashed forward, keeping his head low, only to find himself torn between commandeering the launch controls and attacking the starcraft directly. Or perhaps he needed to remove Jor-El from the equation?

His momentary indecision was his downfall. A well-aimed shot from Jor-El's rifle reduced Zod's sidearm to slag. Grunting in pain, he hurled the super-heated weapon away from him.

It splattered upon the floor.

"Lara!" Zod called out, hoping that she was more amenable to reason than her deranged husband. The Lara Lor-Van he recalled had always been highly intelligent, and she might still be that woman, no matter what depravity Jor-El had forced upon her. "Listen to me! The Codex is Krypton's future!" He appealed to her patriotism and honor. "Abort the launch!"

Then Jor-El was upon him. He pressed the heated muzzle of his rife against Zod, forcing him to his knees. But, as Zod had suspected, he balked at executing the friend of his youth. Instead he merely shouted urgently in Lara's direction.

"Finish it!"

Her graceful fingers played across the illuminated control screen. The starcraft's thrusters flared even more brightly, forcing them to look away. Victory—and the Codex—were slipping away from him.

"NO!!!"

Unlike Jor-El, he had been trained to kill. Moving quickly, while their attention was on the starcraft, he drew a concealed dagger from his boot and drove it into Jor-El's chest, just below his armored breastplate. The carbonized bone blade penetrated Jor-El's skinsuit, piercing the fragile skin and organs beneath.

Jor-El cried out and collapsed to the floor. His rifle slipped from his fingers.

Zod lunged for the fallen weapon, praying there was still time to halt the launch. Leaving his dagger lodged in his friend's chest, he snatched the weapon as he rolled across the floor and scrambled into firing position. He took aim at the departing starcraft...

But he was too late. With a sudden burst of ignition, the capsule blasted off at an angle that took it toward the open ceiling of the observatory. He fired desperately, but the plasma burst fell short of its target, which rocketed beyond the roof and into the dusky red sky.

Frustrated, Zod wheeled around to glare at Jor-El, who lay bleeding upon the floor. His wound was mortal, of course, but a smile played upon the dying scientist's face as he watched the starcraft escape the Citadel. Proud eyes tracked the ship's ascent.

Then they clouded over. Eyes that had once probed the secrets of the universe saw only oblivion.

"Jor-El!"

Lara rushed to his side. She cradled his lifeless body in her arms, sobbing inconsolably. Zod felt a twinge of sympathy for the woman, who had just lost both her husband and her child, but forced it aside in order to focus on the crisis at hand.

"Your *son*, Lara." He spit out the obscenity. "Where have you sent him?"

Tear-filled eyes met his, but they were hard, as well. Her defiant voice held neither fear nor regret.

"Beyond your reach," she replied, her words filled with irony.

We'll see about that, he thought. But as he loomed over the forms of the grieving widow and her dead mate, he was briefly transfixed by the sight of Jor-El's corpse. Remorse threatened to unman him, as the awful weight of this particular killing settled onto his shoulders.

But he shook it off and wiped the blood from his blade. Gathering his soldiers, he moved quickly out of the observatory, leaving Lara alone with her grief.

Let her mourn for both of us, he thought. *For Krypton's future still depends on me, and if I fail, we all will suffer.*

He had to find a way to abort Jor-El's unholy enterprise. Zod raced back to the battle-scarred terrace, where he found Faora and the others staring up in confusion at the ascending starcraft. It was gaining altitude by the instant, trailing a vaporous white contrail as it flew toward space. Within moments it would achieve escape velocity and exit Krypton's atmosphere altogether.

If that occurred, the Codex would truly be beyond his reach, just as Lara had foretold.

"We have to retrieve that ship!" he shouted. "Shoot it down!" Doing so might destroy the object of his desire, but even that was better than letting it vanish into the depths of space. He would have to hope that Jor-El had shielded the Codex sufficiently.

Tor-An relayed the command to a hovering gunship. Zod watched anxiously, wishing that he could personally man the weapons controls as the craft turned and accelerated. It was almost within firing range when a coruscating particle beam blew the craft apart.

What the—?

Flaming wreckage rained down on the Citadel, forcing Zod and the others to dive for cover.

A blinding searchlight found them where they crouched. Peering up into the glare, shielding his eyes with one hand, he spied a huge hammerhead frigate descending toward them. The immense ship dwarfed his smaller fighters. A commanding voice boomed from the behemoth.

"SAPPHIRE GUARDS! DROP YOUR WEAPONS!"

Platoons of heavily armed guardsmen and women dropped from the hammerhead onto the debris-strewn terrace. Faora leapt forward, ready to fight to the death, but Zod held her back. A wise general did not waste his forces on suicidal displays of bravado.

Glancing around at what remained of his band of rebels, he realized that the game was up... for now. Surrender was the only option. Slowly he raised his hands above his head.

Peering past the searchlight, he watched grimly as the fleeing starcraft carried the Codex away. By now, the vessel was only a glowing speck high in the sky.

A prismatic distortion field enveloped it as it reached the upper atmosphere. Space-time rippled around the craft, wavering like a mirage, before it blinked out of existence, passing into another dimension.

Gone, Zod thought. *But to where?*

He offered no resistance as the guards took him into custody. Without the Codex, Krypton's future was lost. There was no point in fighting for a doomed world.

Not today.

But perhaps someday, a new battle might be waged...

CHAPTER FIVE

The walls of the Council Chamber opened like the petals of an enormous ceramic flower, revealing the night sky—and the ominous prison barge hanging just above the exposed amphitheater.

The *Black Zero* resembled a gargantuan cephalopod, with three huge tentacles hanging down from its bulbous black mantle. Each tentacle was nearly as long as the council tower was high. The ship's massive shadow fell over the arena where Zod and his top lieutenants awaited judgment.

The prisoners had been stripped of their armor and uniforms, so that they wore only stark black skinsuits. Energized shackles bound their wrists and ankles. They stood before the Council of Five, much as Jor-El had done only a few days before.

A new solon had been elevated to replace the martyred Ro-Zar. Lor-Em had taken his predecessor's place as High Eminence. His saturnine countenance offered no promise of mercy.

"General Zod," he said with stentorian gravity. "For the crimes of murder and high treason, the Council has sentenced you and your fellow insurgents to three hundred cycles of somatic reconditioning."

Gasps arose from some of the prisoners, as well as from a small party of onlookers gathered at the perimeter of the amphitheater. Zod spotted Lara among them, representing the House of El. In the tumult surrounding the aborted insurrection, Jor-El's own transgressions—including the theft of the Codex—had been hushed up in order to avoid troubling the populace any further. Even the existence of his unnatural offspring had been kept from the public. Lara herself had escaped prosecution, so far.

She was dressed formally, wearing a silken red cloak over an elegant gown—in marked contrast to the humiliating prison garb to which he had been reduced. Zod tried to catch her eye, but she steadfastly refused to look at him.

"Have you any last words?" Lor-Em demanded.

Zod regarded the Council with scorn. He alone would speak the truth, even if these craven figureheads lacked the courage to do so.

"Krypton is dying," he replied. "And you respond by clinging to *protocol*?" He scoffed at their farcical pretenses, and confronted them with the unpalatable reality they seemed unwilling to acknowledge. "The Phantom Zone is a death sentence! Who will be left to release us when our 'conditioning' is done?"

Lor-Em scowled down from his throne.

"We are discussing your punishment today, Zod. Not your release."

Zod gave this cowardly evasion all of the derision it deserved.

"You won't kill us," he said. "You wouldn't sully your hands… but you'll damn us to a black hole for eternity."

He spit upon the floor. "Jor-El was right. You're a pack of fools. Every last one of you!"

Apparently Lor-Em had heard enough. He signaled the master jailer to carry out the sentence. Cryostasis cells, composed of shimmering force fields, rose from the floor, encasing each of the conspirators in an individual sarcophagus.

Preservative gel began to fill the cells, spurring the condemned rebels to panic. Tor-An pounded uselessly at the translucent walls of his sarcophagus, while Faora screamed in rage. Nam-Ek required a larger cell than the others, but even his mammoth fists were unable to break through the rectangular force field that contained him.

Zod wheeled about to confront Lara while he still had the chance. He hadn't forgotten her role in banishing the Codex to space, nor the child to which she had obscenely given birth…

"And *you!*" he snarled. "You believe your son is safe, but—" He took a menacing step toward her, but the energized walls of his cells held him back, even when he shoved against them with all his strength and fury. "—I *will* find him! I will reclaim what you've taken from us."

She flinched at the vehemence of his words. Her hand went to her chest, which bore the emblem of the House of El.

The gel rose to choke him, stinging his eyes and throat, but he shouted over the screams of his fellow prisoners. He would not be silenced—not by the Council, and not by the accusing eyes of Jor-El's beautiful partner in crime.

"I WILL FIND HIM, LARA! *I WILL FIND HIM!*"

The gel rose past the level of his face, filling the cell completely. He clenched his jaws, stubbornly fighting the effects of the gel, but it was a lost cause. It invaded his nose and lungs. An icy numbness spread through his body, while his senses dimmed. Unable to speak any longer, he could only stare at the translucent gel obscuring his vision.

His world went dark.

His last conscious thought was that he would never again set eyes on his beloved Krypton.

Within seconds, it was over.

Lara watched as the petrifying gel congealed, revealing the rebels, frozen within their cells—as immobile as statues. They were preserved in various states of fear and anger. A look of utter malice contorted Zod's rigid features. His unmoving eyes glared balefully at his captors.

Lara shuddered. She derived little comfort from the awful spectacle that was unfolding before her. Banishing the renegades would not restore her husband or son to her, nor ease her fears regarding Kal-El's uncertain future. She could only pray that the Zone would prevent Zod from carrying out his dreadful threats. The rebel leader had already murdered the love of her life.

She didn't want him in the same universe as her son.

The next stage of the process began. With the prisoners secure in their solid-energy cells, the circular platform on which they stood lifted off from the floor, moving toward the prison barge that hung above the Council. An airlock opened in the underside of the *Black Zero*'s plated black hull. Craning her head back, Lara glimpsed the gloomy hibernation bay that was waiting for the new prisoners. Empty niches would hold the cryostasis cells, perhaps for all eternity.

Honest executions might have been kinder, Lara thought.

She shivered, and drew her crimson cloak more tightly about her. Had her own crimes been exposed, she could have easily found herself in a cell of her own, facing the same endless purgatory.

There but for the grace of Rao…

The levitating platform approached the open airlock. Robotic loading arms received the frozen prisoners. Zod was the last of the rebels to be loaded aboard the *Black Zero*. The airlock door shut, sealing the prisoners from view, while the transport platform descended to its original position on the floor of the amphitheater.

It's almost over, Lara thought. *He's almost gone.*

A ceremonial klaxon blared, proclaiming to all of Kandor that the rebels' banishment was underway. The *Black Zero* rose vertically into the sky, its lower tentacles still pointing down toward the planet. The fully loaded prison barge ascended into orbit, where the Phantom Zone projector awaited.

The projector had been devised by Jor-El. He had done so back when he was still in the Council's good graces, and acclaimed as Krypton's greatest scientist. It was a triangular, shield-shaped jumpgate kept in geosynchronous orbit above Kandor. When dormant, the gate consisted of a single satellite. But as the *Black Zero* rose toward the it, the device split into three parts, with each point of the triangle heading off in its own direction.

Lines of energy connected the points so that they formed a much larger triangle over a far greater expanse. A distortion field manifested within the triangle. Phase-shifting colors blurred together like the prismatic optics of a soap bubble. Space-time rippled and fractured, forming a gateway to another plane of reality.

The Phantom Zone.

The *Black Zero* rose into the distortion field, threading the needle between the points of the triangle. The distortion effect washed over the ship. Solid matter particularized before vanishing into the two-dimensional plane of the portal. Within moments the entire ship had vanished, removed from the universe, taking its condemned cargo with it.

The three points of the projector converged once again, closing the gateway as the device powered down. The shield-shaped satellite floated silently in orbit once again.

The klaxon sounded again, signaling the end of the ritual. In theory, every exile was to be released— eventually—after cycles of solitude and subliminal conditioning had curbed their antisocial tendencies. But Lara knew this was unlikely to happen before Krypton perished. Zod had been right about that at least. He and his people had been condemned to the Zone for all time.

Or so Lara prayed.

CHAPTER SIX

Lara lingered in the Citadel's armory, where Jor-El's battle-scarred armor now hung in tribute to his memory. Dents, scratches, and scorch marks testified to his last, heroic efforts on behalf of their departed child. She intended to carry the memory of his sacrifice for as long a time as remained to her. It struck her as cosmically unjust that this tribute—along with the rest of Krypton—would soon be ashes.

It's not fair, she thought. *We should have grown old together.*

Her finger traced the crest embossed upon the damaged breastplate. Although scarred, the sinuous glyph was still legible, reminding her of Kal-El's heritage—and his future beyond the stars.

Hope, she thought. *As long as he lives, there is always hope.*

She had lost her ability to track her son's starcraft once its phantom drives had activated. The drives warped both space and time, taking the tiny ship beyond the scope of her instruments. By the time it reached its destination on the other side of the galaxy, millennia would have passed from her perspective.

That ice age she had glimpsed would be ancient history long before Kal-El arrived at his new home. And those primitive savages should have progressed considerably.

Will they accept you, my son… she wondered. *Or will you always be alone?*

Another tremor shook the Citadel, reminding her that her own time was short. She turned away from the armory and sought out the upper terrace. She had draped a fur-lined cloak over her shoulders, despite the heat of the evening. Lara found that she was often cold these days, regardless of the temperature. Grief and solitude brought little warmth.

She stepped out onto the terrace, which had also been marked by the battle against Zod and his terrorists. Kelor had started to coordinate the necessary repairs, but Lara had not seen the point. The damage inflicted by the war was nothing compared to what was upon them now.

An apocalyptic vista stretched as far as the eye could see as she gazed out upon the end of her world. Volcanic eruptions, spewing radioactive green magma, tore apart the landscape. Kandor's distant towers toppled as the capital was flattened by never-ending quakes. A pyroclastic cloud large enough to engulf an entire city surged across the veldt, setting the grasslands ablaze. Panicked wildlife stampeded for their lives, but there was nowhere to run—all of Krypton was ripped asunder by cataclysmic convulsions.

Herds of frantic Rondors tumbled headlong into gaping chasms that cracked open the surface of the planet. Desperate birds took flight, only to burst into flame as blasts of super-heated air ignited their wings. Artificial ponds and reservoirs boiled over, sending scalding plumes of steam high into the dark night sky. Lara watched stoically as the devastation spread toward the Citadel, which was already being rocked to its foundations.

Bioengineered masonry that had withstood the passage of centuries broke away and tumbled down the sides of crumbling granite cliffs. Avalanches spilled havoc and death on the burning natural preserve below. Clouds of ash and smoke blotted out the moons' light.

"*Lady Lara.*" Kelor joined her on the terrace. "*Shouldn't you find refuge?*"

Lara valued the robot's concern, but she shook her head sadly.

"There is no refuge, Kelor," she said, then she looked out again. "Jor-El was right. This is the end." She turned her gaze upward, away from the catastrophe, toward the stars that lay beyond the storm. Her words were a prayer.

"Build a better world than ours, Kal."

A nuclear volcano, eradicating Kandor in an instant, sent a tidal wave of heat and sound screaming toward the Citadel, which was instantly reduced to atoms by the ferocious blast. No eyes survived to witness the destruction.

Not a single relic endured.

Krypton itself soon followed. Vast tectonic plates buckled, venting mountainous sheets of glowing ejecta into the upper atmosphere and beyond. Continents crumbled and seas boiled over, as the planet's contaminated core built to a critical mass. A series of global detonations overcame the tremendous gravity that held the planet together.

And then Krypton blew apart in a final, apocalyptic paroxysm that could be seen from light-years away.

Doomsday had come.

The blast-wave from the planet's destruction extended out into the surrounding solar system. What remained of the atmosphere spread in all directions, buffeting the Phantom Zone projector and sending it spinning end over end. Krypton's moons were knocked loose from their orbits, becoming cosmic orphans. Lifeless satellites without a world to call their own.

Sparks flared from the projector. Space-time rippled around it.

Light-years and millennia of relativistic time away, a forgotten starcraft re-entered the universe.

Following a preprogrammed course, it sped past a large ringed gas giant toward the local system's inner planets, which were warmed by the radiance of a shining yellow star. Although many times smaller than Rao, the young sun burned much hotter. It was still in the prime of its existence, which would last for another five billion years or so.

The rocketing vessel passed through an asteroid belt, successfully avoiding any collisions with the orbiting space debris. Then it arrived at the third planet from the sun—a medium-sized blue world distinguished by two ice caps, expansive oceans, and several continents, as well as an atmosphere conducive to organic life.

Electromagnetic signals, radiating from the planet's surface, indicated the presence of a rudimentary degree of technology.

The planet's gravitational pull was significantly lighter than Krypton's, but proved sufficient to capture the approaching starcraft. Ceramic heat shields boiled away as the ship entered the atmosphere, blazing through the upper reaches like a falling star.

It hurtled above a sizable landmass—at present enveloped in darkness—located in the planet's northern hemisphere, then descended toward the wide central plains found in the mid-western region of the continent.

Elements of the terrain below registered on the craft's sensors as it searched for a suitable landing site. Winding rivers of fresh water cut through vast stretches of undulating prairies. Population centers dotted the surface. Primitive radar transmissions bounced off the ship's protective plating.

The craft slowed as it dropped lower in the night sky. The light of a single moon shone down on fields of cultivated plants. The rush of its passage spun the sails of a modest wooden windmill.

Finally the capsule came in for a landing, bearing an alien gift...

CHAPTER SEVEN

THIRTY-THREE YEARS LATER

Surging waves washed over the ice-covered rails of the *Debbie Sue,* a two-hundred-foot fishing boat rolling atop the frigid waters of the Bering Sea, just off the coast of Alaska.

Captain Ivar Heraldson watched from the wheelhouse as the soaked deckhands scrambled atop the slippery deck below, racing the fading daylight as they hauled heavy metal cages, laden with captured crabs, onto the deck. It was October, king crab season, which meant that they only had four or five hours of daylight this far north.

Crabbers wearing wet-weather gear and rubber boots defied biting winds to hook the pots to a sturdy metal crane, which then swung the cages over the deck, where hundreds of pounds of crustaceans were dumped onto the sorting table. Rider crabs clung to the sides of the cages.

Heraldson kept a close eye on the proceedings. Theirs was a dangerous vocation, and a moment's carelessness—or just cussed back luck—could lead to injury or death. The captain had lost men to drowning and hypothermia, and had seen skulls fractured by swinging hooks or cages. Manipulating several hundred pounds of cage and crabs was difficult enough. Throw in choppy seas, heavy winds, lack of sleep, and an icy deck littered with ropes, coils, buoys, and other hazards, and you had a recipe for disaster.

It was estimated that at least one man a week was killed every season. Heraldson sometimes marveled that the number wasn't higher.

At the moment, however, everything seemed to going smoothly, despite the massive swells that were tossing the *Debbie Sue* about. Most of his crew consisted of veterans who knew the ropes well enough.

Then his wary eyes sought out the sole exception.

A greenhorn kid who had joined the crew in Dutch Harbor stood off to one side, coiling the buoy lines while the more experienced crewmen hauled in the pots. The hood of his insulated rain slicker partially obscured his face, but Heraldson glimpsed a rugged young face hidden behind a scruffy black beard. The youngster's thoughtful blue eyes took in the hectic activity on deck. As a greenhorn, he was entitled to a smaller share of the profits, yet so far he had handled the long hours, backbreaking work, hellish conditions, and merciless hazing without complaint.

Which was more than could be said of plenty of first-time crabbers who found the job more than they could handle. Heraldson had been impressed by the young man's strength and endurance. The kid didn't even seem to mind the cold.

A wrenching noise yanked the captain's attention over to the crane, which was swinging another pot over the rail. The jarring din came from the hydraulic winch, where a tangled rope had caught. Smoke rose from the straining block and, with a sound like a cannon going off, the line snapped abruptly, sending more than a thousand pounds of cage and crab plummeting toward the oblivious greenhorn. Directly below, the young man was staring off into space, as though his thoughts were miles away. He was only a heartbeat away from being flattened.

At the last possible moment the boat's deckboss—a burly fisherman named Byrne—shoved the greenhorn out the way. The loose pot crashed onto the deck. Frantic crabs scrambled inside the cage, climbing over each other as they sought a way out. Heraldson let out a sigh of relief. For a moment there, he'd thought the greenhorn was a goner.

"Watch it, dumbass!" Byrne barked. "Keep your eyes open or you're gonna get squashed!"

The greenhorn accepted the rebuke. His deep voice held a hint of the Midwest.

"Sorry."

"Where the hell'd they find you anyway?" Byrne stormed off, shaking his head. The crew went back to work, scrambling to salvage the haul from the fallen cage. Crab season was getting shorter ever year, and they couldn't take time off just because a rookie almost got killed. Even the greenhorn returned to coiling the lines, seemingly unshaken by his near brush with death.

Didn't he realize how close a call that had been?

The captain contemplated the young man, who radiated a quiet confidence that belied his age and inexperience. Not for the first time, he wondered what had possessed him to sign on a green young kid who never talked about his past. Byrne was right for questioning why the kid was on the boat in the first place.

Where had he come from anyway?

MAY, 1981

"Martha Kent?"

The nurse escorted Martha and her husband into the examination room. It was a busy day at the Smallville pediatrics clinic, and the waiting room was packed. An anxious-looking brunette in her late twenties, Martha cradled her adopted son in her arms. The baby looked like any other infant. He bawled noisily.

"He won't stop crying," Martha said apologetically.

The nurse just shrugged. She was surely used to crying children.

"The doctor will be right in," she said.

Waiting tensely in the doctor's office, Martha hoped they weren't making an awful mistake. She and Jonathan had been reluctant to let anyone examine little Clark, but his nonstop crying had left them no choice. Besides the fact that neither of them was getting any sleep, she couldn't help worrying that there might be something seriously wrong.

What do we really know about him? she wondered for what seemed like the millionth time. *Or what he needs to survive?*

After a few minutes, Dr. Whitaker joined them in the office. The avuncular silver-haired pediatrician was a fixture in the Kents' small rural community. Bifocals rested upon his nose as a concession to his aging eyes. He had delivered most of the babies of the Smallville, with the notable exception of Clark.

He took the wailing infant from Martha and placed him gently on the examination table. Martha gripped Jonathan's hand as the doctor conducted a routine inspection, checking out his heart, lungs, and reflexes. Peering into Clark's throat and ears, he didn't appear to find anything alarming.

"It's colic," he pronounced. "Newborns have a built-in mechanism for tuning out sights and sounds. When that mechanism falls away, some babies become overwhelmed. Clark's probably just more sensitive than most."

But how sensitive? Martha fretted.

Dr. Whitaker produced a portable electronic device with a cord that was attached to a small earplug. He sterilized Clark's ear with a cloth wipe, then inserted the tip of the probe into it.

"This is a test to measure hearing response," he explained. "Don't worry, it's completely painless—lots of babies sleep through the procedure."

Jonathan Kent frowned. His tanned, weathered features bespoke a life spent working outdoors. A few years older than his wife, he eyed the test apprehensively.

"I'm not sure that's a good—" he began.

The doctor flicked a switch, activating the apparatus, which sent an acoustic signal into the baby's ear. In theory, the device would measure the ear's response to the sounds.

But not Clark.

The baby's screams increased in volume. A deafening shriek shattered every window in the office—and beyond. Out in the waiting room, a gumball machine cracked open, spilling candy-colored spheres onto the floor. The nurse's coffee mug came apart in her hand. An aquarium full of colorful fish exploded, flooding the reception area. Staff and patients rushed to rescue the gasping fish, which were tossed into paper cups filled with tap water. Broken glass crunched beneath their feet.

Car alarms went off outside. Storefront windows up and down Main Street shattered and spilled onto sidewalks. Windshields disintegrated into cubes of safety glass. The town's one traffic light exploded in a shower of sparks.

I was afraid of this, Martha thought. *We should have known better.*

She cautiously uncovered her ears, which nevertheless kept on ringing. Dr. Whitaker stared speechlessly at little Clark. His glasses were askew, the lenses cracked. But the baby was smiling now, as if entertained by all the commotion.

Martha shared a look with her husband, who nodded in response. Before the doctor could collect his wits— or ask any unwanted questions—they reclaimed their son and hustled him out of the doctor's office. Martha cringed at the mess in the waiting room, but didn't stop to talk to the nurse or receptionist, who were busy coping with the chaotic aftermath of the event.

The Kents hurried out onto Main Street, where they found even more broken glass and other property damage.

Dear Lord, Martha thought. *Did Clark do all this, just by crying?*

The baby gurgled happily in her arms.

The waves were higher, the weather rougher, but the *Debbie Sue* hadn't made her quota yet, so there was still work to be done. Down on the icy deck, the men were launching empty pots, baited with herring, into the sea. They leaned precariously over the rails as the freezing wind and spray pelted their faces.

Floating buoys marked the location of the pots.

"Mayday!" The radio in the wheelhouse squealed into life. *"This is the* Bright Aurora *calling all ships in the vicinity. We've had an explosion and the platform is on fire. Numerous survivors are in the water!"*

Captain Heraldson scowled. The *Bright Aurora* was an offshore oil rig only a few nautical miles away. An explosion at the massive platform was seriously bad news. He grabbed a mike and shouted to his men over the boat's loud hailer.

"Lock it up! Just got a distress call from a rig due west of us."

The emergency was going to cost them a day's fishing, maybe more, but Heraldson didn't hesitate. An oil platform like the *Bright Aurora* could house more than two hundred souls, all of whom might be in mortal danger. The code of the sea—and common sense—demanded that he respond to their SOS.

He hoped it wasn't already too late.

To their credit, his crew battened down the cages and gear in record time. Heraldson opened up the throttle, pushing the *Debbie Sue* to her limits as the boat ploughed through the waves. Locating the burning rig wasn't a challenge—the smoke and flames were soon visible from miles away. And it was as bad as he had feared.

The enormous drilling platform, which loomed hundreds of feet above the surging waves, was engulfed in flames. With its towering derrick and one-hundred-and-fifty-foot tall cranes, the imperiled platform resembled a large industrial factory on fire, which was essentially the case.

Terrified oil workers could be seen dashing around the rig's various decks, fleeing the flames and explosions. Some had no choice but to leap from great heights into the frigid water, taking their chances with the sea rather than facing the blazing inferno. Lifeboats bobbed on the whitecaps, fishing survivors out of the oily waters. Gargantuan fireballs blossomed on the upper levels of the platform.

The *Debbie Sue* joined a flotilla of boats coming to assist in the rescue efforts. Heraldson spotted several of his competitors in the choppy waters around them. Fishing crews hurried to pluck burned and drowning roughnecks from the sea. Coast Guard rescue 'copters buzzed overhead, braving the rising smoke and flames. Turning the wheelhouse over to Byrne, the captain joined his own crew at the rail, searching the waters for more survivors.

Along with the rest of the men, the young greenhorn stared in horror at the disaster. Strong winds carried the choking odor of burning gas and oil. Heraldson covered his mouth and nose.

"Dispatcher says there's still men trapped inside," he informed the others. He doubted that anything could be done for those poor bastards, but maybe he and his crew could still rescue the desperate souls who had made it into the sea. He struggled to spot any survivors amidst the foaming swells. "Greenhorn, go fetch my binoculars!"

The kid failed to acknowledge the order. Heraldson turned irritably, only to discover that the youth was nowhere to be seen. A discarded orange slicker lay atop the deck.

What the devil?

CHAPTER EIGHT

The violent sea thrashed the underside of the platform. A thirty-foot wave crashed against one of the massive steel legs supporting the rig. Churning white water briefly hid the rusty metal spider deck that lay below the main complex, just above the surface, but when the wave subsided, a solitary figure was left clinging to the leg.

Clark dug his bare fingers into solid steel. Icy water streamed from his dark hair and beard. The wave had done him a favor, carrying him up out of the water and onto the platform. Despite swimming through the Arctic waters, he wasn't even shivering. Cold didn't bother him the way it did other people.

Neither did fire.

He took a second to get his bearings. The deck modules containing the control rooms and living quarters were still levels above him. His eyes probed the sprawling metal structures, seeing beyond the painted steel. He heard men screaming and cursing and praying. Everything smelled of gas and smoke.

There was no time to lose.

He tensed his muscles, and then hurled himself

upward at the module above. He smashed through the floor of the lower deck, exploding into a smoke-filled corridor. Emergency lights flickered weakly. Blaring sirens competed with the ferocious roar of a rampaging fire. Random explosions rocked the floor. Straining girders moaned in agony. The air reeked of gasoline.

The enclosed deck was a dark, claustrophobic maze. An ordinary man might have found it impossible to navigate, but Clark ran through walls of flame without hesitation, unaffected by the scorching heat. Heavy steel bulkheads got in his way and he barreled through them as though they were made of balsa wood.

The fire was spreading rapidly, peeling the paint of the walls and blocking fire exits. Walls and doors were too hot to touch, at least for most people.

Clark wasn't most people.

Bursting into the smoke-filled hallway, he found a handful of desperate engineers and roughnecks trying to make their way to safety. Soot blackened the men's faces. They clutched rags to their mouths, but were coughing and choking anyway. Burns, bruises, and broken limbs slowed down some of them, so they were being helped along by their equally frightened comrades.

Clark could hear their hearts pounding in fear.

A flashlight shone in his face.

"Are there any others?" he asked.

The men were too intent on escaping to question his presence.

"Forget 'em!" a limping hardhat shouted. Guilt and anguish contorted his sooty face. "They're dead!"

Clark listened harder. He heard what the other men couldn't. An explosion knocked out the lights, plunging the hallway into darkness.

"No," he said. "They're not."

His headlong tear through the module had ripped open an escape path for the men to follow. A flashlight probed a busted bulkhead. Once they started along the cleared route, Clark trusted them to find their way to the lifeboats or helipad. There were others who needed him more now.

Without another word, he re-entered the smoky blackness, following the almost inaudible cries of those still trapped inside the burning module. His route took him rapidly through the drilling chamber at the center of the platform. The vertical drill string, suspended from the derrick, stabbed down into the erupting well. A high-pressure stream of oil gushed from a ruptured pipe.

Clark rushed through the stream, dousing himself in the flammable liquid. Flames ignited the oil, setting Clark ablaze. He kept on running, covered in flames, as his clothes burned away—but not his hair or skin.

Fire and smoke filled the pitch-black corridor outside the mess hall and galley. A red-hot fire door closed off the entrance to the galley. Clark's eyes narrowed in concentration as he peered past the flames that were still engulfing him. His vision shifted along the electromagnetic spectrum so that he could see through the steel walls and into the chamber beyond.

Dozens of men, trapped inside, appeared to him as living X-rays. Even over the roar of the flames and the groaning metal, he could hear the despair as they wept and begged for their lives. Others made their final farewells to loved ones they never expected to see or hold again.

Clark figured differently.

He ripped the door off its hinges with his bare hands and tossed it aside. He rushed into the galley, eliciting startled gasps from the men. They stared at him with varying combinations of shock and wonder. A few backed away fearfully, and Clark realized how he appeared to them—like a fiery angel, burning brightly.

"What *are* you?" a man asked.

Clark didn't have any good answer for him. Ignoring the question, he raced across the mess hall and hammered a wall with his fists, popping it free like the door of a bank vault. Open air showed on the opposite side of the breached surface, offering a way out.

"Go!" Clark bellowed, and he stepped aside to let the men through.

Diminished flames danced upon his bare skin as he hustled them out onto a swaying metal catwalk, hundreds of feet above the frothing sea. An exterior stairway led to the main deck and helipad. Clark was relieved to see that the landing area was still relatively free of flames. Scanning the sky, he spotted a Coast Guard helicopter hovering nearby. He waved his arms above his head to get its pilot's attention. The endangered roughnecks jumped and shouted as well. The 'copter was their best shot at getting away from the burning rig.

The chopper pilot spotted them. Clark heard the pilot barking into his headset.

"I've got some guys on the helipad!" he said. "I'm gonna try for them!"

Braving the smoke and flames, the chopper came in for a landing. The wash from the 'copter's spinning rotors temporarily dispelled the choking smoke. Clark shouted above the noise as he herded the men into the chopper.

"Go, go, *GO!*"

More explosions erupted from the engine rooms. The entire rig seemed on the verge of collapse. The drilling derrick, towering over a hundred feet above the main deck, listed to one side as its overheated steel trusses began to give. It leaned precariously over the helipad, threatening to crash down on the 'copter even as the last of the men clambered aboard.

In the cockpit, the pilot fought the control stick, trying to keep the chopper level amidst the explosions. The 'copter tilted sideways, almost dumping the rescued roughnecks back onto the deck. A hardhat called out to Clark, who was still standing on the rig, clothed in flames and smoke. He stretched out his hand to rescue his rescuer.

But an instant later Clark was gone. Dashing away from the helipad, he threw himself against the toppling derrick. He pushed back against the tower, fighting gravity and thousands of pounds of red-hot steel. Straining with all his might, he managed to halt the derrick's momentum long enough for the chopper pilot to guide his craft out of danger.

Unable to hold the structure up any longer, Clark rode it down as it slammed into the helipad with the force of a giant's hammer. The seismic impact in turn set off a volcanic explosion that sent the entire platform crashing into the sea, taking him with it.

Countless tons of steel and concrete drove him into the water, through thousands of gallons of burning oil. The flames licking his body, however, were doused as the sea swallowed him.

He sank beneath the waves. Compared to the fiery pandemonium above, it was surprisingly cool and tranquil down below. The curtain of flames spreading across the surface felt very remote and far away, almost as though they belonged to a different universe. Stunned, Clark basked for a moment in the peace and quiet. He found it tempting to just stop fighting, stop searching, and vanish into the endless depths.

Then a whalesong broke the silence of the deep. Complex vocalizations, punctuated by clicks, echoed beneath the sea. Three humpback whales, their sleek bodies gliding gracefully through the water, converged on him. The whales circled him in fascination, as though sensing something different about him.

The largest one nudged Clark with his snout and began pushing him toward the surface. He floated among the gigantic mammals, even as his mind drifted backward...

SEPTEMBER, 1988

"Clark? Are you listening, Clark?"

It was the first day of school at Weisinger Primary. Ms. Rampling, Clark's homeroom teacher, approached the boy's desk while his classmates looked on.

"I asked if you could tell me who first settled in Kansas."

Only nine years old and small for his age, Clark cowered at his desk. Wide blue eyes stared in horror at the thirtyish woman who regarded the mute child with confusion.

"Are you all right, Clark?" she asked.

The other children giggled at his discomfort. They couldn't see what he saw—the inside of Ms. Whitaker. The teacher's skin and clothes had gone transparent, revealing the bones, organs, and arteries beneath. He could see the blood coursing through her veins, watch her heart beat rhythmically. Her lungs expanded and contracted like fleshy balloons. Chewed-up food made its way through her digestive tract. She looked like the "visible man" model he'd seen in the Sears catalog, but life-sized and pulsing with animation. Exposed muscles, resembling strips of raw meat, covered her bones. Eyeballs rolled in the sockets of her skull.

He looked away from her, only to discover that his

classmates had turned into living anatomy lessons as well. Even worse, he could hear all of their heartbeats, which were pounding like kettledrums—and growing louder by the second.

Clark threw his hands over his ears, but it didn't do any good. He could hear *everything*. Even the ticking of the wall clock sounded like a jackhammer going off right in his ears.

It was unbearable.

Unable to stand it any longer, he shoved his chair back and jumped to his feet. The other children laughed thunderously, sounding like a million howling coyotes, and he ran in terror from the classroom.

"Clark! Come back here!" Ms. Whitaker called.

The skinless teacher chased him down the hallway, but Clark didn't slow down. His own heart was racing in panic. He didn't know what was happening to him. There was something wrong with his eyes—the world kept shifting in colors and degrees of perception. One minute, people were glowing red pockets of heat. The next, they were walking skeletons.

Steam pipes, hissing like giant rattlesnakes, glowed behind solid walls, which turned clear as glass, revealing the playground and sidewalks outside the school. He could see all the way across Smallville...

He tried to hide from the world in a janitor's closet. Huddling among the mops and brooms, he locked the door from the inside right before Ms. Whitaker caught up with him. She knocked on it loudly enough to make him cover his ears again. Her knuckles rapped against the unyielding wood. It sounded like a tractor ramming into a barn, over and over again.

"Clark!" she called, her voice raised. "Come out of there!"

She tried the knob, wiggling it noisily.

No! Clark shouted inwardly. *Leave me alone!*

Panicky eyes turned red as hot coals. Incandescent beams shot from his pupils to the knob, raising its temperature. Through the door, Clark saw his teacher yelp and yank her hand away. She stared in shock at her scorched fingers, then backed away from the closet.

Ms. Whitaker ran to find the principal.

For a time, Clark had the closet to himself, but its cramped confines provided little refuge from the clamorous world outside, which continued to bear down upon his overwhelmed senses. His hands still over his ears, he squatted in a corner, squeezing his eyes shut as tightly as he could. There was too much to see, hear, smell—and all of it louder or more intense than he could possibly handle. It was as though someone had turned up the volume on the entire world.

Make it stop! he thought frantically. *Please!*

The booming racket made it hard to pick out individual sounds, but eventually, after what felt like forever, a familiar voice broke through the din. He heard his mother rushing down the hall.

"Clark, it's Mom," she said. "I'm here." She didn't shout. She knew she didn't have to.

A crowd of teachers and students, gathered outside, parted to let her through. She knelt in front of the door. Her gentle voice penetrated the fragile wood that stood between them.

"Will you open the door?" she asked.

Clark hesitated, afraid to let in the scary world. He tried to focus on just his mother's voice, but he could hear every other word being whispered out in the hallway. His classmates' voices ganged up on him.

"He's such a freak. He's always doing stuff like this."

"His parents won't even let him play with other kids."

The hurtful words were almost worse than the avalanche of noise. Only his mother's voice, soft and soothing, provided any comfort.

"Clark, please, sweetie. I can't help you if you won't let me in."

His longing for his mother helped him overcome his fear, at least a little. He slowly cracked the door open. His heart sank as he saw through her skin, too. All he could recognize was her caring brown eyes.

Tears filled his own.

"The world's too big, Mom."

She nodded, understanding.

"Then make it small."

"I can't!"

"Yes, you *can*," she promised. "Just focus on my voice. Pretend it's an island. Can you see it? Out in the ocean?"

He closed his eyes and tried to do as his mother said. It was hard, with all those living skeletons screaming at him from all directions, but he forced himself to imagine an island, far out in the water, where strange horned beasts roamed and giant dragonflies buzzed beneath a huge red sun. There was something oddly familiar about it.

"I can see it…"

His mother's voice encouraged him.

"Then swim toward it."

He visualized himself swimming out to the fantastic place, leaving all the jarring sights and sounds of the world behind. His own heart slowly settled, and the overpowering din began to fade away. He opened his eyes cautiously, ready to squeeze them shut again if he saw too much. But, to his relief, his mother looked more like Mom at last. Tanned skin covered her face just like it was supposed to. The shifting colors stabilized, going back to normal. The world became reassuringly solid again. The volume got turned down.

It's over, he realized. *For now.*

He rushed out of the closet, into his mother's arms. She held him tightly as he sobbed on her shoulder. Even though he was better, he couldn't forget what had just happened. Or what the other kids had said.

"What's wrong with me, Mom?"

CHAPTER NINE

Clark awoke underwater, surrounded by whales. He found himself drifting naked beneath the sea, his clothes having been burned away by the inferno. The humpbacks nudged him toward the surface, their lilting songs echoing in his ears. They, at least, seemed to want him to keep going.

Fair enough, he thought.

He shook the cobwebs from his mind, and poked his head above the waves. The burning platform was now several miles away, spewing clouds of black smoke into the sky. Eavesdropping on the Coast Guard and other first responders, he got the impression that the worst was over. Everybody who could have been evacuated from the collapsed platform had been. Numerous survivors, many seriously injured, had been fished from the water and were now receiving medical care. All that was left was the cleanup—and mourning the dead.

I couldn't save everyone, he realized. *But I made a difference.*

Bobbing upon the waves, he knew that he couldn't return to the *Debbie Sue*. There would be too many questions he couldn't begin to answer, questions that had haunted him his entire life. The words of that dumbstruck roughneck, back in the galley, echoed in his memory.

"*What* are *you?*"

Clark wished he knew.

Glancing around, his extraordinary vision located a small Aleutian island only a few nautical miles away. He swam toward it, speeding through the water even faster than his cetacean rescuers. Powerful arms and legs carried him through rough waters that would have defeated even an Olympic swimmer. Hypothermia wasn't an issue.

His bare body was still steaming as he emerged from the sea onto a rocky shore populated by a large group of sea lions. The barking mammals were the only witnesses to his arrival. A disturbing thought occurred to Clark and his hand went to his chest, where a spiky black key hung on a chain around his neck. The unusual pendant had survived the fire that had torched the rest of his clothes.

Good, Clark thought. *I didn't lose it.*

A small fishing village occupied the island. A cannery dominated the remote community, which also boasted a post office, general store, and church. Painted wooden structures fought a losing battle against the elements. Boats were docked at the pier. Moving stealthily, Clark spotted clothes hanging on a line outside a weathered log cabin. A pair of muddy boots rested on a stoop.

Sorry, friend, he thought as he furtively helped himself. He felt bad about stealing, but what else was he to do? Walking around naked would attract too much attention. Crouching behind a rusty dumpster, he pulled on a flannel shirt and jeans. To his relief, the stolen clothes and boots fit, more or less. He tucked the black metal spike beneath his collar.

As he emerged from behind the dumpster, a bright orange school bus rolled down a gravel road nearby. Rowdy kids made faces at him through the windows. The bus looked just like the ones he'd ridden back when he was a kid in Smallville.

OCTOBER, 1992

Thirteen years old, Clark rode in the back of the bus as it rumbled down the interstate. Rain pelted the windows and highway. The Red Hot Chili Peppers leaked from a classmate's Sony Discman. Another kid was playing *Mortal Kombat* on his Sega Game Gear.

Clark was just trying to mind his own business, although he was acutely aware of the presence of Lana Lang across from him. He'd had a crush on the pretty girl for as long as he could remember, but he'd never had the nerve to do anything about it. For all he knew, she thought he was weird—like everybody else did.

"I can't see Favre ever dominating like Majkowski," Pete Ross argued in the seat ahead of Clark. The big redhead wasn't talking to him, of course. "The guy fumbled *four* times against the Bengals."

Pete's buddy, Whitney Fordham, looked back over the seat at Clark. A smirk betrayed his ugly intentions.

"Hey, ass-wipe, what do you think?"

Clark's heart sank. He'd been hoping that Pete and Whitney would leave him alone for once. He stared out the window and tried to ignore them, not that that had ever helped before. Up ahead, just few minutes away, a bridge spanned the flooding Arkansas River, which meant that the bus still had a ways to go.

Just my luck, he thought glumly.

To his surprise, Lana came to his defense.

"Leave him alone, Pete."

"What are you, his *girlfriend*?" Peter asked with a sneer. He leaned back over the seat to get in Clark's face. "I wanna hear what ass-wipe thinks."

"I don't really follow football," Clark mumbled.

That wasn't good enough for Pete.

"What *do* you follow, dick-splash?"

An explosive bang, coming from beneath the bus, distracted everyone. Clark was momentarily relieved, until he realized that the bus had blown a tire. It hydroplaned across the wet highway, swerving toward oncoming traffic. The panicked driver yanked hard on the wheel and the bus swung to the left, straight into the bridge's safety rail. Teenaged passengers screamed as the bus crashed through the rail and plunged down into the frothing river many feet below.

The driver and kids were thrown from their seats even before the bus hit the water. Pandemonium erupted aboard the sinking vehicle as everyone shouted and scrambled frantically, in fear of their lives. They clambered over one another to get to the exits.

Freezing water flooded the interior of the bus, adding to the chaos and desperation. Loose backpacks and injured students clogged the aisle.

Only Clark wasn't afraid—at least not for himself. He turned his gaze toward the rear of the bus, which was sinking faster than the front. Lana was trapped in her seat, neck-deep in the water. Blood streamed from a nasty gash on her forehead. She gasped fearfully as the water rose toward her mouth.

And she wasn't the only one in danger.

Clark knew what he had to do. He swam through the gushing deluge to the submerged rear exit, and kicked it open. More water invaded the bus, but he pushed against the current, diving headfirst into the river outside. The muddy water was dark and agitated, but he could still see what he was doing.

He grabbed onto the bus and kicked.

Lana thrashed wildly as the water rose past her mouth, her nose, and her head. She held her breath to keep from drowning. The freezing water numbed her body. She was running out of air...

And then, miraculously, the water began to recede. Within seconds, it sank beneath her head and she gasped hungrily for air. Confused, she looked to the rear of the bus—where she saw Clark framed in the rear doorway. Straining, his face a mask of concentrated effort, he pushed the bus up and onto the river bank. Torrents of water, escaping the bus, spilled past him.

Lana's eyes widened.

"How?"

Clark couldn't have explained if he'd wanted to. Shifting position, he braced himself against the back of the bus and shoved it further ashore. A choking noise caught his attention and he glanced back at the murky river. His eyes narrowed in concentration.

Hang on, he thought. *I'll be right there.*

Letting go of the beached vehicle, he dove back into the raging river.

He saw Lana watching as he disappeared beneath the waves. Along with the other kids, she'd managed to extricate herself from the bus and stumbled out onto the shore. Wind and rain buffeted her, making it hard to see, but she scrambled to the river's edge. Anxious eyes searched the water.

Clark saw her staring when he climbed out of the river, carrying Pete in his arms. The bully—who must have been washed out of the bus at some point—was unconscious, but he was still breathing.

Emergency sirens signaled approaching rescuers, but it was the shocked expression on Lana's face that concerned him the most. She backed away from him apprehensively.

How on earth was he going to explain this?

"My son told me what Clark did."

Clark sat on a swing outside the Kent family farmhouse. It was late afternoon and it was already starting to get dark. Barns and silos rose behind him. A windmill turned in the autumn breeze. Fields of corn waited to be harvested. Even though he was outdoors, he could easily see and hear his parents talking with Mrs. Ross in the living room.

Pete's mom sounded pretty worked up.

"Pete was under an enormous amount of stress, Helen," Jonathan Kent said. "Everyone was. I'm sure what he thought he saw—"

"—was an act of God, Jonathan." She had her arm around Pete, who was more subdued than usual. He stared at the floor, not speaking. "This was *Providence*."

Martha Kent refilled a coffee cup.

"I think you're blowing it a little out of proportion." she said calmly.

"No, I'm not," Mrs. Ross insisted. "Lana saw it, too. And the Fordham boy. And this isn't the first time Clark has done something like this."

He flinched at her strident tone. He didn't want to listen anymore.

Clark was long gone by the time the swing stopped swinging.

His father found him out by the cornfields, not long after their visitors had left. Clark was seated on the open tailgate of a pickup truck. He braced himself for another lecture.

"I just wanted to help," he said defensively.

"I know you did," his dad said. "But we talked about this. You *have* to keep this side of yourself a secret."

"Was I just supposed to let them die?"

His father hesitated before answering. His face wrestled with conflicting emotions.

"Maybe."

Clark stared at him in surprise. He couldn't mean that, could he?

"There's more at stake here than our lives," Jonathan said, trying to explain, "or the lives of those around us. When the world finds out what you can do, it's going to *change* everything. Our beliefs, our notions of what it means to be human. Everything." He shook his head solemnly. "You saw how Pete's mom reacted. She was scared, Clark."

Clark didn't understand. He had saved Pete's life. Her son would have drowned if not for him. She should have been grateful that he could do what he could.

"Why?"

"People are afraid of what they don't understand," his father said.

He could see that. Clark didn't understand his own abilities either, and that scared the heck out of him. He'd spent his entire life trying to figure out what made him different from everyone else.

"But is she right?" he asked. "Did God do this to me?"

Jonathan paused, biting his tongue. His jaw tensed from the effort of keeping silent. Clark could tell he was holding something back.

"Tell me," he pleaded.

The expression on his father's face showed that he had come to a decision. He nodded gravely, and led Clark to the old threshing barn out back. The modest, dilapidated structure had long ago been rendered obsolete by a bigger barn that could handle the new combine. His parents had declared the smaller barn off limits years ago, "for safety reasons," they said. Clark had always respected their wishes.

Maybe that had been a mistake.

Night was falling, cloaking the old barn in darkness. Rusty metal doors guarded the storm cellar that lay beneath. At his dad's request, Clark threw open the heavy doors. Jonathan stepped forward and shone a flashlight into the murky cellar.

The beam exposed a large, roundish object, partially covered by a dusty tarp. Clark gaped at the oddly organic looking curves of the object, which resembled no piece of farm equipment he had ever seen. What was this buried secret, and what did it have to do with him?

He cast a puzzled glance at his dad as they descended into the cellar. Jonathan Kent yanked off the tarp, exposing... what?

The object, which was the size of a tractor, looked like a cross between a space capsule and a piece of abstract art. An empty cavity rested inside a bulbous shell molded out of a slick, pearly material. The capsule's outer plates were scorched and blackened, as though they'd been through a crash landing—or been burned in a fire.

"We found you in this," Jonathan explained. "At first we thought maybe the Soviets sent it up. We were sure the government was going to show up at our doorstep." His gaze turned inward, as though he was looking back through time. "But no one ever came."

Clark tried to process what he was seeing and hearing. It was almost more than he could take in.

His parents *found* him?

In a *spaceship*?

What does that mean? he wondered. *Where* did *I come from?*

Turning away from the capsule, Jonathan guided Clark to a work area that had been set up at the back of the cellar. He shined the flashlight beam over the wall above the workbench. Dozens of Xeroxed articles and newspaper clippings were pinned up there, many of them faded with age. Clark quickly scanned them. It didn't take long to pick out the common thread.

UFOs.

There were articles on the Roswell incident. And a sighting in Delphos, Kansas back in 1971, which left a luminous ring on the ground afterward. And glowing red fireballs seen above Manitoba, Canada, for several weeks in 1975 and 1976. Every article was about some sort of alleged extraterrestrial encounter.

"We kept searching for evidence of someone like you," Jonathan said, "but we never found any."

What are you saying? Clark thought, too stunned to speak. *That I'm an alien?* But try as he might, he couldn't give voice to his questions.

His father pulled out a drawer and took a small object swaddled in oil-cloth. He unwrapped the object, exposing a palm-sized black spike or nail, and handed it to Clark.

"This was in the chamber with you," Jonathan said. "It was fitted into a slot, like a key. I took it to a metallurgist at Kansas State. He said whatever it was made from didn't even exist on the periodic table."

Wondering briefly how his father had persuaded the scientist to keep quiet, Clark held the object up to the flashlight. It refracted the beam in ways that were strange even when seen by ordinary vision. The spike felt peculiar, too—more like a horn or shell than metal, but somehow different. It had a texture like nothing he had ever touched before.

"Just think, Clark," he father said. "The fact that you're here means we're not alone in the universe." He smiled warmly. "You're a miracle."

Clark knew his dad was trying to put a positive spin on things, but it was no good. He felt dizzy. His whole world had just turned upside down. All this time, he had thought he was human—sort of—but that was a lie.

"I don't want to be," he said. Tears welled up in his eyes. His throat tightened.

"I don't blame you." Jonathan placed a reassuring hand on Clark's shoulder. "It'd be a huge burden for anyone to bear. But you're *not* just anyone, Clark. And I have to believe that you've been sent here for a reason. All these changes that have been happening to you, one day you're going to think of them as a blessing. And when that day comes, you'll have to make a choice whether to stand proud in front of the human race, or not."

He sounded like he'd been thinking about this for a long time.

"Can't I just keep pretending I'm your son?" Clark asked.

His father pulled him close.

"You *are* my son," he said emphatically. "But somewhere out there, you've got another father, too. Who gave you another name. He sent you here for a reason, Clark, and even if it takes you the rest of your life, you owe it to yourself to find out what that reason is."

Another father? On another planet?

Clark wasn't sure where to begin. His dad's answers had only left him with a brand new set of questions. He turned the odd spike-like object over in his hands, examining it from every angle. Was this nameless artifact the key to his origins? The beam of the flashlight fell upon the triangular head of the key, revealing a symbol inscribed there.

It looked like a capital "S."

CHAPTER TEN

The Bearcat was a rough-and-tumble bar outside of Yellowknife, catering mostly to truckers and miners. Several semi-trailers were parked outside, alongside a couple of light utility vehicles belonging to the Canadian Armed Forces. Clark was bussing tables when he heard another big eighteen-wheeler pull up to the bar.

The door swung open, letting in a chilly gust of wind, and a hefty truck driver stomped across the threshold. Stubble carpeted the man's surly features. The bartender called out a greeting.

"Evening, Ludlow," Weaver said. "What can I get you?"

Clark went back to his work. It was after five and the bar was packed with heavy drinkers determined to put a dent in the Bearcat's liquid inventory. Raucous laughter and dirty jokes competed with the Edmonton Oilers game on the TV behind the bar. Sawdust coated the floor, soaking up spilled drinks. Clark stooped to pick up some empty bottles. A greasy apron shielded his flannel shirt and jeans.

He paused as his ears picked up on one particular conversation, a few tables away, where three uniformed

Canadian airmen were chatting in the corner. Most people wouldn't have been able to eavesdrop on the discussion, especially through the noisy din, but Clark had no trouble listening in.

"—found something strange on Ellesmere. AIRCOM's been making runs out there all week."

"That rat-hole? You gotta be kidding me."

"I know, crazy," the first airman agreed. "But the Americans are there, too. A *lot* of them. Space Command. NASA—"

Another conversation, much closer at hand, distracted Clark. He looked up to see the newly arrived trucker hassling one of the waitresses, a tired-looking brunette in her early twenties. He pawed at her blouse.

"—c'mon, Chrissy. Give me a peek."

She pulled away from him, balancing an empty tray.

"Back off, Ludlow," she said. "I'm *serious*."

A leer and a snort indicated just how little he cared what she thought. He grabbed her backside, eliciting a roar of laughter from his drinking buddies. Clark scowled. Chrissy was just trying to make a living. She didn't deserve to be manhandled by an obnoxious trucker. Still, he tried to concentrate on what the airmen were saying.

"—they're calling it an 'anomalous object,' whatever that means."

Like a UFO? Clark wondered. *Like the ones my folks found?*

"Knock it off!" Chrissy protested.

She slapped Ludlow's hand away and took a step backward, but he grabbed her wrist to keep her from leaving. He yanked her back toward the table.

That's enough, Clark thought. He'd hoped to avoid to getting involved, but he couldn't ignore this any longer. He straightened up and headed over to Ludlow's table.

Reaching it, he cleared his throat to get their attention.

"Let her go."

Ludlow sneered at him, like every bully Clark had ever known.

"Or what, tough guy?"

"Or I'm going to ask you to leave."

The trucker shoved Chrissy aside. He lumbered to his feet, obviously spoiling for a fight.

"I've been coming here for fifteen years," he said. "I'll leave when I'm ready." He snatched a foaming glass off the table and hurled the liquid in Clark's face. "But my buddy here needs a new beer, so why don't you help us with that?"

Beer ran down Clark's face. His expression darkened and he clenched his fists at his sides. Ludlow had no idea who—or what—he was messing with.

The trucker snickered at Clark's anger.

"Hey, Weaver!" he called out to the bartender. "I think your busboy's about to go postal."

The bartender shrugged and kept on wiping the bar counter. He weighed the value of a busboy against a steady customer.

"You're fired, kid," he said casually.

Ludlow grinned triumphantly. Laughter spread across the bar. Even the airmen looked amused by the episode. Nobody came to the Bearcat expecting good manners and a tranquil atmosphere. Brawls were considered a good night's entertainment.

"There," Ludlow gloated. "Crisis averted." He nodded toward the exit. "Now *out*!"

Meaty hands shoved Clark in the chest. He seethed, wanting nothing more than to pound the crap out of the trucker. Solar fire smoldered behind his furious blue eyes, ready to be unleashed. A hush fell over the bar as the staff and patrons waited to see what the humiliated busboy would do next. Was he going to stand up to Ludlow after all?

"It's not worth it, sweetie," Chrissy said, looking worried.

He knew she was right. Even though it killed him, he backed down and unclenched his fists. He tossed his beer-stained apron onto the floor and headed for the door.

Ludlow lobbed an empty beer can at him. It bounced off Clark's back.

"Here's your tip, asshole!"

Ludlow was still chuckling at his own wit later on, when he decided to get back on the road. He stood up from the table and tossed a handful of greasy singles next to a half-eaten meal. Then he belched loudly

"This food sucks!" he announced for everyone to hear. "I'm calling the health department."

Chrissy kept her distance as he pulled on his hat and exited the bar. He strolled across the parking lot, fumbling for his keys, only to stop in his tracks.

His jaw dropped.

His eyes bulged.

"What the *hell*?"

Ludlow's eighty-thousand-pound rig was nothing but a heap of mangled metal. The cab was smashed flat, while the entire trailer had been twisted into a smoking pretzel. The smell of burnt rubber polluted the air.

He wasn't going anywhere tonight.

Clark trudged along the side of the highway. A duffle bag was slung over his shoulder. Snow and ice crunched beneath his boots. The road wound through densely wooded hills.

The Northern Lights glimmered on the horizon.

He smiled for a moment, imagining Ludlow's reaction when he saw what was left of his eighteen-wheeler. Then he put The Bearcat behind him and kept on hiking north… toward Ellesmere Island. The conversation he'd overheard in the bar played over and over again in his mind.

What sort of "anomalous object" had been found up north?

A truck approached from the south, heading his way.

Clark stuck out his thumb.

CHAPTER ELEVEN

From above, it looked as though the Ice Age had never left Ellesmere Island. Vast ice caps and glaciers covered the mountainous Arctic island, which was barely more than five hundred miles south of the North Pole. Global warming had taken its toll on the thick ice shelves that extended beyond the island into the sea, but Ellesmere was still forbiddingly white, and barren in appearance. It was said to be one of the most remote places on Earth.

Lois Lane hoped the trip was worth it.

The Sikorsky S-61 helicopter touched down on a landing field at the northeastern tip of the island. Lois braced herself for the bitter cold as she exited the 'copter. A heavy parka and boots provided a degree of protection against the harsh polar climate. Her long auburn hair was tucked beneath the hood of the parka. Not the most flattering outfit she had ever worn, but Lois didn't care about that.

If anything, she sometimes regarded her own—admittedly—striking good looks as an impediment, getting in the way of her career. She wanted people to pay attention to her byline, not her eyes or figure.

A two-man welcoming committee was waiting. The older of the men, who was obviously in charge, came forward to meet her.

"Ms. Lane? I'm Jed Eubanks with Arctic Cargo." His breath frosted in front of his lips. "We're a private contractor augmenting NORTHCOM on the operation."

US Northern Command had been established in the wake of 9/11, to defend and secure the United States and its interests. Although the island was under Canadian rule, NORTHCOM was authorized to coordinate efforts with America's allies. In recent years, Lois knew, budget cuts had led to the privatization of various support services on Ellesmere.

"Got it," she said. "How far's the station?"

He indicated a distant ridge. Snow and ice covered the rugged hills and valleys. They were far above the timberline, so there was no vegetation or wildlife in sight. Sunlight glinted off rolling expanses of white.

"Camp is just over yonder," he said. "I'll walk you there. Joe can get your bags." He turned toward his associate, a strapping young man with a scruffy black beard. "Help her out, Joe."

Lois briefly checked Joe out. He wasn't bad-looking, in a hunky *Ice Road Trucker* kind of way. He nodded to her and began unloading cargo from the helicopter. As he did so, he reached for her overstuffed duffle bag.

"Careful," she said. "That one's heavy."

He lifted it easily. Lois was impressed.

Guess they grow them strong up here, she thought.

Leaving Joe to deal with the luggage, Eubanks escorted Lois away from the landing field.

"Gotta confess, Ms. Lane," he said, "I'm not a fan of the *Daily Planet,* as such. But those pieces you wrote when you were embedded with the 1st Division were mighty impressive."

She appreciated the good review, especially after what she'd survived to get those stories.

"What can I say?" she responded. "I get writer's block if I'm not wearing a bulletproof vest."

"So what brings you to the ass-end of nowhere?" he asked. "Ellesmere's not exactly your standard vacation spot."

That was putting it lightly. The Alert Station at the tip of the island was the northernmost permanent settlement on the planet. The base had been established as a weather station back in the fifties, and had served as a joint US/Canadian listening post during the Cold War. Today it also hosted a handful of environmental science facilities, but nothing worth writing headlines about—until recently.

"Same thing that brought a few hundred assorted Army personnel," Lois said. "Word is their climatologists found something under the ice."

Eubanks neither confirmed nor denied her words, but the view from the ridge lived up to the rumors Lois had heard.

The remote outpost, which rarely housed more than fifty residents at a time, had ballooned into a miniature city supporting hundreds of US and Canadian troops. Temporary structures consisting of insulation draped over steel and aluminum frames had been erected in the snowbound valley. Barracks, garages, hangars, and mess halls had sprung up practically overnight. Mechanical earth movers had been employed to carve out a large settlement out of the permafrost.

And at the center of the base was a deep pit, where a thermal meltdown generator was being used to bore through the packed ice. Steam rose from the borehole.

Lois could only imagine the money and logistics that had been required to set up an operation this massive in the middle of a frozen, barely habitable wasteland. NORTHCOM wouldn't have gone to such lengths unless they'd had a very good reason—one she was determined to ferret out. She could practically *smell* a scoop.

The station's tactical operations center was located within walking distance of the pit. Eubanks led her into the hut, where he handed her off to the folks in charge. They didn't look happy to see her. That was fine with Lois. She hadn't expected them to be.

The commanding officer stepped forward and introduced himself.

"I'm Colonel Nathan Hardy with US NORTHCOM," he said brusquely. He had a receding hairline and a stern disposition. His ramrod bearing practically screamed "career military," as did the eagles on his uniform. He gestured toward the man beside him. "This Dr. Emil Hamilton with DARPA."

The Defense Advanced Research Projects Agency specialized in developing new scientific technologies for use by the military. Hamilton certainly looked the part of an egghead scientist. He was a professorial type, in his sixties, with a bald pate and neatly trimmed goatee. Lois could easily envision him puttering in a lab somewhere, working on various hush-hush projects.

"We were expecting you tomorrow," Hardy said gruffly.

She just shrugged.

"Which is why I showed up *today*," she replied.

Hardy scowled, but Lois refused to be intimidated. She took off her hood and laid her cards on the table.

"Let's get one thing straight, okay, guys? The only reason I'm here is because we're on Canadian soil, and the appellate court overruled your injunction to keep me away. So if we're done measuring manhoods, you want to tell me what your knob turners found?"

Hardy looked as if he would have preferred to assemble a firing squad, but orders were orders, so he and Hamilton led her over to a bank of sophisticated computers and monitoring equipment, where they introduced her to Staff Sergeant Sekowsky. Unlike his tight-lipped superiors, the curly haired technician seemed eager to talk about what his crew had discovered.

"NASA's EOS satellites pinged the anomaly first." He pointed to computer screens cycling through false-color portraits of the seabed and nearby glacial topography. The glacial ice was rendered in shades of blue, while the ocean appeared as green above the rocky gray sea floor. Layers of snow were, appropriately, white. "The ice shelf plays hell on the echo soundings... but there's definitely something down there."

Lois squinted at the screens. She wasn't an expert on interpreting images of this sort, but it was evident that that there was a large solid object embedded deep beneath the ice.

"A submarine, maybe?" she speculated. "Soviet-era?" That would be interesting, but not quite the front-page story she was hoping to find.

"Doubt it," Hardy said. "At three hundred meters, that's considerably larger than anything we know they built back then."

Lois did the conversion in her head. Three hundred meters was roughly a thousand feet long.

That would be an awfully big sub.

Dr. Hamilton asked Sekowsky to call up an "aerial reflection radiometer view." Lois made a mental note to look that up later, and observed that the image on the screen appeared to have been taken from orbit.

"And then there's this," Hamilton said. "You'd expect a sub to be buried in the seabed, but this thing's lodged one hundred feet *above* sea level, at the base of this tidewater glacier."

Lois saw his point. How would a sub end up frozen in the ice, a significant distance above the ocean?

Unless it dropped from the sky.

"Could an earthquake have moved it?" she asked.

"Maybe," Sekowsky said. "But that's not the spooky part. The ice surrounding it is nearly *twenty thousand* years old."

Twenty thousand years?

Lois was still processing that as Colonel Hardy marched her across the encampment to her quarters. The Arctic sun had dipped below the horizon, taking with it what passed for warmth. Shivering in her parka, Lois decided she would never complain about Metropolis winters again.

"Here it is," Hardy said, like a grumpy innkeeper. Joe tagged along behind him, still carrying Lois's duffle bag. Hardy opened the door to the shelter, then realized that Lois had lagged behind. "Ms. Lane."

Despite the cold, she had paused to take in the view. Steam rose from the excavation site where the meltdown generator was living up to its name. The Aurora Borealis shimmered high overhead, spreading across the night sky in rippling curtains of green and red. Pristine sheets of ice reflected the aurora.

"Try not to wander," Hardy said impatiently. "Temperatures drop to minus forty at night. And if a whiteout rolls in, we won't find your body until next spring."

Lois tore her eyes away from the heavenly lightshow.

"What if I need to tinkle?"

"There's a bucket in the corner."

Lois entered the shelter, which turned out to resemble an industrial cargo container more than a cozy bed-and-breakfast. Sure enough, the accommodations consisted of a cot, a sleeping bag—and a bucket.

Hardy smirked before taking his leave. Joe, the hunky baggage carrier, gave Lois an apologetic shrug as he put the duffle bag down, then left without a word. Lois found herself alone in a glorified shack in the middle of an Arctic wasteland.

Could be worse, she thought. *Somebody else might be onto this story.*

She waited long enough to let her babysitters to get out of the cold, then cracked open the door of the shelter and peeked outside. As she'd hoped, there wasn't a guard posted. Where was she supposed to go anyway? Hardy clearly expected her to stay inside, where it was safe and warm.

How little he knew her.

Getting the official story wasn't enough. If she wanted to find out what was *really* going on, she needed to shake her handlers and poke around on her own.

Slipping outside, she zipped up her parka as far as it would go, then crept down toward the excavation site. Nobody in their right mind was outdoors after dark, so she managed to get a good look at the meltdown generator, which resembled a large steel top hanging from a chain. Hot water circulated through copper lines wrapped around the tip of the machine, which was melting the ice below at a slow but steady rate.

Pumps cleared the melted ice water from the borehole.

Lois recalled that a similar gadget had been used to uncover a long-buried WWII fighter plane in Greenland several years earlier. She was hoping for an even bigger discovery here.

Twenty thousand years?

Fishing a digital camera from her pocket, she snapped a few shots of the excavation site. She was looking around for something else worth photographing when she spotted a lone figure moving across a snowy ridge outside the camp. She zoomed in on the figure, using the camera's telephoto lens, and was surprised to see Joe the baggage handler disappearing into the Arctic wastes.

"Where the hell are *you* going?" she whispered to herself. Intrigued, she took off after him, following his tracks through the snow. It was a daunting trek, through one of the most inhospitable environments she could have imagined. But it never once crossed her mind to turn back. Her reporter's instinct told her there was a story to be had, and she wasn't going home without it.

Hopefully it would be worth a touch of frostbite.

She trudged across a huge shelf of floating ice, hugging herself to keep warm. Ellesmere Island, her research told her, had the largest ice shelves in the world, some of them extending for more than a hundred square miles. She assumed Joe wasn't planning that long a hike, since nobody human could stay out in this cold too long. But where did he think he was going?

The aurora barely provided enough light to see by. She lost sight of her quarry amid the rolling hills and depressions, but his tracks led her on. Rounding a stony outcropping, she spied an enormous glacier looming ahead. A bright ruby light, not unlike a laser beam, glowed at the base. Clouds of steam obscured her view.

What have we here? she wondered. *Another excavation site?*

Her face seemed frozen and she couldn't feel her toes anymore, but she made her way to the base of the glacier. A crystalline white cliff, glistening darkly in the night, towered above her where the glacier wall met the ice shelf beneath her feet.

A tunnel entrance, which looked as though it had been newly carved, stood before her. Rivulets of fresh water dripped from the ceiling and ran down the slick walls, continuing the length of the tunnel. Her boots splashed through puddles of slush.

The sloping tunnel appeared to lead deep beneath the glacier. Despite her professional curiosity, Lois hesitated before entering. She didn't feel like getting buried in the ice for another twenty millennia or so, like some long-dead Siberian mammoth.

But she had come too far to turn back now. She swallowed hard, took a deep breath, and started down the tunnel.

All right, Joe, she thought. *Let's find out just what you're up to.*

CHAPTER TWELVE

Clark's eyes glowed like twin red suns. Scalding clouds of steam billowed around him as his fiery gaze melted away the thick sheets of ice. The tunnel he had drilled had brought him to a huge cavern far beneath the ancient glacier. Now only a final layer stood between him and what had he had come so far to find.

His eyes dimmed and the steam cleared, revealing…

An immense alien spacecraft, many times larger than the one in which his parents had found him. The size of a cruise ship, the vessel was distinctly organic in appearance, resembling the fossilized shell of some gargantuan horseshoe crab. Icy water tricked down its flowing contours. Although longer and more streamlined, it was unmistakably akin to the capsule hidden beneath the old barn.

Clark stared in wonder at the ship, which had been buried under the ice for millennia. Alien glyphs were etched into its smooth, ceramic hull. The exotic characters were unfamiliar to him, except for one that resembled a capital "S." Excitement surged through his veins as he fished out the strange black key his father had given him, so many years ago. He compared the symbol on the head of the key to the mark on the spaceship's hull.

It was a match.

He couldn't believe it. Might this forgotten starship actually hold the answers he'd been searching for all his life? Was he finally about to discover the truth about his past—where he came from? *You have another father,* his dad had told him. *Another name.* At long last, the truth seemed within reach.

Clark didn't know whether to be thrilled or terrified. *Maybe a little bit of both.*

Working up his nerve, he stepped forward and touched the hull of the sleeping vessel, then jumped back in surprise as polished ceramic plates slid open before him. He peered inside the silent ship, then gulped and stepped inside.

The interior had the same oddly organic appearance as the craft that had brought him to Smallville. Walking through its ribbed corridors was like exploring the fossilized remains of some gigantic mollusk, or crustacean. Curved arteries, disdaining right angles, branched off in unexpected directions, including up and down. The further he went, the more convinced he became that this ship had originated somewhere light-years away. The unearthly architecture was strange, unsettling, and alien.

Just like me?

He'd assumed that he had the empty ship to himself, but suddenly he heard servomotors whirring behind him. He spun around in time to watch a robot drop from a valve in the ceiling. The metallic creature wasn't humanoid in appearance—it resembled a large rectangular lantern, and had an illuminated three-dimensional display screen at the center of its chest. Glowing tendrils sprouted from its base.

Some sort of automated sentry?

Clark backed away cautiously as the levitating mechanoid scanned him with a beam that shone from its central monitor. He raised his hands, showing empty palms, in what he hoped would be seen as a universal signal of peaceful intentions.

It didn't work.

The robot zipped toward him aggressively, lashing out with its white-hot tentacles. Clark moved to defend himself, and a tendril whipped around his upper arm, burning right through his winterwear to sear the pink flesh underneath.

He cried out as he experienced something almost entirely new to him.

Pain.

A welt formed across his arm. He panicked and stumbled backward, glancing about frantically for a way he might protect himself. His desperate gaze fell upon a small diamond-shaped port in the wall above his head. It was shaped like the S-shield on the head of his key.

Still the hostile robot advanced toward him.

Acting on instinct, Clark jumped up and plugged the key into the slot. It slid in effortlessly, fitting perfectly. The port pulsed in response—and the robot froze in mid-air, halting its attack.

Clark gasped in relief, thanking his lucky stars that he had held onto the key all this time. He clutched his arm, which was still stinging like blazes. Was this what ordinary people felt, whenever they were hurt? His heart went out to them. He had never quite realized what it felt like to be... vulnerable.

Dropping back down, he circled the immobile sentry warily. He kept his guard up, but apparently the ship's long-dormant security system had recognized the key, proving beyond a shadow of a doubt that he was somehow connected to the vessel.

Now what? he wondered. *Where do I look first?*

A flicker of movement appeared in the corner of his eye. Another robot?

Turning quickly, he glimpsed a tall, bearded man, standing at the end of the corridor. He wore a textured robe over what looked like a blue, skintight wetsuit. Clark started toward him, but the figure ducked silently around the corner, vanishing from sight. He shifted his vision to peer through the walls and find him, but the alien substance resisted him along the entire spectrum, from infrared to ultraviolet. Further evidence that it was not of this world.

"Hello?" he called. Clark chased after the man, his mind awhirl with questions. This ship had been buried for twenty thousand years. How could anybody still be alive aboard?

He raced down a long curved artery and into a large vaulted chamber. In front of him stood a clear barrier, behind which lay a chamber filled with a translucent fluid of some sort. Feathery branches, like giant ferns, drifted slowly within the liquid. Empty globules budded along the branches. A phosphorescent green radiance permeated the water.

With his enhanced sense of smell, he detected a distinct saline odor.

Moving slowly now, he was taken aback by the chamber's bizarre contents. He had no idea what he was looking at. A hydroponic garden?

Or something far more alien?

* * *

Words failed her.

Lois was a journalist. Prose was her profession, and over the course of her lifetime—first as an Army brat, then as a reporter—she thought she'd seen it all. That nothing could surprise her.

But at that moment she gaped in shock at what appeared to be an honest-to-goodness *alien spaceship*, hidden away in an underground ice grotto. It had to have been there since caveman days, at least.

This was more than just a scoop. This was the biggest story in human history.

An open airlock called out to her. She wasn't sure how the ship had been thawed out, or what had happened to the guy named Joe, but *no way* was she going to pass up an opportunity like this.

So she stepped inside the buried UFO, hoping that somebody had turned on the heater.

Her footsteps echoed in the empty corridors. The flash from her camera lit up curved walls that were made of a smooth, pearly material she couldn't begin to identify. She found herself wishing that Dr. Hamilton was around to give her a guided tour. Maybe he could make sense of all of this. Lois Lane was definitely out of her element.

Motors whirred behind her. Her brow furrowed.

Joe?

She turned around to see where the mechanical noise was coming from.

It wasn't Joe.

An elevated platform overlooked the liquid-filled chamber. Cylinder-shaped consoles rose like coral from the floor of the deck, which looked as if it might be the bridge of the nameless ship. Cracked tiles and screens showed signs of damage. Clark inspected the controls, hesitant to touch anything. The robot sentry had proved that at least some of the ship's systems were still active.

Four heavily padded couches were arranged in the center of the bridge. Clark guessed that the seats were intended to protect the crew from heavy gravitational forces or a crash landing. Three of the couches were occupied by humanoid skeletons wearing full-body suits of some unknown material. The fourth was empty.

Had there been a survivor?

The bearded stranger appeared again, beneath the arch of a doorway. He lingered just long enough for Clark to spot him before darting around a corner once again. It was as though he was deliberately leading him on.

Clark scowled. He wasn't here to play games.

Once again he chased after the mystery man, this time into an armory of sorts. Sturdy hard-shell space suits, clearly meant to withstand hostile environments, were mounted in closet-sized niches. Further on he found form-fitting bodysuits of different sizes and hues. His fascinated gaze was drawn to one suit in particular—it was a deep steel-blue, and bore a familiar "S" emblem embossed upon the chest.

The "S" was rendered in red against a yellow shield. A matching red cape was attached to the collar. The emblem was identical to the one on his key.

He reached out to touch it.

Blaring alarms echoed throughout the ship. For a second, he was afraid that he had set them off somehow.

Then he heard Lois Lane screaming.

* * *

She ran madly through the alien ship, pursued by a freaking *robot*, of all things. Ear-piercing sirens let her know that she was trespassing. She raced for an open doorway, only to have it slam shut in front of her. She changed course, heading the other way, but a second door cut off her escape.

Cornered, she turned to face the robot, which zipped toward her. Glowing tentacles writhed beneath its mainframe. The circular monitor on its chest scanned her face, producing a three-dimensional replica on its display panel, like some kind of futuristic mug shot.

Lois decided that turnabout was fair play. She raised her camera and caught the hovering robot in the viewfinder. The flash went off.

Good, she thought. *Now at least I have a record of what's happening to me.*

But apparently the robot didn't like having its picture taken. One of its luminous tentacles lashed out, knocking her backward into a bulkhead. Agony burned across her ribs—it was like being whipped by liquid fire. She sagged against the wall, clutching her wounded side.

The robot approached menacingly, ready to finish her off. Its white-hot tentacles flicked through the air.

This is it, she realized. *Perry had damn well better give me a good obit.*

She was mentally composing her own eulogy when, all of a sudden, Joe came rushing in from nowhere. She started to call out a warning, but the husky baggage handler was already punching the robot. His bare knuckles slammed into the thing's central display panel.

Sparks flared and the injured robot squawked electronically, but Joe kept right on pounding it. Holding onto it with one hand, he smashed it to pieces with his fist.

How strong is he?

But even that thought couldn't distract her from the pain. She slid down the wall, holding her side. Blood seeped through her parka where the tentacle had sliced through it.

Joe tossed aside the pulped remains of the robot and turned toward her. She flinched at his approach, not quite sure whose side he was on, or how he'd managed to trash the alien robot with his bare hands.

"It's all right," he said. "I just want to help."

She stared at him in confusion.

"Who are you?"

Kneeling beside her, he peeled back her scorched parka for a better look. His eyes narrowed in concentration, almost as though he was seeing past her skin to examine her from the inside out. Concern showed behind his scruffy beard.

"You're hemorrhaging internally," he said. "If I don't cauterize the bleed, you'll die."

She didn't understand. "How—?"

"I can do things other people can't," he said simply. His fingers found hers, squeezing gently. "Hold my hand. This is going to hurt."

His eyes glowed like burning coals. Ruby beams shot from his pupils to penetrate her ribcage just above her liver. Lois cried out in pain. Her mysterious benefactor was right about one thing.

It did hurt… a lot.

The procedure was over in a second, though. His eyes dimmed back to normal. Shock caught up, though, and she felt herself passing out. The last thing she saw, before everything went dark, was him smiling down at her, like she was going to be okay.

She guessed his name wasn't really "Joe."

* * *

Staff Sergeant Sekowsky yawned and rubbed his eyes. Seated before his bank of monitors, he wondered what he'd done wrong in order to pull a double shift. Multiple screens provided thermal views of the generator and the mystery object that was embedded in the glacier. He'd been watching them for so long that he barely saw them anymore. He groped for his coffee cup, only to find it empty.

Figures, he thought.

All at once, the needle on the seismograph danced, signaling ground motion nearby. An alarm went off and he snapped alert. No longer needing caffeine, he stared in surprise at the thermal imaging monitors, which were suddenly registering massive amounts of activity. The entire glacier was cracking, venting record amounts of steam into the atmosphere. The meltdown generator began to topple as the ice around it broke apart. It swung into the side of the collapsing borehole.

Sekowsky heard shouts outside, and sirens. Heedless of the cold, he bolted from the science station and ran outdoors, where he found the rest of the base's personnel watching the event with their own eyes. Tremors rocked the sprawling Arctic outpost as the ice above the pit fractured, and then vaporized. Startled scientists and soldiers were driven back by the steam.

A glow emanated from deep beneath the ice, so bright that Sekowsky had to avert his eyes.

Colonel Hardy and Dr. Hamilton came running from the VIP quarters. Shielding their eyes from the heat and light, they gaped along with Sekowsky as a huge object broke free from the glacier and took to the sky.

It only took a few moments for the truth to register. It was a ship—and it wasn't from planet Earth. Shedding tons of ice water, the immense UFO ascended toward the Northern Lights. Globular thrusters, mounted to the underside of the object, glowed brightly.

The ship roared past the base, vanishing over the horizon.

Daylight—and the barking of seals—woke Lois.

She found herself sprawled upon a rocky shoreline somewhere on the island. Jagged ice floes washed against the beach. An Army helicopter hovered above her, and was in the process of lowering down a rescue officer on a winch. Her side throbbed, but she guessed she was going to live.

Sitting up, she looked around, but "Joe" was nowhere to be seen. The rising sun suggested that she had been out for hours.

She wondered what she'd missed.

CHAPTER THIRTEEN

"What various military experts surmised to be a Soviet-era submarine was actually something much more exotic. An isotope analysis of the surrounding ice bores suggests that the object had been trapped within the glacier for over 18,000 years.

"As for my rescuer? He disappeared during the object's departure. He was working with one of the private contractors assisting in the operation, but a subsequent background check revealed that his work history and identity had been falsified. Representatives from the Department of Defense declined to comment, other than to say 'an investigation into the matter is currently on-going.'

"I understand the military's cautious approach. The questions raised by my rescuer's existence are frightening to contemplate. But I also know what I saw. And I have arrived at the inescapable conclusion that the object and its occupant did not originate on Earth."

Lois read aloud from her laptop. Reaching the end of the article, she looked up from the computer and awaited the verdict.

Perry White, editor-in-chief of the *Daily Planet*, sat behind his desk in the corner office. A glass partition allowed him to keep an eye on the busy bullpen outside. He was a veteran newsman, whose dark hair was graying at the temples. His sleeves were rolled up to his elbows.

A pained sigh escaped his lips.

"I can't publish this, Lois," he said. "You could've hallucinated half of it."

But she had anticipated his response.

"What about the civilian contractors who corroborated my story?"

"The Pentagon is denying there was a ship," he countered.

"That's what they're *supposed* to do!" she replied. "Come *on*, Perry. This is me we're talking about. I'm a Pulitzer Prize-winning reporter—"

"Then act like one." He kneaded the bridge of his nose, as though he felt a headache coming on. "Our circulation is getting hammered, and you bring me this crap?"

Lois sympathized, but she would not be silenced. This story was too big to bury.

"Print it or I walk," she said flatly.

"You can't. You're under contract." He leaned forward. "Drop it, Lois. There's no way I'm running a story about an 'alien among us.' It's never going to happen."

She recognized the stubborn tone in his voice. He wasn't going to budge.

Fine, she thought. *I have other options.*

"One Old-Fashioned for the lady."

The bartender placed a tumbler down in front of her. The Ace O'Clubs was a waterfront dive in the bad part of town. Ordinarily, Lois wouldn't be caught dead in a place like this, unless she was on the track of a story. But she was working the gutters tonight. She removed a thumb drive from her purse and slid it down the bar to the sleazeball sitting next to her.

"This is the original article," she said, keeping her voice low. "My editor won't publish it, but if it happened to leak online…"

Glen Woodburn picked up the drive. He was a scuzzy, middle-aged newshound who reeked of booze and tobacco.

"Didn't you once describe my site as 'a creeping cancer of falsehoods'?"

"I stand by my words, Woodburn," she said, "But I want this story out there. So if you post this, I'll feed you more."

He eyed her suspiciously, trying to figure out her angle. "Why?"

She decided to stick with the facts.

"Because I want my mystery man to *know* I know the truth."

Whatever that was.

A polar bear loped along the Arctic mountain range where the alien spaceship had come to rest. Half buried beneath windblown snow, the ship was anchored to the remote, inaccessible summit like a fortress. The bear growled at the object, and then gave it a wide berth.

Inside the craft, Clark heard the bear amble by. With any luck, that would be the only visitor to stumble upon the ship's location. A short flight had carried it hundreds of miles away from Ellesmere, or any other human settlement. In theory, he finally had time to explore it at his leisure, now that he had left NORTHCOM—and Lois Lane—behind.

He hoped he hadn't scared her too much.

Pushing thoughts of the attractive reporter out of his head, he inspected the lifeless bridge. A port matching the one he'd used to deactivate the mechanical sentry was located on what appeared to be a control cylinder. He took his key, which he'd retrieved from the other port, and moved to insert it experimentally into the console.

Here goes nothing, he thought.

Once again the key fit perfectly. A glowing three-dimensional display appeared above the trunk-like cylinder. Streams of alien code spiraled across the screen as the console booted up. Clark braced himself for liftoff, just in case the ship decided to take off again. He still wasn't quite sure why the ship had launched the first time, or chosen to set down here in the Arctic.

To his relief, it didn't happen again. Instead, a three-dimensional figure materialized upon the bridge. Clark recognized the bearded man as the stranger who had led him on a chase before, through the bowels of the ship. He realized now that the man was actually some kind of holographic projection.

Not a survivor then, he thought. *I'm still alone.*

The hologram smiled fondly. His deep voice was strangely reassuring.

"You made it," he said. "We prayed you would, but actually *seeing* you here, grown into an adult." He smiled ruefully. "Gods, I wish Lara could have witnessed this."

Clark stared at the figure, who seemed know him.

"Who are you?"

"I am your father, Kal. Or rather," he corrected himself, "a shadow of him. His consciousness... and conscience. My name was Jor-El."

You have another father.

Another name.

Clark was staggered by the revelation—overcome with emotion by the sight of his birth father. This was far more than he had ever expected to find.

"And… Kal-El? Is that *my* name?"

The holographic figure nodded. "It is."

"I have so many questions," Clark said, unsure where to begin. "Where did I come from? Why did you send me here?"

The hologram, which was apparently tied into the ship's computers, gestured broadly and an array of virtual display screens surrounded them. Alien text and images scrolled past. A colossal red sun appeared, and Clark shaded his eyes.

On another screen, horned beasts with armored hides roamed an unearthly landscape. Humanoid figures rode upon flying creatures that looked like a cross between a seal and dragonfly. A domed citadel was rooted to the top of a high cliff, much as the ship was currently anchored to the mountain. Multiple moons shone in the sky.

"You came from Krypton," Jor-El continued. "A world with a much harsher environment than Earth's."

City-states spread across alien continents like time-lapsed images of growing coral colonies. Mighty starships, not unlike the one in which he stood, were built and launched into space. Their thrusters lit up the endless black.

"Long ago, in an era of expansion, our race spread out through the stars, seeking new worlds to settle upon. This scout ship was one of thousands launched into the void."

A vast interstellar armada spread out across the galaxy, leaving Krypton's red sun behind. Clark watched, rapt, as the history of a people he had never known played out before his eyes.

"We built outposts on other planets, using great machines to reshape the environments to our needs."

Kryptonian explorers, sealed inside rigid space suits, set foot on distant planets, some inhospitable to life. Gargantuan World Engines, resembling immense walking oil rigs, set about transforming alien environments into something more suitable. Skies changed colors. Land masses shifted. Icecaps melted into oceans...

"For a hundred thousand years, our civilization flourished, accomplishing wonders." At that moment, Clark caught a trace of melancholy in the hologram's voice.

"What happened?" he asked.

"Space exploration was abandoned," Jor-El explained. "We exhausted our natural resources. As a result, our planet's core became unstable. Eventually, our military leader—General Zod—attempted a coup. But by then, it was too late."

Civil war erupted across the myriad screens. A paramilitary force, armed with futuristic weapons and aircraft, turned on the government, which had its own defenders. The alien gunships resembled flying crustaceans—scarabs, trilobites, and crabs.

Bursts of white-hot plasma streaked a dim red sky. Explosions and crashing ships wreaked havoc on an alien metropolis where curved domes and spires reflected the biology-based architecture of the scout ship. Clark was saddened to see that his hidden history was one of war and destruction. It sounded as if Krypton was no better than Earth, in some respects.

It had its bullies, too.

The planet itself began to come apart on the screens. Veins of glowing green magma—most likely radioactive—broke through the crust, erupting all across the globe. It was like Krakatoa or Vesuvius, times one billion.

"Your mother and I, however, foresaw the coming calamity and took steps to ensure your survival. I knew the ancient scout ships were still out there. Left to rust on worlds we'd once considered colonizing."

Like Earth, Clark realized. *Twenty thousand years ago.*

Jor-El crossed the bridge, leading him past the three-dimensional screens to the platform overlooking the large, liquid-filled compartment. Clark was briefly distracted by the reference to his birth mother, but focused his attention on what the hologram was saying.

"This is a Genesis Chamber. Every scout ship came equipped with one. In the past, all Kryptonians were conceived in chambers such as this. Every child was designed to fulfill a predetermined role in our society as a worker, a warrior, a leader, and so on. Zod had his own vision for the future, one that only included the bloodlines he deemed worthy. But your mother and I envisioned something even *more* revolutionary."

Jor-El turned away from the chamber to look at Clark.

"We believed that Krypton had lost something precious," he continued. "The element of choice, of *chance.* What if a child dreamed of becoming something other than what society intended for him? What if he aspired to something greater? We wanted to restore that possibility. We wanted to eliminate the class distinctions entirely."

He gazed proudly at his son. His brown eyes held both warmth and wisdom.

"*You* were the embodiment of that belief, Kal. Krypton's first live birth in centuries. That's why we risked so much to save you."

It was a lot to absorb. Clark wasn't sure how he was supposed to feel about all of this.

I'm not just an alien, he thought, *I'm a special alien. One of a kind?*

Alone?

Lost in thought, he followed Jor-El to the armory

he had visited before. The space suits and skintight garments were still hanging in their nooks. Fashions from a dead planet.

"Was anyone else saved?" Clark asked. "What about you? My mother?"

"My memories extend only up until the moment your ship was launched. Beyond that, I can know nothing." His voice held sympathy, yet little in the way of hope for those left behind. "Given the enormity of the disaster threatening our world, it seems unlikely that *anyone* could have survived."

Clark gathered that the real Jor-El had downloaded this virtual version into the key found in the starcraft that had brought him to Earth as a baby. He must have planned that "Kal-El" would be drawn to the buried scout ship.

"Why didn't you come with me?" Clark asked.

"We couldn't, Kal. No matter how much we loved you, we were a product of our world's failures as much as Zod was, tied to its fate. Trapped in ancient tribal divisions. We knew that."

His sad, thoughtful tone reminded Clark of his dad, Jonathan Kent, who had also fretted about his son's future—and what it meant for Earth.

"So I'm alone," Clark said.

Jor-El shook his head.

"You are not. You're as much a child of Earth now as you are of Krypton. You can embody the best of *both* worlds. The dream your mother and I gave our lives to preserve.

"The people of Earth are different from us, it's true," he continued, "but I believe that's a good thing. They won't make the same mistakes we did. Not if you guide them, Kal. Not if you bring them hope."

He gestured at the big red "S" on the blue suit, then

drew back his own robes to reveal the same "S" embossed on his own uniform.

"That's what this symbol means. That's what you can bring them."

Hope.

CHAPTER FOURTEEN

Clark emerged from the Fortress feeling like a different person.

I probably look like one, too, he mused.

The steel-blue suit, which had once belonged to a distant ancestor, fit him perfectly. The crest of the House of El was emblazoned in crimson upon his broad chest. A gust of Arctic wind lifted the red cape that now flowed from his shoulders. The colorful outfit was like nothing he had ever worn before, but felt natural upon his frame.

His face was clean-shaven. Now that he knew where he came from, he didn't feel a need to hide his features any longer. It felt as if he was becoming somebody new.

But who?

He stopped and stood framed beneath the arched entrance of the space craft, lit from behind by the bright interior lights. The incandescent glow cast his shadow across the snowy mountain peak. Jor-El's voice echoed in his memory as he lifted his eyes to the clear blue polar sky. As it did, he recalled his own urgent questions.

"Why am I so different from them?" he had asked.

"Earth's sun is younger, brighter than Krypton's was,"

Jor-El had explained back in the armory. *"Your cells have drunk its radiation, strengthening your muscles, your skin, your senses. Earth's gravity is weaker, its atmosphere more nourishing. You've grown stronger here than I ever could have imagined."* He indicated the blue-and-red skinsuit. *"The only way to know* how *strong is to keep testing your limits."*

With that thought, Clark turned toward the sun. He felt its light and heat upon his face. He looked out across the desolate mountain range, full of dramatic peaks and crevasses. The looming mountains made the giant oil rig seem like a kid's climbing gym, by comparison. An icy ledge ended in a steep precipice several yards away. A matching ledge rose up again in the distance.

He took a deep breath to steel himself.

I can do this, he thought. *Jor-El says I can do this.*

Throwing caution to the wind—and possibly himself, as well—he ran toward the ledge and leapt over the gaping chasm, landing on the other side in a single bound. His heart filled with exhilaration and he repeated the feat, again and again, each leap propelling him higher and higher, until he was practically flying.

Jor-El's words urged him on.

"You will give the people of Earth an ideal to strive toward."

But he was just getting warmed up. *Almost* flying wasn't good enough, not any more. Balling his fists, he threw his arms out in front of him and launched himself up, up, and away—into the open air.

Despite his enthusiasm, it was an ungainly flight. Screaming out loud, like a passenger on a roller coaster, he corkscrewed through the sky, losing control. Powerful wind currents buffeted him.

He began to lose altitude.

"*They will race behind you. They will stumble. They will fall.*"

A snowy slope seemed to rush up to meet him. He crashed into the side of a mountain, setting off an avalanche. His body bounced and skidded across the rocky ground and over gaping crevasses. Momentum carried him for miles. Unlucky boulders were pulverized by the impact.

Finally he came to rest at the bottom of a freshly carved crater. The ravaged mountainside looked as though a meteor had hit it. Wincing, he rose to his feet and brushed off the snow and powdered stone dusting his skin and uniform. A quick inspection revealed that the Kryptonian skinsuit was just as durable as Jor-El had promised—his crash landing hadn't even scratched it, so that it appeared good as new. Even the flowing red cape was still in one piece.

Clark chose to accept that as a positive omen.

I actually flew, he realized. *Not very well, but…*

He couldn't wait to try again. So he turned his eyes skyward once more, drawing strength from the golden daylight. Then, without hesitation, he hurled himself back into the sky. Ice and rock shattered beneath the force of his leap.

"*But in time, they will join you in the sun, Kal,*" Jor-El had said. "*In time, you will help them accomplish wonders.*"

The last son of Krypton soared above his adopted world, higher than any bird or plane. Slowly getting the hang of it, he flew smoothly through the sky, gazing in awe at the Arctic wilderness that now lay so very far below. For perhaps the first time, he felt comfortable using his unique abilities, as though he was finally doing what he was always meant to.

Tears stung his eyes. No longer earthbound, he jetted across the planet at more than supersonic speed. He could go anywhere now, do anything, be anyone.

Even a superman.

Leaving the barren polar region behind, he zipped across the ocean to Kenya, where he cruised above a grassy savannah, barnstorming a herd of stampeding zebras. He whooped in delight as the hot African sun filled him with speed and energy. He waved good-bye to the animals as he rocketed back up into the jet stream, heading west toward America.

Miles sped by in seconds. A cool ocean spray pelted his face as he skimmed across the Atlantic—by focusing, he could allow himself to feel it, to *enjoy* it. The salty air was fresh and invigorating, adding to his exuberance. If only his friends the humpback whales—not to the mention the captain and crew of the *Debbie Sue*—could see him now!

Reaching North America faster than any commercial jet, he took an aerial tour of Monument Valley, Utah. Testing himself, he wove through the rusty limestone buttes and mesas jutting up from the desert floor. His fist stretched out in front to control his flight, he banked and rolled like a fighter jet. He took a corner too quickly and clipped the edge of a towering rock formation, sending a loose boulder plummeting toward the cacti that grew on the desert floor.

Oops.

He dived after the dislodged rock, catching it with one hand before it hit the ground. He placed it safely on top of a convenient mesa before continuing on his way, climbing higher and higher into the sky. A thick layer of clouds hung before him, but he punched through the misty barrier and emerged into the sunlight.

The bright, yellow sunlight.

How do you find someone who's spent a lifetime covering his tracks?

Lois began back at Ellesmere, where she showed around a blurry surveillance photo of "Joe." The military personnel wouldn't speak to her, naturally, but at least she got Jed Eubanks to talk a little bit about his former employee.

Off the record, of course.

Returning to Metropolis, she looked for the urban legends that had sprung up in the mystery man's wake. A wild story, posted on the internet, led her to a trucker bar in Yellowknife, where a sweet young waitress named Chrissy shared an amazing story about a scruffy young busboy—and an eighteen-wheeler that got reduced to scrap under mysterious circumstances. The rig had belonged to a trucker called Ludlow, but he hung up on Lois every time she got hold of him.

Even so, it was a clue.

One of many.

The threads were tenuous, to be sure, and it was difficult to tell fact from fiction. Friends of friends of friends claimed to have seen "Joe," or somebody who looked a lot like him. Lois followed every lead, all the way to the port of Dutch Harbor where the captain and crew of a crabbing boat—the *Debbie Sue*—told her about an enigmatic young greenhorn who apparently had been washed overboard.

It had happened around the time an indestructible "burning angel" had rescued several endangered roughnecks from an exploding oil rig. Captain Heraldson, the skipper of the boat, conceded that the missing greenhorn *might* be the man in the photo Lois had showed him.

His engineer, Byrne, was sure of it.

As she worked her way back through the years, a profile began to emerge, albeit a murky one. For some, he was a guardian angel. For others, a cipher... a ghost who never quite fit in.

Like the one who used to live in Smallville.

Lois drove her rental car down the town's main drag. When compared to Metropolis, the place certainly lived up to its moniker. A water tower bearing the name of the tiny rural community was the closest thing they had to a skyscraper. A large American flag was painted on the side of the local VFW. Pickup trucks were parked in front of the Sears department store. Old men sat on benches, watching the world go by. A banner advertised an upcoming church bake sale.

A strolling couple even stopped to clean up after their bulldog.

It seemed nice enough, as hick towns went, but all in all, it struck her as an unlikely home for the laser-eyed man of steel she had encountered in the Arctic. She would have expected him to come from Roswell, at least.

Here's hoping this isn't a dead end, she thought. *I've come a long way to leave empty handed.*

She pulled into a gas station to refill her tank and ask for directions. The friendly attendant pointed her to the pancake house down the road. Lois didn't feel like pancakes at the moment, but she parked her car and went in search of the restaurant's manager. He was a round-faced redhead in his early thirties.

"Pete Ross?" she asked. "I'd like to talk to you about

an accident that occurred when you were young. A school bus that went into the river."

No surprise, he remembered the incident vividly, as well as the quiet, reclusive classmate who had saved his life.

A boy named Clark Kent.

The Kent family farm lay just outside the town, at the end of a long dirt road, and was surrounded by acres of cornfields. From the looks of things, the place had seen better days. The barns and silo needed painting. The blades of a rickety windmill rotated slowly in the breeze. A swing hung from a branch of an old maple tree. Chickens clucked in a pen.

Lois got out of the car and approached the farmhouse. A dilapidated wooden porch creaked beneath her feet. She knocked on the front door, which rattled under her fist. A handsome older woman, wearing an apron over a floral dress, opened the door. She eyed Lois warily.

"Mrs. Kent," she said cheerily. "My name is Lois Lane. I'm with the *Daily Planet*." Everybody knew the *Planet,* even out in the sticks. "I'd like to talk to you about your son."

Martha Kent's face fell—try as she might, she was unable to conceal her reaction. She inhaled sharply, and her hand went to her heart. Lois got the impression that the woman had been dreading this moment—most likely for more than three decades.

Looks like I've come to right place after all, she thought.

CHAPTER FIFTEEN

The Smallville cemetery was located on a gentle hillside overlooking the town. A spiked iron fence enclosed the peaceful graveyard. Weathered headstones of varying age jutted from a well-tended lawn. Fading flowers rested atop the more recent graves, and many of the older ones as well.

Twilight was falling as Lois contemplated the inscription on a modest granite marker.

JONATHAN NATHANIEL KENT
1951–1997
Beloved Husband and Father

A sudden wind rustled the branches of an old oak tree. Fallen leaves blew past her ankles. Footsteps sounded behind her, then stopped.

She turned around to find Clark Kent, a.k.a. "Joe," standing there. Although he had shaved off his beard, she instantly recognized the enigmatic baggage handler who had saved her life up north.

I'd know those x-ray eyes anywhere.

She wasn't surprised to see him. In fact, she'd been expecting this.

"I figured if I turned over enough stones, you'd eventually find me," she said. "Once I knew what to look for, I started seeing a pattern. There'd be some kind of disaster. An earthquake, an oil rig failing... And a Good Samaritan would show up, doing things no human could possibly do."

He didn't deny it. He just watched her silently, as if waiting for the inevitable questions, which she was eager to supply.

"Where did you come from?" she said, and then the words just seemed to tumble out. "Why are you here? Let me tell your story."

But he remained wary.

"What if I don't want my story told?"

"It's going to get out eventually," she argued. "Someone's going to photograph you. Or figure out where you live."

Like I did, she thought.

"Then I'll just disappear again," he said.

"The only way you could disappear for good is if you stopped helping people altogether." She looked him over, remembering how he'd saved her from that killer robot, and tended to her injuries afterward. "And I sense that's not an option for you."

He frowned. Clearly, she had touched a nerve.

"How'd you know that ship was there?" she asked.

"I'm not sure," he admitted. "I just had a *feeling*. Something always drawing me north." He gazed down at the tombstone before them. "My dad used to keep these clippings of UFO sightings..."

She could guess which ones. She had been researching the topic pretty thoroughly since her experiences on

Ellesmere Island. She kept quiet, though, letting him talk as he finally started to open up.

"I was born on another world. I think you know that. But the Kents found me and raised me as their own. They taught me how to be human. How to do right by people." He looked at her, his eyes piercing. "If you keep going down this road, you'll make it harder for me to do that."

He leaned over and brushed a fallen leaf off the tombstone.

"My father believed that if the world found out who I really was, they'd reject me out of fear. And then I'd never be able to fulfill my purpose. He *died* because of that belief..."

APRIL, 1997

"I need to be somewhere I can do some *good*, Dad."

The Kent's sturdy Jeep Wagoneer cruised down the highway. Clark, all of seventeen years and aching to get on with his life, rode shotgun beside his father. His mom was in the back seat with Shelby, their terrier pup, resting his furry head in her lap. They were taking I-35 to Wichita to visit relatives. Afternoon sunlight warmed the flat green terrain along the interstate.

"The Army's not the right place for you, Clark," Martha said from the back. "I don't know what you're thinking, anyway. You'd never even pass the physical."

"She's right," Jonathan agreed, keeping his eye on the road. "There's too much scrutiny."

"And there's not *here*?" Clark sulked in his seat. "Half the town's already suspicious of me."

It had been years, yet Lana had barely spoken to him

since the bridge incident. People still walked on eggshells around him, when they weren't giving him a hard time for being different.

"Fine," Martha said. "Then go to college. We talked about that. Kansas State's a safer bet, anyway—"

"I'm tired of 'safe'." He felt like he had been hiding forever. "I want do something *useful* with my life."

His father bristled behind the wheel.

"So farming, *feeding* people, that's not useful?"

Clark groaned and looked out the window. Not this old argument again…

"I didn't say that," he muttered. But it was too late. His dad launched into an all-too-familiar lecture.

"Our family's been farming for five generations, Clark."

"*Your* family, not mine," Clark said sullenly. "I don't even know why I'm listening to you. You're not my dad. You're just some guy who found me in a field."

"Clark!" his mom protested.

"No, he's right," Jonathan said stiffly. He looked away from the road long enough to give Clark a stern look. "We're not your parents. You *don't* have to listen to us. We're doing the best we can. And we're making this up as we go along. So maybe our best isn't good enough anymore."

Clark already regretted his harsh words. The last thing he wanted was to hurt his parents' feelings, no matter how confused—and frustrated—he felt sometimes. He knew his folks were just trying to protect him.

"Look, I'm sorry. I just—"

"*Hold on*!" Jonathan said sharply as he hit the brakes. Traffic had slowed to stop all along the highway. Dozens of cars and truck were backed up across multiple lanes. Hail fell from the sky, bouncing off pavement and windshields.

Uh-oh, Clark thought. *This doesn't look good.*

His parents shared a worried look. Tornado season

had just begun, and they were smack dab in the middle of "Tornado Alley." Anybody who grew up in Kansas knew what a sudden change in the weather could mean. A storm, and a twister, could arrive from out of the blue.

A car was no place to be during a tornado. Worst came to worst, you were better off in a ditch than an exposed vehicle. Clark and his folks scrambled out of the SUV, joining hundreds of other travelers on the highway, which was now nothing but an endless parking lot.

The air was muggy and still, full of warm, moist air. Everyone was staring to the southwest, where ominous black storm clouds were racing toward them. The low-hanging clouds flattened along the tops, so that they resembled a blacksmith's anvil. A wall of gray hung beneath the billowing, black thunderheads.

Then a funnel cloud dropped toward the vulnerable terrain below, snaking above the ground in a classic "stovepipe" shape. Tornado sirens sounded, warning everyone in the vicinity to seek cover.

Easier said than done, Clark noted. Terrified drivers and passengers alike dashed back to their cars, but they weren't going anywhere. The traffic was hopelessly snarled. Clark looked around for shelter. A solid building or structure was the best place to be during a tornado.

"Go for the overpass!" his father shouted, pointing at a concrete structure several yards up the road. "*Take cover!*"

Most people had the same idea. A tide of panicked humanity swept the Kents toward the overpass, even as hailstones continued to rain down on them. Chunks of ice, some as large as fists, crashed into the parked vehicles, denting hoods, cracking windshields, and setting off car alarms. A hailstone bounced harmlessly off Clark's scalp, but others weren't so lucky.

He saw people stumbling as the hail assailed them. A

little girl, who had somehow gotten separated from her family in the crush, cried forlornly. Jonathan scooped her up before she could be trampled.

The funnel cloud touched down, turning into a full-fledged tornado. A vortex of spinning air churned up a thick cloud of dirt and debris, and was bearing down on the highway at terrifying speed. Trees and highway signs whipped back and forth. Sparks erupted as power lines were ripped loose. The twister looked like it was an F-4, maybe even an F-5.

Clark knew that a tornado could travel thirty miles an hour or faster, which meant it was going to hit them in a matter of moments. Could they reach the overpass in time? And would it be enough to protect them? He wasn't worried about himself, but the danger to everyone else was all too real.

His mother froze and looked back at their Wagoneer. A look of dismay came over her face.

"We forgot Shelby!"

Clark remembered the puppy sleeping the back of the SUV. He heard the terrier barking frantically.

"I'll get him!" he shouted, turning back.

"No!" Jonathan thrust the scared little girl into his arms. "Get your mom to the overpass. You have to protect her."

Clark watched as his father raced toward their truck. He wanted to chase after him, but he had to protect the girl, and his mother, too.

The tornado was almost upon them; he could hear it roaring like a runaway train. Flying grit bounced off his face. The wind whipped his hair. He had to get the others to safety.

Hurry, Dad, he thought anxiously. *It's coming!*

Along with dozens of others, they reached the overpass

and crowded beneath it. Clark looked back, hoping his father was right behind them. He saw his dad reach the truck and reach inside for the panicked terrier. Jonathan tucked Shelby under his arm and started to back out of the truck.

Hurry! Clark thought, still holding onto the lost toddler. *You have to get out of there!*

A compact car, caught up by the swirling vortex, fell from the sky onto the Wagoneer, crushing its cab. Shelby escaped from the crash, running for the overpass as fast as his four little legs could carry him, but Jonathan was trapped inside the smashed SUV.

He struggled to free himself.

"DAD!"

Jonathan managed to wriggle free from the wreck. He made it onto the shoulder of the highway—just as the tornado touched down on top of him. A spinning cloud of uprooted dirt and debris whirled around him at hundreds of miles an hour, while the sky-high funnel cloud stretched overhead, all the way to a looming black thunderhead. Lighting flashed across the funnel, from one side to another.

The air was gassy and hard to breathe.

Clark spotted his father inside the twister. Handing the crying girl over to his mom, he shoved his way through the packed crowd, determined to rescue his father before it was too late. If he could save an entire school bus of kids from drowning, surely he could he snatch his dad from a tornado.

But Jonathan must have guessed his son's intentions. He locked eyes with his son, and shook his head grimly. The message was clear.

No. Don't expose yourself.
Not for me.

In that moment Clark hesitated, torn between his instincts and his father's wishes. The lesson Jonathan had tried so hard to teach him—to hide his true nature from the world—slowed him a moment too long.

The twister swept Jonathan up, carrying him away.

"DAD!"

"I let my father die because I trusted him," Clark said, standing before Jonathan Kent's grave. "He was convinced that I had to wait, that the world wasn't ready." He lifted his gaze from the tombstone and looked into Lois's eyes. "What do you think?

She didn't know what to say. She was no stranger to sob stories, having interviewed more than her share of refugees, political prisoners, and victims of crime, but she was deeply moved by what she had just heard. This man was carrying a lot on his broad shoulders. Maybe more than she could possible imagine.

Then he walked away, leaving her alone with her thoughts—and a dilemma.

What was she going to do with his secret?

CHAPTER SIXTEEN

"You better watch out, Lois."

Steve Lombard cornered her in the *Daily Planet's* hectic bullpen. Rows of cubicles stretched all the way to the elevator banks. Framed front-page headlines, mounted on the walls, paid tribute to the paper's illustrious history. Reporters tapped away at their computers while working the phones and internet. Deadlines and caffeine produced a constant buzz of activity.

"Perry's gunning for you," Lombard said. An aging ex-jock, he had parlayed a brief, undistinguished career in the NFL into a cushy stint at the sports desk. His dark hair was thinning, while his once-toned body was losing its battle against junk food, booze, and Father Time.

"He knows you're Woodburn's anonymous source and he can't wait to rip you a new one." He grinned at the hot water Lois had landed in. And for once, Lombard probably had his story straight.

Lois approached Perry's office like a condemned prisoner walking the last mile. Jenny, the chief's new intern, was posted at a desk outside the office. She was a pretty brunette studying Journalism at Metropolis University.

"Good luck," Jenny said, lowering her voice. "Don't listen to Lombard. He's an ass-clown."

The girl clearly had the instincts of a born reporter.

Lois gave her an appreciative look before heading in to face the music. She didn't have to wait long. Perry let her have it with both barrels.

"I *told* you not to run with this," he growled. "And what did you do? You let Woodburn shotgun it all over the net." He paced back and forth behind his desk, too worked up to sit still. Each time he stopped, he glared at her accusingly. "The publishers want to sue you!"

Lois glanced through the glass partition at the bullpen, where a smirking Lombard drew a finger across his throat. "Ass-clown" was putting it mildly, she decided.

Then she concentrated on calming her boss.

"Well," she said, "if it makes any difference, I'm dropping it. The alien, Ellesmere Island. Everything."

Perry hadn't been expecting that. He stopped pacing, and peered at her over the tops of his glasses, making no effort to conceal his skepticism.

"Just like that?" he asked suspiciously. "What about all your leads?"

Lois shrugged.

"They didn't pan out. The story's smoke."

"Really?" He still didn't sound convinced. "Or did it just not gain traction like you hoped it would?"

She didn't comment, knowing she was already on thin ice. *Please, Perry*, she thought. *Don't press me on this. I have my reasons.*

Trust me.

He scrutinized her for what felt like forever. Then his expression softened somewhat, and he sat down behind his desk, like a judge preparing to pass sentence.

"Two weeks' unpaid leave," he pronounced. "That's

your penance. And if you do something like this again, you're done."

Lois tried not to look too relieved. She figured she was getting off easy.

"Fine," she said.

His eyes narrowed.

"Make it *three,* then. Since you were so quick to agree."

"Perry—!"

He shut her up with a look.

"I *believe* you saw something, Lois," he said, and she could tell that he meant it. "And I'm not buying for a second that your leads ran cold. But whatever your reasons for dropping this, I'm glad you're doing it."

Now it was her turn to be baffled. Perry was an old-school newsman with printer's ink in his veins. Yet he wanted her to turn her back on the story of the millennium.

"Why?"

A pensive expression came over his face, replacing his usual hard-ass routine. His sober tone conveyed years of hard-won experience, and too much firsthand knowledge of what human beings were capable of doing, when frightened.

"Can you imagine what it would mean for Earth?" he asked her. "Knowing that someone like him was out there?"

Then she knew what he meant. Maybe Jonathan Kent was right.

Maybe the world wasn't ready for a superman.

Clark found his mother on the front steps of the house, planting geraniums in a window box. Dusty, the Border Collie who had succeeded Shelby some years ago, heard him coming a mile way, and started barking.

"Hi, Mom," Clark called as he headed up the walk to the house.

Dusty bolted to greet him. Clark knelt to pet the excited canine, who gave him an enthusiastic lick across the face.

"More geraniums, huh? I could never stand the smell of them."

"Me neither," she confessed, "but they're hard to kill."

He glanced around at the once-familiar setting, feeling guilty that he hadn't visited more frequently. He scanned the venerable farmhouse, which was showing its age. His eyes narrowed as he studied the eaves above the porch.

"There's dry-rot in the joists up there," he reported. "You want me to fix them? I can get it done in a day."

His mother shook her head.

"Just because you can doesn't mean you should," she said.

"What's that supposed to mean?"

"It means it'd look suspicious, getting done so fast." She stripped off her gardening gloves and put them aside. He could tell from her worried expression that the time for small talk was over. "A reporter showed up here."

"She's a friend," he replied. "Don't worry."

Calling a Lois a friend was probably a bit of stretch, but she had kept his secret—so far. He felt as if he could trust her.

His mother frowned. She seemed less than thrilled by the prospect of Clark sharing his secrets with a "friend." And he couldn't blame her. She'd spent most of her adult life guarding those secrets—and Dad had given his life for them.

But he hadn't come here to talk about Lois.

"Mom, I have to tell you something."

His tone let her know right away that this was serious.

She waited apprehensively, visibly bracing herself for whatever he had to say.

"I *found* them," he said. "My parents, my people—" He tried to contain his excitement, deliver the news gently, but it burst out of him. "I know where I come from now." As he spoke, she relaxed, and a new look crossed her face.

"That's wonderful, Clark," she said softly. "I'm so happy for you."

She hugged him warmly, yet he could feel her trembling, too. He knew she meant it, that she was truly happy for him, but he couldn't miss the fact that she was clearly troubled, as well. Her anxious eyes gazed nervously into the distance.

"What?" he asked her.

"It's nothing," she insisted. "I just... when you were a baby, I used to lay by your crib at night, listening to you breathe. It was hard for you at first. You struggled. And I worried all the time. The doctors thought it was asthma, but your father and I knew the truth. You were adapting to our world."

Clark remembered Krypton's red sun and emerald magma. His homeworld had indeed been very different from Earth. He tried to imagine the challenge they had faced, raising a child from another planet.

"So what did you do?"

"We prayed you wouldn't get sick," she said. "And when you did, we never took you to the same doctor twice. We wouldn't let them x-ray you or take blood. God knows what they would have found if they had."

He nodded. "You were worried the truth would come out."

"No," she said forcefully, making sure he understood. "The truth about you is *beautiful*. We saw that the moment we laid eyes on you. And one day the world will, too." She wrung her hands. "I just worry they'll take you away from me when they do."

Clark could feel the love radiating from her like the rays of the sun. He pulled her close.

"I'm not going anywhere, Mom. I promise."

CHAPTER SEVENTEEN

NORTHCOM's main operations center put their Arctic base to shame. A small army of analysts were arrayed in front of the "big board," a wall of state-of-the-art monitors presenting real-time data and visuals from all over the planet—and beyond. Smaller screens were positioned at every desk and workstation. Telemetry command systems collected data from orbital spy satellites and monitored the positions of suspect aircraft and ocean-bound vessels.

The assembled personnel sat up straighter as a five-star general entered the room, accompanied by a female aide. Both were in full dress uniform.

"General Swanwick, sir," Dr. Hamilton greeted the center's commanding officer. Being a civilian, he wasn't obliged to salute.

Swanwick nodded curtly. His stern features looked as though they had been carved out of dark brown granite. He examined the main screen, which depicted a time-lapsed view of a large dark object moving across familiar constellations. He assumed that this was the UFO that had demanded his presence tonight.

"What am I looking at, Doc?" he asked. "A comet? Asteroid?"

Hamilton shook his head, a frown appearing on his face.

"Comets don't make course corrections, General."

Swanwick understood. This was not a natural phenomenon. Someone—or something—was guiding it.

"Have you tried communicating with it?"

The scientist nodded.

"So far, it hasn't responded," he said. "The ship *appears* to be inserting itself into a lunar synchronous orbit directly between the earth and the moon." He stroked his goatee thoughtfully. "Though I have no idea why."

Swanwick hazarded a guess.

"I'm just speculating," he said, "but I think whoever's at the wheel of that beast is looking to make a dramatic entrance."

Monitors captured satellite shots of an alien vessel. Its silhouette resembled a gigantic tripod, descending across the face of the moon. Three immense legs or tentacles hung beneath the bell-shaped mantle of the ship. Its size and ominous black shape made it impossible to miss—which may have been the idea. All eyes were on the unidentified vessel as it actually *eclipsed* the moon.

Swanwick frowned.

Shock and awe, he thought. *That's military thinking.*

"*Re-supply toner,*" the laser printer blinked annoyingly. Lois resisted the urge to kick the recalcitrant machine. How was she supposed to make her deadline if technology refused to cooperate? She stormed out of her cubicle and into the hall. Tomorrow's paper had yet to be put to bed, so the bullpen was still abuzz with activity. She looked around to find somebody who would assist her.

"Anybody know where the toner cartridges are——?" she said.

But nobody paid any attention to her. Instead she saw Lombard and Jenny rushing across the bullpen. They looked as if they had a lot more than toner on their minds. Even Steve looked excited, and maybe a little scared.

Lois didn't like being out of the loop.

"What's going on?" she asked before they had passed.

"It's on the news!" Jenny called out. "Everyone's talking about it!"

Talking about what? Lois hurried after them to the other side of the room, where she found Perry and the rest of the staff staring at a bank of TV monitors, tuned to every major station. As much as the *Planet* regarded broadcast journalism as the competition, they still needed to monitor breaking stories as they happened.

Every channel—Fox, CNN, even the major networks—was running the same footage, showing what looked like a giant, three-limbed octopus hanging in front of the full moon. Lois stared wide-eyed at the ominous UFO. More than anyone else in the room, she knew that Earth was sometime visited by vessels from other worlds.

Could this have anything to do with Clark? Or that ship they'd found buried beneath the ice?

She glanced out a window and was stunned when she saw the lights of Metropolis going dark, borough by borough, block by block. Before she could say anything the wave hit the *Daily Planet* building and the power went out, throwing the bullpen and offices into darkness. Startled gasps and even yelps came from the group—even Perry. People stumbled and bumped into each other.

Lois reached out to steady herself against a cubicle wall. *This isn't a coincidence,* she thought. The alien ship had to be responsible for the sudden blackout. *But are they doing it on purpose?*

And what did they want?

Barely more than a hundred miles above the Earth, a disabled spy satellite drifted out of orbit. The high-tech hardware, pulled into space at an ever-increasing speed, crashed full-tilt against the *Black Zero*'s dark unyielding hull. It crumpled to pieces, yet the prison ship's dense plating remained unscratched by the collision.

Far below, the entire continent was going dark, from the eastern seaboard on through to the west...

Clark was in the kitchen, drying dishes while watching a Kansas City Royals game on TV, when the lights went out. Puzzled, he stood in the dark for a moment before he heard his mother cry out in alarm.

"Clark!"

Abandoning the dishes, he raced out onto the front porch of the farmhouse, where his mother was gazing up at the sky with a frightened expression on her face. Moonlight shone down on the farm—despite the unearthly black silhouette drifting between Earth and its satellite. Clark couldn't believe his eyes.

Another ship?

His eyes narrowed as his vision brought the mysterious vessel into closer focus. It appeared much larger, and was differently configured than the scout ship he'd found in the Arctic, but the bio-organic look of it definitely hinted at Kryptonian origins.

Had someone else survived the destruction of Krypton—and found him at last?

Suddenly he wasn't sure how he felt about that.

"It's a ship," he told his mom.

Before he could say anything more, the TV set in the living room squawked and blinked back on, even though the rest of the house remained dark. Clark and Martha went back inside and cautiously contemplated the glowing TV screen, which provided the only illumination. Electronic snow filled the screen. Then a nameless, faceless voice emerged from the speakers.

"YOU ARE NOT ALONE. YOU ARE NOT ALONE."

Clark knelt before the TV set and switched from channel to channel. The same visual static—and the same repetitive message—was on every channel.

"YOU ARE NOT ALONE. YOU ARE NOT ALONE."

A chill ran down his spine. He was an alien, and even *he* found this creepy. He could only imagine how ordinary men and women were coping with it. Was this the beginning of a new era of extraterrestrial contact—or the end of life as they knew it?

Clark wished he had the answers.

At the *Daily Planet*, Lois and her colleagues were transfixed by the unprecedented communication. Every monitor was obscured by static. The anonymous voice issued from every speaker.

Lombard had retreated to his cubicle.

"It's coming over the RSS feeds, too!"

"Same with my phone!" Jenny reported.

Every computer in the office had been hijacked by the ominous message. It was on Twitter, Facebook, YouTube, the message boards, even the *Planet*'s own interactive web page.

"—NOT ALONE. YOU ARE NOT ALONE."

* * *

Then the message changed, and a voice addressed the world. Somehow it was translated into every language.

"MY NAME IS GENERAL ZOD," it said.

At NORTHCOM Ops Center, General Swanwick listened warily. He stood with his trusted aide, Captain Carrie Farris, an up-and-comer with short dark hair and a no-nonsense attitude. The static-filled screens of the big board were the only lights in the op center, giving it the dim, nocturnal atmosphere of a submarine's control room.

Dr. Hamilton stared at the glowing screens, rapt with fascination. He had been waiting his entire life for an encounter like this. The rest of the staff, however, looked more apprehensive than intrigued.

"I COME FROM KRYPTON, A WORLD FAR FROM YOURS."

The sun was rising in Nepal as nomadic herders flocked around a single jury-rigged television set inside a tent made of hides. Nervous yaks lowed at the moon. The herders listened anxiously as the voice spoke in their native tongue.

"WE HAVE JOURNEYED ACROSS AN OCEAN OF STARS TO REACH YOU."

Busy pedestrians, shoppers, and commuters froze in the streets of Shinjuku, Tokyo, which was ordinarily a bustling commercial district. They gawked at the many large video screens adorning the skyscrapers, all of which were broadcasting the same message in fluent Japanese. A sunny sky stood in ominous contrast to the frightening announcement.

"THE MESSAGE WE BRING IS ONE OF GREAT URGENCY."

The sun had not yet risen in Moscow, but the crisis had driven confused and frightened Russians onto the streets. Speechless Muscovites gathered in front of a popular electronics store, staring at the big screen TVs on display in the window. Cyrillic text scrolled across the screens.

"FOR SOME TIME, YOUR WORLD HAS SHELTERED ONE OF OUR CITIZENS."

Two wide-eyed teenagers sat on a couch in a basement rec room. Their Xbox controls rested forgotten in their sweaty palms as their screen was captured by an unknown controller.

"WE REQUEST THAT YOU RETURN THIS INDIVIDUAL TO OUR CUSTODY."

At a busy international airport, jetlagged travelers crowded around banks of monitors that no longer displayed the usual departure and arrival times. Instead the screens announced the unexpected arrival of a flight from another world. The pilot of that flight had new instructions for the travelers.

"FOR REASONS UNKNOWN—"

A night game at a crowded football stadium had come to an abrupt halt. Dumbfounded players stood on the field, staring up in unison at the Jumbotron screen now bearing Zod's message. In the stands, thousands of cell phones received identical communications.

"—HE HAS CHOSEN TO KEEP HIS EXISTENCE A SECRET FROM YOU."

Locals clustered around a beat-up, secondhand TV in the squalid Nigerian shantytown, while casting nervous glances up at the sky. Plywood homes with corrugated metal roofs, assembled from scrap materials, suddenly seemed more fragile than usual.

"HE WILL HAVE MADE EFFORTS TO BLEND IN. HE WILL LOOK LIKE YOU."

Clark wrapped his arm around his mom. He alone recognized the name of the speaker—a name Jor-El had associated with violence and rebellion. General Zod had launched a bloody civil war, back on Krypton…

"BUT HE IS *NOT* ONE OF YOU."

Lois's gaze remained glued to the static-filled screens. She feared that she knew *exactly* who Zod was talking about, and so did Perry. They shared a worried look. Perry's scowl deepened.

"TO THOSE OF YOU WHO MAY KNOW OF HIS CURRENT LOCATION—THE FATE OF YOUR PLANET RESTS IN YOUR HANDS."

Lois gulped. Perry watched her carefully.

"COMPLY WITH OUR REQUEST, AND WE WILL REWARD YOU IN KIND."

Tearing her gaze away, Lois walked to the window. The ship hung before the lambent moon, visible to the naked eye. The absence of the usual city lights made its silhouette all the easier to see.

She wondered what it looked like from Smallville.

"TO KAL-EL, I SAY THIS: SURRENDER WITHIN TWENTY-FOUR HOURS. OR WATCH THIS WORLD SUFFER THE CONSEQUENCES."

Standing in the Kent family living room, Clark listened to the ultimatum. His mother shuddered in his arms. He had already shared his Kryptonian birth name with her, so she understood the decision he faced now— as well as the fact that his alien heritage had brought all this upon them.

The transmission ended abruptly. The faceless static vanished, to be replaced by the Emergency Broadcast signal. The lights came on so suddenly that Martha jumped in surprise. The power surge caused a bulb to pop overhead. He heard her heart skip a beat.

Clark did his best to comfort her, but his own thoughts were consumed by a name that should have never been heard on Earth. A name that should have been lost with the destruction of Krypton.

Zod.

CHAPTER EIGHTEEN

The lights came back on at NORTHCOM, where General Swanwick was already on the phone with the White House. Numerous monitors continued to track the "Kryptonian" vessel.

"Yes, sir," the general said. "We're activating the Joint Emergency Evacuation Plan, but I'd advise against using Air Force One. I'm not sure the skies are safe."

To be honest, he wasn't sure *anywhere* was safe.

Lois stood at the window of her cluttered third-floor apartment, gazing up at the unnatural black shape that loomed high in the sky. Zod's ship was still visible, even by daylight, and it didn't look like it was going anywhere.

Not without Clark.

She had tried calling Smallville, leaving numerous messages on Martha Kent's voicemail, but so far she hadn't managed to get hold of Clark or his mom. She guessed that he was dealing with bigger things than returning her calls. She just wished she had a better idea of what exactly was at stake.

Who was this *Zod*? And what did he want with Clark? Her TV droned in the background. She half-listened as Woodburn—of all people—discussed the crisis with David Rowland, a network talking head with more phony gravitas than journalistic chops. He was barely a step above Woodburn when it came to professional ethics.

"I think the question everyone is asking this morning is, who is this guy? And why has he kept his existence a secret from us for so long? I mean, we hardly know anything about him. Isn't that right?"

"We know nothing," Woodburn declared. *"And that's why I'm speaking out right now. He could be a criminal for all we know. And if he is, why should we pay for his crimes?"*

"Aren't people innocent until proven guilty?" Rowland asked.

"Sure," Woodburn conceded. *"But this guy's not human."*

Lois frowned, afraid that too many other people would feel the same way. She trusted Clark, and owed him her life, but to the rest of the world, he was just a scary alien infiltrator, posing as a human—and maybe a fugitive to boot.

She moved to turn off the TV, but her phone rang before she could locate the remote. She picked up her phone instead, and as she did, Woodburn kept right on with his rabble-rousing.

"Kal-El, or whatever his name is… if he doesn't really mean us any harm, he should turn himself in to his people, and face the consequences. And if he won't, then we should. Lois Lane knows who the guy is. She's the one we should be questioning."

"Terrific," Lois muttered. She should have known he'd rat her out like that, just to get a little extra air time.

Annoyed and distracted, she answered the ringing phone.

Perry spoke before she could even say hello.

"Are you watching this crap?" he asked. She could imagine him pacing back and forth in his office, watching the same channel on his snazzy LCD screen. Lombard and Jenny and the rest were probably glued to the tube, as well.

"It's been running all day," Perry continued. "And for once, I actually agree with Woodburn. Where is he, Lois? Do you know?"

"Even if I did, I wouldn't say," she replied.

"The entire world's been threatened," he argued. "This isn't the time to fall back on journalistic integrity."

"I'm not, Perry," she said, struggling to keep her cool. "This isn't about me grandstanding. He said he's here to help us. And I *believe* him."

The conviction—and passion—in her voice startled even her. When did she become the president of the Clark Kent Fan Club? When he carried her bags through the snow, or when he healed her busted insides with his laser eyes?

"Lois, listen to me. This is serious." He lowered his voice. "The FBI's here, interviewing everyone. And they're throwing around words like 'treason.'"

She heard brakes squealing outside. Cranky Metropolis motorists honked in protest. She dashed to the window and looked to see what the commotion was, afraid that she already knew the answer.

"You need to get yourself a lawyer immediately."

Black vans pulled up at the curb outside the building. Men in dark suits piled out of the vehicles, accompanied by a paramilitary unit in full body armor. The Feds clearly weren't taking any chances.

"I gotta go, Perry!" she said quickly. Hanging up,

she scooted out of her apartment and sprinted to the stairwell at the end of the hall. She ran down four flights of stairs, wincing at the sound of her own footsteps, until she reached the basement.

Washing machines and dryers churned in the laundry room. She ran past the tenant storage units to the back stairs, which led to a back alley that ran behind the building. Rusty dumpsters crowded the narrow way. A cool autumn wind blew litter into a tiny whirlwind.

She started down the alley, only to spot some G-Men at the end of the block. Changing direction, she speed-walked toward the opposite end, hoping she could make herself scarce before the Feds surrounded the entire building. As a rule, she preferred *asking* the questions, rather than being interrogated herself.

Just a few more yards, she thought. *Then maybe I can track down Clark and find out what the real story is.*

"Hey!" A voice shouted behind her. "Stop where you are!"

Damn, Lois thought, and she broke into sprint. The agents chased after her, shouting louder and more urgently. She prayed they weren't authorized to use deadly force.

"*Stop where you are!*"

She'd almost reached the end of the alley when another black SUV jumped the curb, cutting her off. Agents in suits and soldiers in body armor poured out of the van, brandishing automatic weapons. They swarmed toward Lois.

"On the ground! *On the ground, now!* Hands behind your back!"

So much for making a discreet exit. She dropped onto the filthy pavement and they surrounded her. Immediately her wrists were cuffed behind her back. Then the agents in suits yanked her to her feet and dragged her toward the waiting vehicle, where a familiar face nodded at her.

Colonel Nathan Hardy, from Ellesmere.

Lois wondered if she would get a bucket this time.

Trinity Lutheran Church was a refuge from the fast-paced streets of Metropolis, a place for prayer and solemn contemplation. Sunlight illuminated the stained-glass windows and cast a heavenly glow on the altar below. Incense flavored the tranquil atmosphere.

But not even the church could escape the impending threat from the heavens. Father Daniel Leone listened anxiously to the radio as he swept the front of the sanctuary. The alarming reports were enough to shake anyone's faith.

"*—the alien ship hovering above Metropolis has remained silent. In response, the President has declared a nationwide state of emergency—*"

Father Leone looked up from his work. Evening services were still hours away, so the pews were largely deserted, save for a troubled-looking young man seated in the back. The priest did not recognize the visitor as one of his usual parishioners, but observed that the stranger appeared to be deep in thought.

He wondered if his visitor was as worried as he was.

MARCH, 1992

"Come on! Fight back!"

Ken Braverman shoved Clark backward into a chain-link fence at the edge of the park. His backpack slipped from his shoulder and fell to the ground. Books spilled at his feet. Mocking laughter assailed Clark.

A crowd gathered to witness his latest humiliation.

Another year, another group of bullies.

It was a sunny day in Smallville, and Clark had hoped to get in a little outdoor reading while his dad was picking groceries up in town. But it looked like Braverman and his pals had other ideas. Even after what had happened, they were still tormenting him. It was as if they didn't believe it—as if they were *testing* him.

Maybe they were actually starting to forget…

The toughs were fifteen and sixteen—a couple of years older than Clark, but he spotted several of his own classmates among the audience—including Pete Ross who stood sheepishly at the back of the crowd, looking uncomfortable. There were also a fair number of girls watching, which made the embarrassing spectacle a hundred times worse.

"Get up, Kent!" Braverman said.

If only I could fight back, Clark thought, seething in frustration. He wanted nothing more than to punch his tormenters all the way into the next county, show them what he was *really* capable of. But then he remembered the alien space capsule, hidden on his parents' farm—and the secret that needed to stay hidden, as well.

No matter what.

Braverman feinted a punch, forcing Clark to flinch like any ordinary person would. The other boys laughed uproariously and, even worse, some of the girls giggled behind their hands. Playing to the crowd, Braverman upended Clark's backpack, causing the books to tumble out again. He snatched one up at random and scornfully read the title aloud.

"Plato's *The Republic*." He snorted, as though reading Plato—or even just reading—was for losers. "What a fag!"

Like you even know what it's about, Clark thought, but he bit his tongue. He even grabbed onto a fence post to hold himself back. Maybe Braverman would get bored and leave him alone soon.

No such luck. The other kid got right in Clark's face, smirking the entire time.

"So that's it?" he taunted. "That's all you got?" The bully poked Clark in the chest, but not hard enough to break his finger. "C'mon, Kent..."

Clark's grip tightened on the steel post. For a second, he was sorely tempted to teach this gang a lesson they would never forget. Ruby fire hid behind his angry eyes. His muscles tensed.

It would almost be worth it.

But instead, he turned his eyes downward, refusing the challenge. The teenage audience, hoping for a fight, groaned in disappointment. Girls tittered loudly enough that Clark could have heard them from a thousand miles away. His cheeks burned hotly.

Braverman just shook his head in disgust. He bounced the book off Clark's chest, but he still couldn't get a rise out of his meek, mild-mannered target. So he drew back his fist, this time for real, only to balk when he spotted Jonathan Kent approaching the park, carrying a bag of groceries.

He lowered the fist, apparently thinking twice about beating Clark up right in front of his father.

"Whatever," he muttered, and he turned away.

Likewise the crowd dispersed, seeking other entertainment. Clark didn't know whether to be relieved or mortified by his dad's timely arrival.

I'm thirteen years old, he thought, *and I'm not even allowed to stand up for myself.*

He let go of the post, which was crimped where he'd

grabbed it. His fingers had left deep impressions in the metal. Part of Clark wished that he'd left his mark on Braverman instead, even if that might have led to questions, and investigations, and everything his parents had worked so hard to avoid, all these years.

He bent to pick up his books. To his surprise, Pete Ross came forward to help him. He picked up Plato's *The Republic* and handed it back to Clark, still unable to meet his eyes.

Jonathan stopped a short distance away, and waited.

"I wanted to help," Pete mumbled, "but, you know—"

He had changed since Clark had saved him from drowning. He was less cocky, and more inclined to leave Clark alone.

"It's okay," Clark said, and he meant it. He didn't expect Pete to fight his battles for him. Any small kindness was appreciated. The boy recovered another book, handed it to him, then drifted away.

Clark hoped Pete wouldn't be too hard on himself for not coming forward. It was enough that he hadn't joined in the tormenting.

His father waited until Pete was gone before stepping closer.

"Did they hurt you?" he asked.

"You know they can't," Clark said bitterly.

"That's not what I meant," his dad said. "Are you all right?"

Clark wasn't sure. He looked into his father's eyes.

"You want the truth," he replied. "I hate them. I wanted to hit him *so bad*—"

"I know you did," Jonathan said. "Hell, part of me even wanted you to. But then what? Would it make you feel any better? They pick on you because you're different. That's what people do. We're hard-wired that way. You want to hit back. I get it. It's *easy*… especially for someone like you.

"But showing mercy?" he added. "That actually takes character. That takes real strength."

I know, I know, Clark thought. *But it still sucks… big time.*

His father wasn't finished. He spoke carefully, making sure Clark was listening.

"You just have to decide what kind of man you want to grow up to be, Clark. Because *whoever* that man is, good character or bad, he's going to change the world."

Right now Clark would have settled for just getting through junior high with a modicum of dignity. But he understood what his father was saying. Like it or not, his special abilities were a burden—and a responsibility—he couldn't escape. He could either use them the right way, like saving Pete and the others, or he could cause a lot of damage, maybe to people like Ken Braverman.

He just wished the Bravermans of the world didn't make that choice so tricky sometimes…

"Can I help you?" the priest asked.

Clark looked up to see the priest gazing down on him with a concerned expression on his face. Memories of Smallville retreated, as his present-day dilemma descended on him like the alien ship hanging in the sky.

"I'm sorry, Father," he apologized, reluctant to burden the man with his troubles. "I just… needed someone to talk to, I guess."

"I'd be happy to sit with you, if you like." He joined Clark in the pew. "What's on your mind?"

Clark doubted the priest had ever heard a confession like this before.

"I don't know where to start."

"Wherever you want."

Clark began cautiously, keeping things vague.

"In my work… I often have the opportunity to save people."

"That's a good thing, isn't it?"

"It is. But sometimes I have to make *choices*—"

Father Leone nodded as if he understood.

"Every time a doctor has to triage a patient, or a dispatcher has to decide where to send a squad car, they're *choosing*, he said. "It's part of life. That's what makes us human."

Clark took the plunge.

"What if I'm not human?"

The priest's eyes widened in surprise. An uneasy expression came over his face. Clark heard the man's pulse speed up.

"The ship that appeared last night," he said. "I'm the one they're looking for."

Clark half-expected Father Leone to run for help, perhaps shout for the authorities, but the priest stayed where he was. Although his body language was considerably warier than it had been before, the father kept on talking to him.

"Do you know *why* they want you?"

Clark shook his head.

"No," he admitted. "I've lived here my whole life. Until last night, I thought I was the only one of my people left. But this General Zod—" He decided to spare the priest a lesson in Kryptonian history and politics, which he still barely understood. "Even if I surrender, there's no guarantee he'll keep his word. But if there's a chance I can save earth by turning myself in, shouldn't I take it?"

Father Leone regarded him with obvious sympathy.

He seemed to understand the tremendous weight of Clark's dilemma. There was so much at stake—including, perhaps, the fate of two very different peoples. How could even a superman know what was best for the world?

"You want me to make the choice for you," the priest said gently. "I can't."

Clark's shoulders slumped. For the first time since learning to fly, he felt trapped. Was this what Krypton's terrible gravity felt like? He wished his *human* father was still alive to counsel him.

"What does your gut tell you?" the priest asked.

"That Zod cannot be trusted," he replied. Zod had launched a civil war on Krypton, and Clark shuddered to think what he had in store for Earth. "Problem is, I'm not sure the people of Earth can be, either."

He realized how harsh that sounded. He hoped Father Leone didn't take it the wrong way, as a threat or a rebuke. Fearing he'd said too much, Clark stood up and started to ease his way out of the pew.

"Look, I'm sorry I bothered you."

The priest waved away Clark's apologies. Then he offered the best advice he could.

"Sometimes you have to take a leap of faith first," he said. "The trust part comes later."

How much did Clark trust humanity?

And how far did he have to go to earn *their* trust?

CHAPTER NINETEEN

"Where is the alien, Ms. Lane?"

General Swanwick leaned across his desk at NORTHCOM HQ. Colonel Hardy and Dr. Hamilton—whom Lois remembered from Ellesmere—were also taking part in the interrogation. A pair of federal agents stood guard by the door, just in case she tried to make a break for it.

Fat chance, Lois thought. She knew better than to try to get past an army of soldiers on high alert. She'd have better odds breaking out of a supermax prison.

"I told you," she said irritably, "I don't know."

"The FBI have your hard drive, your emails," Hardy said, playing bad cop. "They know you were tracking him. Keeping silent doesn't benefit anyone."

Except maybe Clark, she thought. *And everyone who's depending on him.*

"We believe the ship you discovered transmitted a signal that guided the visitors to Earth," Emil Hamilton stated. "The question is, why is this particular individual so valuable to them. Did he ever discuss a motive for his people's journey?"

Lois kept silent, unwilling to reveal anything that might be used against Clark. She stared back at her interrogators without flinching. She wasn't about to let anyone intimidate her—not even a five-star general.

"Be reasonable, Ms. Lane," Swanwick said. "If you're found guilty of treason, you could be given the death penalty."

"I've been threatened with death before, General," she responded. "It doesn't scare me."

"Then what about the aliens that levied this ultimatum?" he countered. "Because they sure as hell scare *me*."

Lois knew how he felt, but she held her tongue. Clark wasn't like them—he wasn't the enemy, of that much she was sure.

"He's not *human*, Ms. Lane." Swanwick pounded on his desk in frustration. "Why are you protecting him?"

"I'm not!" she blurted. "He doesn't need my protection. *We need his*." She tried her damnedest to make them understand. "If we give him up, there's no one left to stop them. They *know* that. That's why they want him!"

The general's aide, Captain Farris, rushed into the office. She was breathless, and very flustered.

"Sir, we've, umm, got a situation out at the North Gate."

Swanwick had read the leaked accounts of Lane's experiences in Arctic. He had been briefed on the alien's alleged superhuman abilities. Even so, as his Humvee pulled up to the gate, he rubbed his eyes in disbelief.

A caped figure, clad in red, blue, and gold, hovered in the air above the base's main gate, brazenly defying gravity. A stylized "S" was emblazoned on the chest of his uniform, while his crimson cape flapped gently in the wind. A dark-haired Caucasian male, the man matched the description of the alien who had infiltrated the base at Ellesmere—and absconded with the buried spaceship.

He looked surprisingly human.

Battle-clad soldiers scrambled in response to the incursion, bringing their weapons to bear, but the floating stranger appeared unconcerned by the battery of automatic rifles, handguns, and missile launchers that were targeting him. Swanwick wondered what he knew that they didn't.

He and Hardy got out of the vehicle. He approached the intruder.

"All right," Swanwick said. "You've got our attention. What do you want?"

"I want to talk to Lois Lane."

Swanwick hedged, testing the intruder's intel.

"What makes you think she's here?"

"Don't play games with me, General," he said without hesitation. "I'll surrender. But only if you guarantee Lois's freedom."

Swanwick weighed his options. Taking the alien into custody seemed worth the risk. He nodded, and the figure descended to the pavement, touching down as lightly as an army chopper—or a dancer.

An armed security team cuffed the prisoner and marched him toward the compound. Experienced military personnel, most of whom had seen combat, nervously watched as he passed by. Nothing in their training had prepared them for a close encounter like this.

The general found himself pining for the good old days, when all he'd had to worry about were terrorists and rogue nations. Not strange visitors from another planet.

* * *

Despite herself, Lois was relieved to see Clark again. He sat opposite her in a sterile white containment cell, his cuffed hands resting in his lap. She assumed they were being monitored by about a zillion cameras, scanners, and recording devices. A long rectangular mirror occupied one wall of the cell, and Lois had seen enough cop shows to know they had a live audience, as well.

"Why are you surrendering to Zod?" she asked.

"I'm not," he answered. "I'm surrendering myself to *mankind*. There's a difference." He sounded certain, as if he had thought long and hard about his decision, and was at peace with his choice. "It's your world. I'm letting you—all of you—decide what happens next."

She glanced at his wrists.

"You let them cuff you."

"Wouldn't be much of a surrender if I resisted." He shrugged. "If it makes them feel more secure, all the better."

She turned her attention to the colorful blue-and-red costume he had donned for the occasion. It was a far cry from the ordinary, civilian attire she'd always seen him in before. Her gaze zeroed in on the emblem on his chest.

"So what does the 'S' stand for?"

"It's not an 'S,'" he explained. "On my world, it means 'hope.'"

"Well, *here* it's an 'S.'" She thought it over, searching for something more headline-friendly. "So how about... Superman?"

He blushed slightly, which she found rather charming.

"Sounds a little showy," he said.

And that suit isn't? she thought. The way she saw it, anything was better than "Scary Alien Guy."

Superman it is, she decided.

* * *

The observation room on other side of the two-way mirror was packed with military brass and scientists, all getting their first close look at the alien as he interacted with Lane. Swanwick wasn't sure what he thought about this whole "Superman" business, but figured it was as good a label as any, at least until they uncovered his true identity.

"He seems so human," Carrie Farris observed.

"The similarities are only skin deep, I assure you," Dr. Hamilton said. He and his fellow brainiacs were hunched over an array of remote-imaging monitors. A battery of sensors had been deployed to probe the alien's anatomy using everything from infrared to ultrasound. "Based on these readings, his muscles and bones are considerably denser than ours."

"What about flight?" Swanwick asked. "How can he keep aloft?"

"I have no idea," Hamilton admitted. "Some kind of bio-electric field?"

Superman turned toward the mirror.

"I don't know how I fly. I just *do*."

Swanwick and the others twitched in surprise. *What the devil*, the general thought. *That cell is supposed to be soundproof.*

"I can hear you just fine, general," the alien said. "Your heartbeats, too. So I wouldn't advise lying to me."

Hamilton leaned forward and keyed the intercom.

"Sir, my name is—"

"Dr. Emil Hamilton, I know." Superman seemed to look straight through the mirror at them. "I can see your ID in your breast pocket. Along with a half-eaten roll of Wintergreen Lifesavers."

The scientist sheepishly checked his pocket. Then he nodded in confirmation.

Superman shifted his gaze, looking directly at Swanwick.

"You should know that I can see those soldiers in the next room, readying that 'tranquilizing agent' of yours."

Sure enough, another monitor showed the soldiers preparing a high-tech injector system designed by DARPA. Swanwick had been assured that even without a needle, the injector would penetrate the alien's skin, no matter how dense it was. At least, in theory.

"You won't need it," Superman said. "And even if you did, I doubt it would work on me."

The alien's confidence was both unnerving and annoying. He had already demonstrated sensory abilities beyond anything they had anticipated. Who knew what other tricks he had up his steel-blue sleeve?

Swanwick irritably signaled his soldiers to stand down.

"You can't expect us not to take precautions," Hamilton stated. "What if you're carrying some kind of alien pathogen?"

"I've been here for thirty-three years, doctor. I haven't infected anyone yet."

"That you *know* of," Swanwick said. "I'm sorry, but your assurances aren't good enough. We have legitimate security concerns." He nodded at Lois, confident that Superman could see him through the mirror. "You've revealed your identity to Ms. Lane here. Why won't you do the same with us?"

Superman rose from the table and approached the mirror. Fearful scientists and technicians backed away from the glass.

"Let's put our cards on the table, general," the alien said. "You're scared of me because you can't control me. You don't. And you never will. But that doesn't mean I'm your enemy."

Swanwick wished he could believe him.

"Then who is?" he asked. "Zod?"

"That's what I'm worried about, yes."

Then we have that in common, Swanwick thought, *if you're telling the truth.* Then he said, "Be that as it may, I have been given orders to hand you over to him."

The general braced himself for Superman's reaction, and Farris placed her hand on her sidearm. But their visitor accepted the news with a stoic expression. If he was disappointed in humanity for acceding to Zod's demands, it was difficult to tell. He just nodded gravely.

"Do what you have to do, then."

CHAPTER TWENTY

Dawn was rising as assault teams massed on an airfield outside NORTHCOM's command center. General Swanwick, Dr. Hamilton, Colonel Hardy and Captain Farris were already positioned behind concrete barriers. All eyes were on Superman and Lois, who were standing by themselves in the middle of the airfield. Spotlights lit up the scene.

"If I don't come back," he said, "I wanted to thank you."

"For what?" she asked.

"Believing in me. Not revealing my identity."

She shook her head glumly.

"Didn't make much difference in the end."

"It did to me."

After a lifetime of hiding, it felt strange and oddly liberating to have revealed himself to the world at last. She squeezed his hand as they watched the sun rise. Finally he lifted his eyes to the sky, waiting. He heard a whooshing sound high above them.

"They're coming," he said. "You should go."

She peered upward, unable to see what he was seeing. She hesitated, clearly reluctant to abandon him.

He appreciated her loyalty, but he wanted her out of harm's way.

"*Go*, Lois." His voice was firm.

She didn't argue the point, thank heavens, and retreated behind the security cordon, where she joined General Swanwick and the others. With any luck, Swanwick would honor their agreement and release her once he was gone.

Superman continued to listen to the approaching spacecraft, which was louder now, and eavesdropped on the NORTHCOM folks from several yards away, as well.

"Do we have a backup plan if this goes pear-shaped?" Dr. Hamilton asked.

"Only the unthinkable one," Swanwick said. "Code words have already been issued."

Superman visualized mushroom clouds exploding above Earth. He prayed it wouldn't come to that. He had met too many people he admired, all across the planet, to wish such a fate on his adopted world.

A light appeared in the sky as a Kryptonian dropship came into view. He recognized the basic design from Jor-El's history lessons. About the size of the *Debbie Sue*, the ship resembled a giant mutant insect with a hard, impervious shell. Delta-shaped, it was aerodynamically designed to travel through both planetary atmospheres and the vacuum of space. Its thrusters flared brightly as it came in for a landing.

Hardened soldiers gasped and checked their weapons. A few crossed themselves or offered up murmured prayers. Despite his apprehensions regarding Zod's agenda, Superman felt a tremor of excitement, as well. These were his people, after all. For the first time in his life, he was about to meet other living Kryptonians.

Maybe this was just a reunion?

The dropship touched down on the tarmac. Segmented limbs served as landing gear. A valve slid open and a solitary figure emerged in a haze of heat vapor. Clearly female, she wore an intimidating suit of jet-black armor. Jagged fins added to the uniform's fearsome aspect. A space helmet, with a visor that consisted of an opaque force field, concealed her features—even from his X-ray vision.

She walked briskly across the runway toward Superman; confidence echoed in her every step. She saluted him with military precision and activated a control on her armor. Her visor went transparent, revealing the striking feature of an attractive female with short dark hair and icy brown eyes. Like Jor-El, she could easily have been mistaken for human.

"Kal-El," she addressed him. "My name is Sub-Commander Faora-Ul. On behalf of General Zod, I extend you his greetings."

She walked past Superman toward the security perimeter. Wary soldiers placed her in their sights, but she stopped before crossing the proverbial line in the sand. She nodded at General Swanwick, who watched her from behind a concrete barrier. Her body language conveyed a disdainful hauteur.

"Are you the ranking officer here?" she asked.

Swanwick nodded. "I am."

She pointed at Lois, who was standing with Swanwick and the rest.

"General Zod would like this woman to accompany us."

Colonel Hardy instinctively stepped in front of Lois. He shook his head.

"You asked for the alien," he protested. "You didn't say anything about one of our own citizens."

Faora arched an eyebrow, clearly amused by Hardy's

defiance. Ignoring the colonel, she spoke directly to Swanwick instead.

"Shall I tell General Zod you are unwilling to comply?" The implied threat could not have been clearer.

"It's all right," Lois said. She squeezed past Hardy. "I'll go."

Swanwick and Hardy both stared at her in surprise, but they were in no position to argue. Swallowing his pride, the general allowed her to cross the security perimeter. Faora turned her back on the military brass and gestured for Lois to follow. They crossed the tarmac toward Superman.

"Lois," he said anxiously. "What are you doing?"

She rejoined him next to the Kryptonian vessel.

"I've been at the center of this story from the beginning," she said, and she shrugged. "I might as well see it through to the end."

Superman didn't like it one bit. He looked Faora in the eye.

"I'm not letting you take her," he said firmly.

Faora smirked, unimpressed.

"I was bred to kill, son of El. As were my crewmates. The specific areas of our brains governing conscience were altered, so that we are genetically incapable of feeling empathy toward our enemies." She tilted her head toward the troops that surrounded them. "Knowing this, do you really wish to see us engage the humans arrayed around us?"

So much for a happy reunion, Superman thought. His worst fears had been confirmed. Zod's people were just as ruthless as Jor-El had suggested. If they possessed the same abilities he did, he could only imagine what they could do to Swanwick and his people. The fragile soldiers wouldn't stand a chance.

He had no choice but to let them take Lois as well.

Faora knew she had the upper hand. She turned the visor opaque once more, hiding her cruel smile behind a faceless forcefield. Superman took Lois's hand as they reluctantly boarded the dropship. As the door slid shut behind them, he glanced back at the human authorities who had delivered him into Zod's hands. He could hear their hearts pounding.

Captain Farris had a guilty look on her face. She looked away, and Swanwick noted her reaction.

"You have something to say, Captain?" he asked.

"Just wondering if we did the right thing, sir."

Swanwick watched the alien ship take off into the sky. "Believe me, so am I."

Lois had always dreamed of being the first reporter in space. This wasn't exactly how she'd imagined it, but she supposed it would have to do. She sat beside Clark—no, *Superman*—in the cockpit of the dropship as it flew beyond the atmosphere and into the vacuum. The ship rolled laterally and Earth came into view through a transparent port. Despite her perilous situation, Lois was overcome with wonder at the sight of the cloudy blue orb rotating below her. She had seen orbital photographs of Earth before, naturally, but that was nothing like looking down on the planet with her own eyes.

Holy cow, she thought. *I'm in space… for real.*

The big question, of course, was whether she would ever set foot on Earth again, now that she had literally been abducted by aliens. Or did it still count as an abduction if you volunteered—even under duress?

Superman took her hand again. Although she knew

he was capable of crushing her bones to powder, his grip was both firm and gentle. To her surprise, he slipped something into her palm before withdrawing his hand.

What's this?

Faora was busy piloting the ship, so Lois risked a peek at the object Superman had surreptitiously passed to her. It was short black spike marked with the S-sigil he wore on his chest.

Hope, she remembered. *It stands for hope.*

She shot him a quizzical look. He responded with a barely perceptible shake his head. She got the message.

Not now.

Wait.

But for what?

The ship rolled again, bringing their destination into view. The gigantic alien vessel, whose televised image had captivated the entire world, hovered before them. The squid-like mothership was easily as tall as the *Daily Planet* building, and several times larger than the huge spacecraft she'd found buried under that glacier on Ellesmere. Three mechanical tentacles hung beneath its immense obsidian mantle. Lois flinched slightly, recalling the tentacled robot that had nearly killed her.

What is it with the Kryptonians and scary pseudopods?

"Behold the *Black Zero,*" Faora said proudly.

The name meant nothing to Lois. Maybe it lost something in the translation.

An airlock slid open in the hull of the larger vessel. Faora piloted the dropship inside and touched down. The door slid shut again.

A reception committee composed of yet more alien soldiers saluted Faora as she exited with the visitors from Earth. Lois was surprised—and a little disappointed— to discover that some manner of artificial gravity was in place aboard the *Black Zero*. Her feet remained squarely on the floor.

Faora removed her helmet. She took a deep breath of the ship's pressurized air.

"The atmospheric composition on our ship isn't compatible with humans," she divulged. "You will need to wear a breather beyond this point."

She wasn't kidding. Lois was already finding it hard to breathe. She gasped, and her lungs burned.

A female Kryptonian, whom Faora addressed as Car-Vex, fitted Lois with a respirator helmet. It was a trifle claustrophobic, but at least she could breathe more easily.

"Are you all right?" Superman asked.

"I'm okay." She didn't want to let on how scared she was.

An inner doorway slid open at the other end of the airlock. Wasting no time, Faora and her underlings marched them into the heart of the ship, which proved to be a very bleak and gloomy environment. Unlike the futuristic white corridors she had envisioned, the Kryptonian vessel was a warren of cramped, claustrophobic tunnels and catacombs, dimly lit, cold, and drafty. The spooky alien milieu gave her goosebumps, and not just because of the uncomfortably low temperature.

Alcatraz was cozy by comparison.

A sickly green bioluminescence provided barely enough light for her to see anything. Shivering, Lois kept her hand closed tightly on the object Superman had passed her.

She knew it had to be important. She just didn't know why.

* * *

The doorway opened onto a cavernous, multistory chamber lined with elevated catwalks. Rows of empty cryostasis compartments lined one wall of the chamber, giving it the feel of a futuristic alien cell block. A handful of Kryptonian soldiers waited for them on a platform overlooking the ground floor of the chamber. It was clear at a glance who was the man in charge.

He stood at the forefront of the assemblage, gazing down at the visitors like a dictator addressing his subjects from a palace balcony. His stern, saturnine features lacked the warmth and gentle nobility of Jor-El, although his shrewd eyes appeared equally intelligent. He was tall and fit, but his deeply lined face looked as if it had been through the wars. Cropped brown hair was graying at the temples. His black and silver uniform, made of the same durable Kryptonian fabric as Superman's own suit, was adorned with stripes and medals befitting his rank. A long black cloak hung from his shoulders.

"Kal-El," he said. "You have no idea how long we've been searching for you."

I'll bet, Superman thought. "I take it you're Zod?"

"*General* Zod," Faora snarled. "Our commander. Show some respect, dog."

"It's all right, Faora," Zod said calmly. He descended a flight of stairs to join them on the lower level. "We can forgive Kal any lapses in decorum. He's a stranger to our ways."

Superman remained suspicious. Zod's graciousness seemed at odds with the way he had bullied Earth in order to get his way. So he kept a close eye on Zod, even as he began to feel oddly dizzy, and then disoriented. His eyes watered. His head felt foggy all of a sudden. He blinked in confusion.

"Please," Zod insisted, "this moment should be cause for celebration, not conflict."

Superman tottered unsteadily. His head was swimming. His eyes burned. Nausea twisted his stomach. He gasped for breath.

"—feel strange... weak..."

The chamber seemed to spin around him. He stumbled forward, then dropped to his knees before Zod. A groan escaped his lips.

Lois rushed to his side.

"What's happening to him?" she asked anxiously, looking up at their captors.

"His body is rejecting our ship's atmospherics." Zod gazed down at Superman, who felt sicker than he had ever felt before. "You spent a lifetime adapting to Earth's ecology, Kal. But you never adapted to *ours.*"

Superman struggled to overcome this unexpected weakness. His head throbbed painfully. His limbs felt like rubber. His vision blurred. Sudden chills alternated with feverish hot flashes, while pressure built within his ears. He heard Lois calling out from what sounded like miles away.

"Help him!" she demanded.

"I can't," Zod replied. "Whatever's happening to him has to run its course."

Superman coughed hoarsely, spraying blood onto the deck of the ship. His face was cold and clammy. A cold sweat drenched him beneath his skinsuit. He could barely keep his head up. He fought to stay conscious, for Lois's sake, even as darkness encroached on his vision.

CHAPTER TWENTY-ONE

Clark opened his eyes. To his surprise, he was no longer aboard the *Black Zero*. Instead he glimpsed a clear blue sky beyond the front porch of his childhood home back in Smallville. He sat up and looked around. Everything was just as he remembered it—the barn, the silo, the cornfields. His old swing still hung from a tree branch in the front yard.

The farmhouse was good as new, not at all as rundown as the last time he'd seen it. The warm spring air smelled of freshly cut grass and fertilizer. Laundry hung on a clothesline.

"Hello, Kal."

He turned around to see Zod standing behind him.

"Or do you prefer Clark?" he continued. "That's the name they gave you, isn't it?"

Clark jumped to his feet. He took a closer look at his surroundings, noticing again how out-of-date they were. His eyes narrowed suspiciously.

"You can access my memories?"

"To an extent," Zod admitted. "Apparently, your unconscious decided these surroundings might put you at ease."

But Clark wasn't feeling at ease. "Where's Lois?"

"She's safe," Zod said. "I'll take you to her soon enough. But I thought you might like some answers first."

That might have sounded reasonable, if not for the evidence of history. So far Zod had given Clark little reason to trust him.

"Why don't you start with why you gave Earth an ultimatum?" he suggested.

"We didn't have time for diplomacy," Zod said. "The survival of our race depended on finding you."

Clark didn't understand.

"I was told I was the only survivor."

"And yet I'm standing here today because of your father's ingenuity."

Jor-El? Clark was caught off-guard. "You knew him?"

Zod nodded solemnly. A note of what sounded like genuine sorrow entered his voice.

"We were friends—until our beliefs drove a wedge between us. I was Krypton's military leader. My officers and I attempted a coup. We were sentenced to the Phantom Zone, a subspace dimension that exists alongside our own. Your father had developed a projector capable opening a gateway into the Zone. And since capital punishment was deemed inhumane on Krypton," Zod said with a bitter edge, "we were shunted into the Zone aboard this prison barge. Our bodies were kept in somatic fugue while our minds were supposedly 'reconditioned.'"

He chuckled bitterly.

"But the destruction of our world damaged the projector and a handful of us were awoken prematurely…"

* * *

MANY LONG CYCLES AGO

"System Failure" messages pulsed across display orbs in the cryostasis containment chamber, where the Kryptonian prisoners served out their sentences in a honeycomb of individual cells. One of the cells folded down from its niche, releasing the prisoner inside. Mobility returned to his body as the preservative gel wore off. His face twitched as he fought his way up from endless dreaming.

His fists clenched.

Zod awoke violently, sitting up straight inside the hold of the *Black Zero*. His plain black skinsuit clung to his reanimated body. He glanced around in confusion, surprised to find himself alert once again. He had never expected to wake from cryosleep.

What's happened? Why have I been freed?

As his vision came into focus, the first thing he was saw was Faora, standing before him. Tears streaked her ivory cheeks. That alone was almost enough to make Zod think he was still dreaming. He had never seen Faora cry before. He hadn't thought her capable of it.

"Krypton's gone," she said.

He had no reason to doubt her, but he clambered from his cell and staggered toward the nearest viewport to see for himself. His heart sank as he beheld nothing but a desolate debris field—strewn with planetary rubble— where Krypton had once been. Flecks of iridescent green glinted amidst the drifting asteroids, which were all that was left of the world that Zod has sworn to protect.

Jor-El had been right all along.

* * *

"We were adrift... destined to float amidst the ruins of our planet until we starved." Zod's voice caught in his throat. He looked away for a moment, overcome by the memory. The illusory Kansas farmhouse was very different from the Kryptonian prison barge that had escaped from the Phantom Zone.

Clark figured there had to be more to the story.

"How did you find your way to Earth?" he asked.

"We took a shortcut," Zod said, "just like you did. We managed to retrofit the Phantom projector into a hyperdrive. Your father made a similar modification to the ship that brought you here."

Zod and his officers stood upon the dark cavernous bridge of the *Black Zero*. No longer a prison, the ship had become an ark, carrying the last survivors of Krypton, save for one other.

The mood was tense. Having only recently escaped the Phantom Zone, the soldiers were understandably nervous about activating the projector again. Zod understood their concerns, but saw no other option. There was nothing left for them here, orbiting the wreckage of their lost world. None of Rao's other satellites could be made habitable, even if they had access to World Engines, which they did not.

If the Kryptonian race was to have a future, it would have to be forged elsewhere, around another star.

Faora and the others took their places in the acceleration couches. Zod signaled Commander Gor— one of the other reanimates—to activate the phantom drive. The man slid a command key into an active port.

All at once, the universe vanished from the viewport, to be replaced by a maelstrom of unnatural lights that didn't belong to any spectrum Zod knew. The colors hurt his eyes, and he heard some of his weaker soldiers react in fear, but he refused to look away, gazing steadily into the Zone.

A moment of turbulence shook the ship, and Zod's stomach turned over, before the *Black Zero* completed the transition and exited into normal space. In theory, they could use the phantom drive to cross countless light-years in a fraction of the time it would take otherwise. The entire galaxy was now open to them.

And so the instrument of their damnation became their salvation.

But the galaxy proved a cold and unwelcoming place. Years passed as they traversed the cosmos, looking for a new home—and perhaps the treasure Jor-El had stolen from them. In desperation, they sought out the old colonial outposts, searching for signs of life.

One such outpost was located on an icy planet of frozen black sand and windswept wastes. It looked unpromising from orbit, after the *Black Zero* materialized above it, returning to normal space, but Zod insisted on leading an expedition to the surface in the hope that some remnant of the lost colony had survived.

Located at the outer rim of its solar system, treacherously far from a cooling white dwarf, the planet was too cold to support life under ordinary circumstances. Endless night and icy winter reigned over the barren world. Its harsh environment required Zod and the others to don protective hardsuits as they trekked across the frozen black desert.

He caught a reflection of his face in the visor of Faora's helmet, and was shocked at how much their bleak odyssey had aged him. His hair was going gray at the temples, while his face was more worn and drawn than he remembered.

Howling winds had carved rocky outcroppings into jagged, twisted formations. A midnight sun—small and faint in the sky—provided only the dimmest glimmers of light. Zod and the landing party needed to rely on searchlights to explore the ruins.

All they found was death. The skeletons of long-dead colonists littered the crumbling structures, which were being eaten away by the relentless winds. Cut off from Krypton after space exploration became a discarded luxury, the abandoned outpost had withered and died, perhaps even before Krypton had. Zod and his followers found no long-lost brothers and sisters.

They were still alone.

Yet the expedition still yielded some benefits. Work crews from the *Black Zero* salvaged everything they could from the dead outpost—armor, weapons, even a massive World Engine only somewhat smaller than the *Black Zero*. The towering mechanism had apparently been left idle after the colonists lost hope, but Zod dreamed of a day when it might finally fulfill its intended purpose on a far more suitable planet.

Thus, in an impressive feat of engineering, worthy of their genetic heritage, his people married the exiled prison barge to the World Engine, creating a vast hybrid dreadnought even larger than the ship that had carried them here. Reduced to scavengers, Zod's soldiers stripped the bones of the forgotten outpost before they resumed their quest for a new beginning. The *Black Zero* searched the cosmos, homeless and without direction, until one day they received a signal from across the galaxy...

* * *

Zod waited impatiently upon the bridge while Tor-An and the others attempted to track the signal to its source. His heart raced with anticipation. In all of their years of weary wandering, he had never forgotten the miniature starcraft that had escaped Krypton before its destruction, carrying Jor-El's barbaric progeny—and their race's best hope for survival.

Could it be that the stolen Codex had finally been found?

Finally Tor-An isolated the signal. A three-dimensional star chart, hovering above the control cylinder, zeroed in on the third planet of a distant solar system. Magnification revealed a watery blue world orbiting a bright yellow star. A pulsing icon pinpointed a location near the planet's northern pole. The image zoomed again, and they saw a rocky island surrounded by icy seas.

"Then we detected a distress beacon, which you triggered when you accessed the ancient scout ship."

Dusk began to fall over the cornfields. Clark listened intently as Zod concluded his tale. He drew nearer, his mien and manner serious, and looked Clark over, as if taking his measure.

"*You* led us here, Kal," he said. "And now you have it within your power to save the rest of our race, as well."

"How?" Clark asked. He sympathized with the trials Zod and his people had endured, but suspected there was a catch. *What exactly do you want from me?*

"On Krypton," Zod explained, "the genetic template of every being yet to be born was encoded in the Registry of Citizens. Your father stole the registry's Codex, just before the end. He stored it in the capsule that brought you here."

This was news to Clark.

"For what purpose?" he asked.

"Isn't it obvious?" Zod responded. "So that Krypton could live again... on Earth."

Clark was stunned by Zod's bold statement. He wanted to think that the other Kryptonians were simply seeking refuge, as would any displaced immigrants. But he feared that Zod had something far more ambitious in mind.

He was about to demand a fuller explanation when an unexpected sight caught his eye, distracting him.

A foreign object dropped from the sky, looking like a shooting star. Far larger than the compact starcraft that had brought him to Earth decades ago, the object struck the rolling farmland less than a quarter-mile away. The impact shook the ground for miles around, almost throwing Clark off-balance. A tremendous plume of debris was thrown into the air, rising higher than a tornado. A billowing cloud of dust obscured the crash site at first, but as the cloud settled, the object rose from a smoking crater.

Clark stared in shock, unable to believe his eyes.

The World Engine towered above the blasted landscape. The colossal machine was supported by three huge legs the size of skyscrapers. Lights pulsed along the engine's armored carapace as it powered up. Clark identified it as the ancient device Zod had salvaged on the ice planet.

But what was it doing on Earth?

"For thirty-three years," Zod said, "you've hidden yourself amongst mankind. But you can't really believe that's all your father intended for you. He knew that Earth, more than any other world we'd ever discovered, was a fitting home for us. He knew there was a Genesis Chamber on the scout ship and he wanted you to *use* it. He sent you here to revive our race."

Clark wasn't so sure. Why hadn't Jor-El said so himself?

"Where is the Codex, Kal?"

Not so fast, Clark thought. "If Krypton lives again, what happens to Earth?"

As if in answer, the World Engine fired a titanic pulse of energy that spread outward across the wide Kansas plains, clearing away everything in its path. Acres of wheat and corn were flattened by the blast. Trees and telephone poles toppled. The blast swept over the Kent farm, instantly obliterating the farmhouse, barns, and silo. Caught in the midst of the disaster, Clark was momentarily blinded by a tidal wave of dust, ash, dirt, rock, and splinters.

In a heartbeat, his childhood home was wiped from the face of the Earth.

The shock wave passed and Superman found himself standing upon a barren plain that had been stripped clean by the World Engine's power. His earthly clothing had been erased, as well, replaced by a forbidding black-and-silver version of the uniform he wore as Superman.

A cold silver "S" was inscribed on the chest of a matte-black skinsuit similar to the ones sported by Zod and his troops. A long black cape hung from his shoulders.

Quakes shook the scoured ground beneath him. Fissures tore open the exposed bedrock. Red-hot lava welled up from below, spewing smoke and flames. Through the haze, Superman saw that the surface beneath his feet was no longer composed of rock or soil, but was instead a bed of human skulls. A heap of charred bones, with empty sockets and death's-head grimaces, lifted him above the coursing magma. A hot volcanic wind lifted his jet-black cape.

"A foundation has to be built upon *something*," Zod said. "Even your father recognized that."

"No!" Superman ripped the black cape from his shoulders. "I can't be a part of this."

He rejected Zod's nightmare scenario, which flickered and began to lose integrity. The scorched wasteland and skulls evaporated as the holographic environment collapsed. Superman found himself bound to an examination table in a sterile science ward somewhere within the *Black Zero*. No longer black and silver, his suit had reverted to its usual colors.

A bright red "S" shone against a field of gold.

Zod stood before him, accompanied by a gaunt Kryptonian male. His pale skin, sunken eyes, and hollow cheeks made him look more like a ghoul than a soldier. He wore a dark burgundy lab coat over a black skinsuit. Superman wondered what the man had done to be exiled to the Phantom Zone.

"Your parents are gone," Zod said. "Mine as well— along with my children, everyone I've ever loved. For decades, the only thing that kept me going was the hope that one day I'd be able to rekindle our race. Are you really going to extinguish that hope for the sake of these people who cast you out? Who were willing to hand you over without hesitation?"

He drew closer to the table and its captive.

"You're an *alien* to them," he said grimly. "They would not show you such concern. They *did not* show you such concern."

That much was true. Superman had been disappointed when the authorities had surrendered him to Zod, but he couldn't blame them for being frightened. The Kryptonians were an even bigger threat than General Swanwick and the White House feared, and, to be honest, they'd had little reason to trust an alien who'd kept his existence a secret for his entire life. What else were they supposed to have done?

And then there was Lois…

"You're asking me to betray them," Superman said. "I can't."

"You already have," Zod declared. "Why do you think we accessed your memories?"

Smallville, Superman realized. *He knows about the farm... and Mom.*

"You still need the scout ship," he said, desperate to keep Zod away from his home. The apocalyptic nightmare he had just witnessed, in which the heartland was reduced to bones and ashes, was still fresh in his mind. He couldn't let that doomsday scenario play out in real life.

"We've known where it was since we first entered the system," Zod stated confidently. He turned to his cadaverous associate. "Continue examining him, Jax-Ur. I want to know precisely how this world's ecosphere has affected him. How he can fly."

The scientist nodded. He regarded Clark with pitiless curiosity, clearly intrigued by the challenge.

Zod began to exit the laboratory. Then paused and looked back at Superman. He contemplated the prisoner.

"Back on Krypton," he said, "in the era of the warring states, if a foe died a noble death, custom dictated that the victor raise his enemy's child as his own." A flicker of guilt played across his face. "Your father acquitted himself with honor, Kal. I would gladly keep that custom alive."

What?

Superman instantly grasped the implications behind what Zod was saying. His fists clenched at his sides and he strained against his bonds. He glared furiously at Zod.

"You killed him."

"I did," Zod confessed with uncharacteristic remorse. "And not a day goes by when I don't think about it. But if I had to do it again, I would. The stakes were that high.

They still are." His face and voice hardened. "I have a duty to my people. And I won't allow *anyone* to prevent me from carrying it out."

Superman tried to break free from the table, but for the first time in his life, his strength met its match. The bonds refused to budge, so that he could only watch helplessly as Zod departed the lab, leaving him to Jax-Ur's questionable mercy.

The Kryptonian scientist set about his work.

CHAPTER TWENTY-TWO

On the big board at NORTHCOM, two red triangles inched their way over an illuminated map of the American Midwest. Dozens of adrenalized threat analysts rushed to interpret the data as General Swanwick rushed back into the ops center, accompanied by Hardy, Farris, and Hamilton. He quickly scanned the numerous video displays upon the wall.

"What's the sitrep, major?" he demanded of the nearest officer.

"DSP pinged two bogeys launching from the alien ship," the man reported.

Swanwick remembered the bug-like dropship that had collected Superman and Lane. What were the aliens after now?

"Retask Ikon-4 and get me a closer look," he ordered. Maybe the spy satellite could shed some light on this latest development. He hoped to God that this wasn't the beginning of an invasion, but knew that he needed to take appropriate action, just in case.

While his people redirected the satellite, he walked briskly to a secure land-line and picked up the receiver.

"Command Victor-Eight-Six-Whiskey-Three," he barked into the phone. "The word of the day is 'trident.' We have two alien craft on aggressive approach. Request SECDEF set DEFCON 1. Put all combat and combat support airborne on Alert 5!"

"Ikon-4 coming online!" an analyst called out.

And none too soon, Swanwick thought. He replaced the receiver, just as real-time images of the Kryptonian dropships appeared on the central screens. The ships—which were identical to the one that had been piloted by Sub-Commander Faora—were flying low over America's heartland. Acres of growing corn and wheat rippled in the ships' wake. They looked like two giant locusts zipping above the amber waves of grain.

"Air speed?" Swanwick asked.

"Three hundred and eighty knots and entering Kansas airspace!" an analyst reported. He adjusted his headset. "They're not responding to our hails!"

Swanwick did some quick mental calculations. He glanced at an illuminated map to see what resources were available to him.

"Get me Fort Anderson," he ordered. "Scramble the closest AWACS." He turned toward Colonel Hardy, who was waiting expectantly. "That's for you, Colonel. I need your eyes on the ground yesterday. And bring me one of those bastards back alive."

Hardy saluted and made tracks. He was good soldier who understood better than most just what was at stake, having been involved ever since the discovery on Ellesmere. There wasn't a better man for the job.

Except maybe the one he had turned over to Zod.

* * *

Superman felt like a lab rat laid out for dissection. Gritting his teeth, he strained once again against his shackles, but was unable to break loose from the examination table. He had never felt so weak, so helpless.

"You're wasting your efforts," Jax-Ur said. "The strength you derive from your exposure to Earth's sun has been neutralized aboard our ship."

The lean Kryptonian scientist approached the table. His gloved hands gripped a bony, segmented syringe that looked more like some sort of petrified parasite than a piece of medical equipment. Razor-sharp pinchers clamped down on Superman's arm while a hollow stinger penetrated his sleeve and skin. The prisoner winced at the unfamiliar stinging sensation—thanks to his parents' studied secrecy, he'd never had blood drawn before. He watched with dismay as the grotesque parody of a syringe extracted a crimson sample.

"Here, in this environment," Jax-Ur said, "you're as weak as any human."

Superman just hoped that Lois wasn't being subjected to similar treatment.

Car-Vex tossed Lois into an empty cell.

Even worse, the female Kryptonian had refused to answer any of her questions. She wouldn't reveal where Superman was, or if he was okay. When she'd last seen him, he was being dragged off by Zod's goons, unconscious and looking like death warmed over. Since then, nobody on this space-age penitentiary had bothered to give her an update.

For all she knew, he was dead.

Fighting despair, she sat in the corner of her cell, staring down and hugging herself to keep warm.

The air-conditioning aboard the *Black Zero* was set uncomfortably low, leading her to guess that Krypton had been a much cooler planet. Shivering, she tried to figure out what to do next.

She'd been in tight fixes before, but being locked up on a chilly alien spaceship populated by superhuman storm troopers was a new one. She couldn't count on Superman to come to her rescue again, either.

Whatever her next move would be, it was entirely up to her.

The air that was being pumped into her cell had been adapted to her needs, so she didn't need a respirator anymore. Lifting her eyes from the floor, she examined her cell more closely. Rounded walls gave it the feel of a hollow cavity inside a living organism, which didn't do anything to reassure her. The polished surfaces were largely smooth and seamless, but her questing gaze fell upon a glowing port set into the wall next to the sealed entrance.

An idea occurred to her, and she retrieved the nail-like object Superman had given her on the way here. Thankfully, Zod's forces hadn't bothered to search her—no doubt they assumed she was incapable of posing a threat.

She compared the head of the object, which bore Superman's trademark "S," to the empty port on the wall. Hope sparked inside her as she confirmed that they matched. Superman had silently hinted that she should hold onto the key until the time was right.

Was this the moment?

Might as well go for it, she thought. *Who knows if I'll get another chance?*

Holding her breath, she inserted the key into the port. It fit perfectly, which she took as a positive omen, and she waited for something to happen. But, much to her disappointment, the cell remained as closed and claustrophobic as ever. The entrance stayed sealed.

Great, she thought glumly. *Talk about a big black zero.*

She turned away from the locked door—only to find a tall, bearded man standing behind her. She yelped in surprise.

"Where did you come from?" she demanded.

"The command key, Ms. Lane," came the reply. "Thanks to you, I'm now uploading a copy of myself into the ship's mainframe."

What does he mean by that? Lois took a closer look at her unexpected guest. He was an imposing robed figure whose regal bearing conveyed a combination of wisdom and authority. His graying brown beard gave him the look of some space-age patriarch.

"Who are you?" she asked.

"I am Jor-El," he answered. "Kal's father."

She hadn't seen *that* coming. Startled, she peered at the stranger's face. On closer inspection, she thought she saw a family resemblance… maybe. He drew back his robes to reveal the "S" emblazoned on his chest.

Like father, like son.

She glanced around furtively, afraid that the entire discussion was being monitored. There were no two-way mirrors in evidence, but maybe the Kryptonians had a more advanced method of surveillance?

So she cut to the chase.

"Can you help me?" she asked.

"I designed this ship," he said. "I can modify its atmospheric composition to human compatibility. And I know how to stop them." Soulful brown eyes implored her. "Will you help me?"

"Yes, of course."

This whole business was getting wilder and wilder, but if there was even a chance of blindsiding Zod and his troops, then she was determined to take it.

Jor-El gestured toward a holographic display pad. Helixes of Kryptonian code spiraled across the screen. Lois couldn't make head nor tail of it.

"We will have to move quickly then," he said. "The crew is already aware of my presence. You can send them back to the Phantom Zone, but you must give my son the following message…"

Lois listened carefully.

The dropships came in low above the cornfields outside Smallville. Their slipstream uprooted the crops and set the fields ablaze. Smoke rose from burning stalks even as the ships descended toward the town.

Ordinary citizens, going about their business, stared in shock at the extraterrestrial aircraft. A mother in a playground, pushing her child on a swing, froze at the sight. Pete Ross, hearing the commotion, dashed out into the parking lot of the pancake house. His jaw dropped as he watched the bizarre objects streak over the water tower. They screamed through the air like banshees.

Pete froze in place. He hadn't been this scared since the bus crash, twenty years ago. And this time, there was no one to rescue him.

Jor-El's data screen blinked off abruptly. The lights went out in Lois's cell, plunging her into darkness. Alarms sounded.

"Remove the command key, Ms. Lane."

If you say so, she thought. Fumbling in the dark, she extracted it from the port.

The cell door slid open. Lois poked her head out and took a cautious breath, afraid that the air would still be too alien for comfort. But Jor-El had adjusted the atmosphere, as promised. She could breathe easily.

That was one less thing to worry about.

She slipped out into the cramped, murky corridor, accompanied by Clark's father. By this time she had figured out that he was a hologram, a computer program who apparently could traverse the ship at will. He looked deceptively solid, but he was as insubstantial as, well, a phantom.

For a brief moment she hoped they could get away undetected, but then Car-Vex spotted her. The female soldier charged, drawing a creepy-looking Kryptonian pistol.

Lois prayed it had a "stun" setting.

Right, she thought. *I should be so lucky.*

But before woman could fire, an emergency blast door slammed down from the ceiling, pinning her to the floor. Her pistol was knocked from her grip and went skidding across the nacreous tiles toward Lois.

Lois glanced sideways at Jor-El. "Did you do that?"

"Yes," he confirmed. "Take her sidearm. Keep moving!"

He didn't have to tell her twice. Scooping the freaky alien gun from the floor, she sprinted after Jor-El, who guided her through a bewildering maze of arteries. Her sweaty palm was wrapped around the grip of the pistol. She had never fired a ray-gun before, but figured there was a first time for everything.

She wondered how long that door was going to hold Car-Vex.

CHAPTER TWENTY-THREE

Blaring klaxons echoed off the walls of the science ward. Jax-Ur looked up from his work, his expression twisted in surprise. He triggered an intercom, but then found himself short of breath. He gasped and clutched his throat.

"What's… happening?" he croaked hoarsely.

Superman smiled.

"It's called a backup plan. Your ship's atmospherics just switched back to Earth levels, which means I've got my strength again." Steely blue eyes, with a hint of solar red, fixed on Jax-Ur. "So if I were you, I'd start running."

Superman tested his shackles again. Straining beyond his limits, he ripped one loose, freeing his right arm. Jax-Ur's sunken eyes grew wide. Coughing painfully, he staggered out of the lab as quickly as he could manage. He clutched the stolen blood sample to his chest.

Superman let him go. He took a deep breath, pulling the Earth-like air into his lungs. He felt his strength rushing back.

That's more like it, he thought.

* * *

Lois hoped Jor-El knew where he was going.

They dashed through curved tunnels that branched out at wild angles—the weirdly biological architecture reminded her of the spaceship in the Arctic, but on a massive scale. Emergency lights provided only dim illumination, but her eyes soon adjusted to the gloom. She spotted another junction ahead.

"To the left," Jor-El instructed. "Fire!"

She spun and clumsily fired the pistol, grateful that the trigger mechanism had been designed for humanoid hands. A white-hot plasma pulse knocked a Kryptonian soldier on his back. Lois grinned in satisfaction, but her momentary victory was cut short by the sight of reinforcements approaching from the corridor on the right. Boots pounded on the floor as they shouted at her to surrender.

Lois wondered how many shots her blaster held. Even though she had seen only a handful of soldiers aboard the ship, she was still outnumbered here.

Jor-El gestured toward the tunnel and another blast door slammed into place, cutting off her attackers. They pounded angrily on the other side of the thick barrier, and Lois decided Jor-El was a pretty handy guy to have around.

"This way!" he said.

She followed his lead, stepping over the fallen soldier. Swiftly they rounded another corner.

"Ahead you will find an escape pod," he said. "Secure yourself. I'll take care of the rest."

A portal irised open, revealing a padded seat inside a spherical cavity. Lois climbed into the seat, which faced the corridor outside. She yelped in surprise as silken restraints automatically strapped her into the seat, and briefly wondered if it had all been a trap.

Then display panels pulsed to life as the pod powered up and was shunted into a long black launch tube. A transparent canopy began to lower. Lois felt as if she was stuck on some futuristic amusement park ride—one which was just about to get rolling.

"Safe travels, Ms. Lane," Jor-El said. "We will not likely see each other again. And remember what I said. The Phantom Drives are the key to stopping them." He paused, as though he had suddenly become aware of something, and offered a final piece of advice. "Shift your head to the left."

Huh?

She quickly did so.

"Oh, shit!" she exclaimed as she realized why.

Car-Vex burst through the hologram's immaterial form. Red-faced and panting, she drove her fist through the back of Lois's seat, just to the right of the reporter's head, missing her skull by only millimeters.

The soldier yanked her fist back, leaving a gaping hole in the seat. Lois gulped.

Strapped in her seat, she was a sitting duck with nowhere to run. She hastily raised the stolen pistol and took aim, but the Kryptonian female snatched it from Lois's grasp. With practiced skill, Car-Vex flipped the gun in her hand and pointed its skeletal muzzle.

She fired point-blank.

At the last instant the pod's exterior hatch crashed down, deflecting the shot. Car-Vex ducked as sparks sprayed from the pod's damaged plating. She swore in Kryptonian.

Lois gasped in relief. That had been way too close.

Before the frustrated soldier could fire again, a sudden burst of acceleration slammed Lois into what was left of her seat. She shrieked, clutching onto it with white knuckles, as the pod zoomed down the launch tube like a rocket sled, leaving Car-Vex behind. Spinning madly, it shot out of the *Black Zero* and into open space.

Then it tumbled toward Earth, hundreds of miles below.

Klaxons blared inside the Kryptonian science ward. Regaining his full strength, Superman tore loose his remaining shackles and jumped off the examination table. It felt good to back on his feet again.

Jor-El appeared before him.

"Father!" Superman exclaimed. "Is it true? What Zod said about the Codex?"

The hologram nodded.

Superman tried to understand.

"Why didn't you tell me this before?"

Heavy footsteps beat a military tattoo outside. He heard a couple of Kryptonian soldiers running toward the lab. Charged plasma rifles were locked and loaded. The soldiers fired through the doorway as he ducked for cover. He hadn't forgotten how that plasma whip had stung him back on Ellesmere.

White-hot bursts scalded the walls and table, and ricocheted wildly around the lab. Superman raised his cape to shield himself from the flying energy.

"We're out of time," Jor-El said. "Strike the panel to your left."

Superman had many more questions, but his father was right—now was not the time for a lengthy discussion. Trusting Jor-El, he punched the indicated panel. A fist of steel tore through a solid bulkhead, puncturing the outer hull of the *Black Zero*.

Hurricane winds roared as the science ward's atmosphere was sucked out into the vacuum of space.

The breach expanded, and loose apparatus vanished through it, caught up by the explosive decompression. It reminded Superman of the tornado that had carried away Jonathan Kent, so many years ago. Pushing the painful memory aside, he dug his fingers into a sturdy bulkhead, anchoring himself against the voracious pull.

Screeching emergency sirens competed with the wail of the cyclone.

Have to hold on, he thought. *Just a few more seconds.*

A metal plate slammed into place, cutting the compromised science ward off from the rest of the ship, while locking out the soldiers on the other side of the airtight barrier. With any luck, that would slow them down long enough for him to escape the *Black Zero*— and for Jor-El to provide some answers.

"We wanted you to learn what it meant to be human first," the hologram said, "so that one day, when the time was right, you could build a bridge between the two races."

That provided the reassurance Superman had needed. He'd known that Zod had to be wrong, that Jor-El had never intended for him to recreate Krypton on Earth, or to betray humanity. Moved by his birth father's faith in him, he reached out without thinking, but his fingers passed through the holographic figure.

Jor-El wasn't really there.

Only his ghost.

"From the moment I first laid eyes on you," the image said, "I knew you were meant for greatness."

And Jonathan Kent once told me I would change the world, Superman recalled. He vowed to live up to their expectations—both of them.

Then a motion distracted him, visible through the rent in the hull. He realized that it was an escape pod, falling toward Earth's atmosphere, heating up as it entered the atmosphere. A fiery glow enveloped its outer plating—it was accelerating out of control, as though its braking systems were malfunctioning.

Even across the void of space, he could see who was inside the pod. She looked scared to death.

"Lois—"

"You can save her, Kal," his father said. "You can save *all* of them."

Superman prayed he was right. He took a deep breath of the escaping air, filling his lungs, and dived though the breach into space. Momentum carried him away from the *Black Zero* and he let Earth's gravity pull him down toward the planet below. His telescopic vision locked onto the glowing escape pod as he pivoted and shifted direction, taking off in a controlled dive.

His fists thrust out before him, he plunged into the turbulent atmosphere.

Hold on, Lois, he thought. *I'm coming!*

The ride was bumpier than Lois had expected. Maybe *too* bumpy.

The escape pod shook violently, rattling her despite the straps that held her fast to her seat. She clenched her jaw to keep her teeth from chattering, and struggled to keep her lunch down. Vertigo assailed her as the pod spun like a carnival ride. It was all she could to do to keep from screaming.

It was getting hotter and hotter inside the confined space, and dangerously so. It felt like a sauna, heading toward a furnace. She was soaked with perspiration. Alarms squealed in her ears. Warning lights blinked frantically all over the control panels.

Car-Vex had fired a blast of plasma at the pod before it ejected. Had the deflected shot done some serious damage?

Something's wrong, Lois realized. *This thing should be slowing down by now...*

The malfunctioning pod was heading in for a crash landing. Its heat shields were barely holding on—the outer plates were melting into slag and peeling away. Gravity tightened its grip, accelerating it to terminal velocity. Even if the heat shields held a few minutes longer, there was no way Lois could survive the impact if and when the pod hit the Earth. Her fragile human body would be crushed to a pulp.

That's not going to happen, Superman resolved.

Racing against time and gravity, he dived after the falling object, increasing his speed, desperate to catch up with it before time ran out. The wind whipped against his face as he plummeted toward the Great Plains. The sun shone down, fueling his flight. His red cape streamed behind him like the tail of a meteor, and his blue-and-red uniform withstood the heat of reentry.

Gaining on the pod, he almost came within reach of it. His arm stretched and his fingers grazed its molten husk, only for it to spin out of his grasp, continuing its deadly freefall. Despite the roar of the wind, he could hear Lois gasping inside the pod. Her heart was pounding frantically. She had to know she was only moments away from crashing.

No! Superman thought. *I can still save her. I can't let her die!*

The Earth seemed to rocket up to meet them. There would be just one more chance, so he dug deep to fly faster than he ever had before. With one last burst of speed, he managed to get a solid grip, sinking his bare fingers into the molten metal. The entry hatch was fused shut, but grunting with effort, he tore it off and hurled it away.

Lois tumbled out, and into his arms.

At first, she didn't realize what was happening. Metal screamed as the door flew off into the clouds and she fell into empty air. A pair of strong arms caught her and a broad blue chest absorbed the impact, cushioning her against a bright red "S." Glancing down, she saw the scorched remains of the pod slam into the ground like a bullet, exploding on impact.

Flames, smoke, and shrapnel rose into the sky, but Superman shielded her with his body, taking the brunt of the blast without even flinching. He held her high above the ground as clouds of thick white smoke billowed around them. He really was a Superman, she realized. A veritable Man of Steel.

And he had just saved her life... again.

Does this count as our second date? she wondered.

He carried her away from the smoking crater, cradling her in his arms, before descending to the Earth with amazing grace and precision. She barely felt a bump as he landed upon the well-tended lawn of the Smallville Cemetery. He gently put her down on a lonely knoll overlooking the town. A cool breeze provided relief after the overheated interior of the escape pod.

"You'll be safe here," he promised. "Are you all right?"

She nodded and looked to the horizon. Unlike the tranquil rural vista she remembered, smoke and flames rose up from acres of burning cornfields. She assumed that Zod was responsible—and felt a twinge of guilt.

"I didn't want to tell them anything about you," she said.

"But they did something to me, looked inside my mind…"

That was why Zod had insisted on having her brought aboard his ship. He had monitored all those news reports linking her to Superman, and had wanted to find out everything she had learned about him.

Is this my fault? She contemplated the conflagration spreading rapidly below. *Did I lead Zod to Smallville?*

"Me, too," Superman assured her. "It's okay."

His eyes narrowed as he looked out over burning fields. She guessed that he was seeing—and hearing—a whole lot more than she did. Judging from his grim expression, things were bad.

"I have to go," he said.

She didn't want him to, and it seemed as if he didn't want to leave her, either. He was more than just a story to her now. She felt a connection between them—and an attraction—that was stronger than gravity. They gazed at each other for a long moment, neither saying what they were feeling.

Maybe it was just the adrenaline rush, but she had never wanted to kiss anyone more than she wanted to kiss Superman—no, *Clark*—right this very minute.

But the moment passed, washed away by the tide of events, and he took to the sky. She watched in wonder as he flew toward Smallville, faster than the eye could follow. Within seconds, he was out of sight.

She wondered if she would ever get used to that.

A siren wailed in the distance. Turning around, she spotted a sheriff's vehicle, its gumball light spinning, speeding toward the crash site. She ran toward the road, waving her arms to flag the car down.

Jor-El had given her a mission. She knew what she had to do next.

CHAPTER TWENTY-FOUR

Dusty barked furiously at the front door. Martha shut off her vacuum cleaner and crossed the living room to see what had the collie so agitated. Worry lines deepened around her eyes and mouth. Her brow furrowed. What if the government had come looking for Clark? Or someone worse was?

She locked Dusty inside and stepped out onto the front porch. A smoky odor alerted her to a fire somewhere in the vicinity. High-pitched squeals heralded the arrival of two exotic aircraft that bore an unmistakable resemblance to the alien space capsule hidden in the barn. The ships descended out of a sunny sky and landed on the yard in front of the farmhouse.

She stepped down from the porch, ready to face their occupants.

Martha had been dreading a moment like this for over thirty years, afraid that Clark's alien kin would show up to reclaim him, but now that it was finally happening, she had no idea what she was supposed to do.

Except protect her son, of course.

Four Kryptonians in armored suits, black capes, and

helmets exited the ships. Unearthly and intimidating, they resembled futuristic gods of war. One of the intruders was a giant who towered over his companions, while another was shaped like a woman. The strangers spread out and surrounded her, but Martha didn't bother trying to flee. If they were even half as fast and strong as Clark, she wouldn't get far.

The leader came forward. She recognized his voice from the broadcast that had panicked the world. A transparent helmet protected his head. A black cape fluttered in the wind.

"The craft he arrived in," Zod demanded. "Where is it?"

She didn't like his tone.

"Go to hell," she said, not knowing if he'd understand the reference.

He scowled behind the shimmering visor of his helmet, then nodded at the statuesque female soldier accompanying him.

"Faora," he said curtly.

The alien amazon grabbed Martha by the throat and lifted her off the ground with one hand. Martha's feet dangled in the air as fingers that felt like bands of steel locked onto her throat. A strangled gasp escaped her lips.

"You raised him," the woman said coldly. "You know what he's capable of. Now imagine that kind of power in the hands of someone who could not care less about you."

With that, she hurled Martha to the ground.

I won't tell you anything, Martha thought angrily. *You're* nothing *like my son!*

But Zod had already lost interest in her. He scanned the farm with eyes that might be able to see as far and deep as Clark's. Martha's heart sank as he squinted at the old threshing barn, which had been converted into a tool shed. He pointed at the building.

"There," he said.

Faora leapt fifty feet into the air, arcing across the farm to crash through the roof of the barn and past its floor as well. Landing in the musty basement, she yanked off the tarp concealing the capsule. Her gloved fingers dug into the blackened hull and she ripped off the canopy. Impatient eyes scanned the interior of the starcraft. Then she snarled in disappointment.

"The Codex isn't here."

Zod yanked Martha from the ground and flung her across the yard. She hit the grass hard enough to knock the breath from her. Her whole body felt bruised and sore. She would be lucky if she hadn't broken any bones.

"Where has he hidden it?" he demanded.

Martha wasn't sure what a "Codex" was. Maybe that spiked black key they'd found in the space capsule? Last she knew, Clark had taken it with him to the Arctic.

She decided to play dumb.

"I don't know what you're talking about—"

"*Don't lie to me!*" he bellowed, losing his temper. An aging John Deere tractor was parked beside the barn. Zod irritably swatted it aside with the back of his hand as he marched toward her. Eight thousand pounds of rusty green metal crashed into the corner of the house. Wooden timbers splintered and a section of roof crumbled. Dusty barked frantically inside, but Zod paid no heed to the frightened animal.

He glared furiously at Martha.

"WHERE IS THE CODEX?"

I wouldn't tell you for all the tea in China, she thought.

He reached for her again, but before he could grab hold, a sonic boom thundered above the farm, rattling the decrepit windmill. Zod and his cronies turned their eyes upward, searching for the source of the boom. Lying on the ground, Martha spotted a red-and-blue blur streaking down from the sky.

Clark?

With the impact of a locomotive, Superman slammed into Zod at hypersonic speed. The force of the blow sent the Zod bouncing across the rural landscape. Superman zoomed after him, determined to carry the fight as far from the Kent farm—as far from his mother—as possible.

They crashed through a grain elevator on the outskirts of Smallville without even slowing down. A cascade of wheat poured from the breached concrete silo, while the heat of their passage ignited the highly combustible grain dust, triggering a chain of explosions that blew off the roof. A tremendous fireball shot into the sky, even as the warring Kryptonians kept on hurtling through the air, leaving the burning facility behind.

Momentum sent them sailing through a 7-Eleven at the edge of the main commercial strip. Glass shattered as they tore in through one wall and out the other. Terrified customers ran screaming into the street, spilling their Slurpees onto the pavement. The roof of the convenience store caved in. Sparks sprayed from broken neon lights.

A gas station was the next victim of their headlong trajectory, which had traversed dozens of miles in less than a minute. The filling station exploded into flames as Superman and Zod barreled through the pumps, ripping them from their foundations. Thick black smoke rose from the inferno. A gassy odor leaked into the air. Debris rained down from sky.

Panicked men, women, and children ran for cover, seeking the dubious safety of the surrounding shops and businesses. Old men fled their benches. Tires squealed as drivers hit the gas, speeding away from the war zone that the downtown had become. A siren wailed from the fire station, as though a tornado was approaching. People hid in barber shops and beauty salons, as well as the bank, drug store, and gym.

The combatants finally came to a stop in the middle of Main Street. Superman was the first to rise to his feet. Anger was written all over his face. He raised his fists.

"You think you can threaten my mother?"

Zod staggered to his feet, shaken and off-balance. Burning gasoline blazed across his cape and he yanked it angrily from his shoulders. His force-helmet was cracked and sputtering, deformed by its collision with Superman's fists. Unable to maintain its integrity, it began to dematerialize.

Zod blinked as he tried to bring his vision into focus. He stared at his hands in bewilderment.

Superman could guess what he was seeing—the same shifting electromagnetic spectrum that had overwhelmed Clark as a small child, the world ablaze with disorienting colors, the deafening cacophony of a million amplified sounds.

Finally Zod's helmet dissolved in a shower of sparks, leaving his face and lungs fully exposed to Earth's atmosphere. Gasping, he reeled away. He threw his hands over his ears in a futile attempt to muffle the sonic barrage. He choked on his words as he glared furiously at his foe.

"What have you done to me?" he demanded, but his

words carried little of the usual command.

"Found your Achilles heel," Superman said. "My parents taught me to hone my senses, Zod. Focus on just the things I *wanted* to see, and tune out everything else."

He advanced on his enemy. It was time to finish this, before anyone else got hurt.

"But without your helmet, you can't focus. You're getting *everything*. And it's too much, isn't it?"

A dropship flared in overhead, coming to Zod's rescue. Plasma cannons fired at Superman, knocking him backward into a parked delivery truck, which crumpled when he hit it. Momentarily stunned, he pulled himself out of the demolished truck even as the ship touched down in the street. One of Zod's lieutenants rushed out and hurriedly dragged his general to safety.

Forget it, Superman thought, determined to stop them from getting away. He started toward the ship, only to be blocked by Faora and another soldier, who suddenly leapt into the street before him.

Superman gaped at the sight of the woman's comrade, who was at least nine feet tall. An opaque helmet concealed the giant's features. Wide in the chest, with fists like anvils, he put any human bodybuilder to shame. He overheard Faora address the brute as Nam-Ek. They looked as if they were spoiling for a fight.

Smack dab in the middle of Smallville.

Superman was acutely conscious of his surroundings, and of the countless innocent lives at risk. He scanned the downtown area with his X-ray vision, noting dozens of scared and helpless people taking cover in the nearby buildings. Parents clutched their crying children. Clerks and customers cowered behind shelves and counters while calling for help on their cell phones.

Doors and windows slammed shut and were locked

as quickly as possible. Gun owners sought out their weapons, never imagining just how futile they would be in the face of the Kryptonian threat. Sobs, curses, and desperate prayers reached Superman's ears.

But he heard something else as well—the whirr of approaching helicopters.

CHAPTER TWENTY-FIVE

Six AH-6 gunships swept in from the east, ferrying Special Forces troops. Spinning rotors sliced through the afternoon sky. The smoke and flames rising up from the small Kansas town and its surrounding farmlands were visible from the cockpit of Colonel Nate Hardy's own "Little Bird."

His blood boiled at the rampant destruction. Before joining the army, he had grown up in a rural community much like Smallville. He took this unprovoked attack personally.

"All players," he barked over the radio. "This is Guardian. I am Airborne Mission Commander. Stand by for words. I have previously encountered and observed the beings we are about to engage at close proximity. They possess technology and capabilities well beyond our own. In addition, at least one of these beings is capable of flight. They are extremely dangerous and we have been authorized by executive order to use deadly force."

He hoped that he'd gotten his message across—that the Kryptonians were significantly more dangerous than any human combatants. But how could even highly trained Special Forces personnel really grasp what they might be up against here?

Hardy had seen Superman fly, witnessed it with his own two eyes. And even now, he could hardly believe it.

Who knew what these other aliens were capable of?

His radio crackled as the lead gunship called in.

"Roger, Guardian. This is Gunslinger 06. Sitrep, Over."

"Gunslinger 06, request you put troops down in LZs One, Two, and Three. This operation is non-permissive."

His order made it clear that they were flying into a hostile environment, presumably under enemy control. This was not how he had ever thought of Kansas before.

"Roger that, Guardian."

The gunships weren't the only birds under Hardy's command. His radio crackled once more as the pilot of an A-10 Thunderbolt fighter jet contacted him for orders.

"Guardian, Thunder-One-One flight. Checking in and stand-by for A/O update."

Hardy scoped out the scene below, spotting Superman, Faora-Ul, and a hulking Kryptonian bruiser. They were facing off in the middle of the town's main drag. He couldn't see any civilians, but they hadn't had the time to evacuate. So he assumed they were taking shelter in the modest commercial buildings that lined the street. A two-story Sears department store made a workable landmark.

"Thunder-One-One, I need you to engage the targets with gun and Maverick. Your field elevation is as needed. You've got three individuals occupying intersection just in front of Sears, marked by laser."

"Copy all, Guardian. Tally three targets. Thunder-One-One Flight in from the east."

A pair of fighter jets rocketed ahead of the 'copters. The twin-engine, straight-wing aircraft, nicknamed

"Warthogs," were equipped with both heavy-duty rotary cannons and six Maverick missiles each, the better to provide close air support for troops on the ground. Hardy figured the Hogs were their best bet at taking out the aliens.

They were built to take out tanks, for Pete's sake.

"Thunder-One-One Flight, you are cleared hot!"

The jets came in low for a strafing run. Powerful 30mm autocannons unleashed a barrage of firepower on the alien trio, spraying more than four thousand rounds a minute. Precision-guided Maverick air-to-surface missiles followed the explosive rounds. Each missile carried a three-hundred-pound warhead.

Hardy felt sorry for Smallville.

Superman spotted the Warthogs as they began firing. He dived out of the way of the air strike, but was tagged anyway. An armor-piercing shell, made of depleted uranium, failed to break his skin, but sent him crashing through the front of a hardware store. The property damage hurt even worse than the ammo—this was *his* hometown that was being wrecked. He knew these people and their businesses.

His father had shopped in this store.

Faora dodged the shells and missiles, but her lumbering comrade, Nam-Ek, didn't even try to get out of the line of the fire. Standing like an alien goliath in the middle of the intersection, he took the full brunt of the attack.

Anti-tank missiles slammed into the armored giant, hurling him down the length of the street. He skidded to a halt some thirty feet back.

Well, that's one down, Hardy thought, watching from the cockpit of his chopper. *At least we got the big guy.*

"Thunder-One-One Flight," he said into the radio. "Good hit. Request immediate reattack."

"Guardian copy," the pilot of the lead A-10 replied. *"We'll be back in one minute."*

The Warthogs circled around for a second pass. Their first attack had inflicted serious damage. Smoking craters pitted the intersection. Charred rubble was strewn everywhere. Water gushed from blasted hydrants and water mains. Broken glass had spilled onto the street and sidewalks. Abandoned cars had been reduced to burning heaps of metal.

"Flight in," the pilot reported. *"Coming from the east."*

The Warthogs screamed in for another run, ready to let loose their devastating firepower once again.

But this time Nam-Ek was ready for them. Climbing to his feet, he leapt to meet the oncoming aircraft. The giant Kryptonian shot through the air and collided with the cockpit of the lead jet. Superman heard its pilot cry out in alarm.

"Thunder, jink! Target off the nose!"

Nam-Ek clung to the front of the aircraft. A mammoth fist smashed into the cockpit. Superman watched in dismay as the A-10 spiraled out of control, taking the Kryptoian with it. The spinning jet crashed into the street, drilling into the pavement.

Only a single heartbeat could be heard beneath the wreckage. Superman knew it wasn't the pilot's.

"Guardian, Thunder-One-Two," the pilot of the second jet reported, his shrill voice unable to hide his shock. "Lead is down! I repeat, lead is down!"

Faora looked eager to bring down an enemy of her own. Flames rose from the burning wreckage as she flung herself through the fire at the remaining Warthog, only to be intercepted in midair by Superman. He clipped her with his shoulder, sending them both tumbling down through the elevated sign of the pancake house and into the dining area of the restaurant.

Chairs and tables went flying as the battling Kryptonians struck like twin cannonballs, leaving a ragged hole in the ceiling. Dust and debris rained down. Superman spotted Pete Ross, of all people, hiding behind the checkout counter. He remembered his mom saying that Pete was the manager here.

To his relief, he didn't see any other customers or employees. He guessed that they had escaped out the back when all hell broke loose, leaving Pete to hold down the fort. Superman wished he had cleared out, too.

But Faora didn't care about innocent bystanders. Recovering quickly from their crash landing, she assailed Superman with a flurry of jabs and kicks to his vital areas. Her vicious hands and feet blurred as they lashed out at his knees, neck, and solar plexus. It was like being beaten up by a schoolyard bully again, except this time he could actually feel it.

"You're weak, Son of El," she sneered. "Unsure of yourself. But I am *not*."

A spinning kick knocked Superman's legs out from under him. She stood over him, gloating.

"The fact that you possess a sense of morality—and we don't—gives us an evolutionary advantage. And if history has proven anything—"

She grabbed onto him and hurled him through two full blocks of solid brick and concrete buildings. Only the reinforced steel door of the Kansas National Bank's main vault arrested his momentum. Dangling electrical cables spewed sparks. Superman braced himself against the dented steel door as he caught his breath.

"—it's that evolution *always wins*."

Her mocking voice rang out as she and Nam-Ek dropped through the roof of the bank. Nam-Ek remained unscratched by the crash that had destroyed the downed A-10. His lumbering tread crushed fallen chunks of masonry to powder. Faora grinned sadistically through her visor.

Outside in the street, army helicopters touched down in three designated landing zones. Uniformed figures swarmed out of the Little Birds, fanning out to evacuate the endangered civilians. The soldiers kicked open doors and climbed through busted shop windows. They hustled trembling families out into the street and toward the waiting choppers, where door gunners manned M2130 chain guns and GAU-19 Gatling guns.

Faora and Nam-Ek converged on Superman, just like the bullies who had ganged up on him on these very streets when he was growing up. But there was a big difference this time around.

He didn't need to hold back anymore.

Like a missile, he shot past Nam-Ek and powered into Faora, driving her out of the bank and into a garbage truck, tearing a hole in its side. A second later, he flung her out of the gap into the imposing stone façade of the bank. The impact cracked the solid masonry.

He took a different route out of the ruined truck. Defying gravity, he shot straight through the roof and into the contested airspace above downtown Smallville. Army choppers shared the sky with him. He heard Colonel Hardy barking orders to the troops below.

"Check fire! All players, ensure clear lines of fire before engaging!"

Superman wasn't worried about the soldiers' bullets.

He zoomed down from the sky to strike Faora squarely with both fists. The collision rattled her, but she fought back furiously. They traded dozens of blows, each of which would pulp an ordinary human. Thinking on his feet, Superman deliberately targeted her helmet, which was starting to sputter and spark like Zod's had.

Good, he thought. *I can work with that.*

Nam-Ek burst through the front of the bank to join the fight, even as the Special Forces opened fire on all three Kryptonians. Snipers took up positions on nearby rooftops and joined in the attack on the alien combatants. The choppers blasted away with their airborne artillery. A symphony of percussive gunfire drowned out the thunderous blows of Superman and his foes.

All-out war had come to Smallville.

Observing the battle from above, Hardy received word from Sergeant Rick Vance, the ground commander.

"Guardian, this is Badger 01," Vance reported. *"We've engaged targets. Negative BDA! We're not even plinking the paint off them!"*

Hardy's own eyes confirmed Vance's assessment. Despite receiving enough firepower to take out a small army, the three aliens were still standing—and fighting amongst themselves. Superman's colorful uniform was easily distinguishable from the intimidating black capes and armor of the other two. And from what Hardy could see, he was barely holding his own.

But he was doing a better job fighting Zod's people than anyone else was. Hardy watched as Superman ducked beneath the giant's armored fist, while jabbing his elbow in the visor of the woman's helmet. She staggered backward, affected more by Superman's strike than by the blistering hail of gunfire targeting all three of them. Then she lunged at him again, murder in her eyes.

They sure don't seem to be on the same side.

Maybe that reporter was right? Maybe Superman wasn't the enemy?

Hardy made a judgment call.

"All players," he ordered. "Do *not* target the guy in blue! He is friendly. Repeat: *friendly*!"

Impossibly, the female Kryptonian seemed to hear his command. She turned her face to the sky, spotting Hardy's helicopter. She nodded at the giant, who turned away from Superman long enough to pick up an abandoned UPS truck. He hefted the heavy vehicle with no effort whatsoever, and hurled it at the hovering 'copters.

The big brown truck sailed through the air, almost nailing a chopper, which pulled up and out of the way with only a second to spare.

"We're breaking right!" the pilot shouted over the radio. *"Breaking right!"*

The airborne truck flew straight at the helicopter that was carrying Hardy. The Little Bird banked sharply to one side, but the truck grazed them anyway, sending the chopper out of control. A door gunner tumbled out of the Little Bird, into the empty air.

The dislodged soldier fell toward the battle-scarred street dozens of feet below.

"Fallen angel!" the pilot barked into radio. "Fallen angel!"

The man was about to splatter all over the sidewalk when Superman intercepted him. Zipping through the air, he scooped up the endangered soldier before he hit the ground. Then the Kryptonian flew off, carrying the man to safety.

Thank God, Hardy thought.

But the fallen gunner might have been the lucky one, because the wounded 'copter was going down.

"Hold on!" Hardy shouted to his crew. "We're auto-rotating! Brace for impact!" Racing against time, he fired off one last radio communication. "All players, Guardian's going off the net—"

CHAPTER TWENTY-SIX

The chopper crashed into the parking lot in front of Sears. Superman wanted to check on Hardy and his crew, but knew that he had to deal with Faora and Nam-Ek first. Nobody would be safe as long as Zod's ruthless lieutenants were on the rampage.

After leaving the rescued gunner on a rooftop, Superman dropped down on Nam-Ek from above and grabbed hold of the silent giant. As far as he could tell, he had one tactical advantage over the other Kryptonians—flight—and he intended to make the most of it.

He launched himself high into the sky, dragging Nam-Ek along with him. Before the startled Kryptonian even knew what was happening, they were hundreds of feet above the ground. Then Superman let go of the giant and hammered him with a haymaker that sent Nam-Ek somersaulting through the air. He crashed to earth several blocks away from Main Street, landing on a railroad spur at the edge of town. Slamming into a group of train cars, he knocked them off the tracks. His armor scraped against the iron rails as he slid to a stop.

That got Nam-Ek clear of downtown, if only for a moment.

But what about Faora?

Miraculously, Hardy survived the crash landing. Bruised and battered, he struggled to extricate himself from the crushed cockpit, which had hit the ground in the parking lot in front of the department store.

Sergeant Vance and his men rushed to secure the downed chopper. Before they reached his location, however, gunfire sounded nearby, and Hardy guessed that he wasn't out of the woods yet.

A sudden thump proved he was right.

Faora-Ul leapt into the parking lot, landing amidst a sea of empty cars. She smirked maliciously as her eyes locked on him.

He was still trapped inside the wreckage.

She seemed to recognize him from their brief confrontation at the NORTHCOM airfield, where he'd objected to the abduction of Lois Lane. She stalked toward him, casually flinging parked vehicles aside.

Vance and his ground troops tried and failed to halt her advance. Automatic weapons fire bounced harmlessly off her Kryptonian armor as she confidently made her way toward the broken Little Bird. Losing ground, the soldiers fell back behind the empty cars and trucks, using them for cover, but she easily flipped the vehicles out of her way, one after another, exposing the men and forcing them to scramble away. A Ford pickup landed upside down on top of a crumpled station wagon.

With gunfire proving ineffectual, the men unloaded on her with grenades. The devices exploded against her, packing enough punch to take out a platoon of hostiles, but she shrugged them off as though they were nothing but a cloud of annoying gnats. The blasts and shrapnel didn't even knick her armor.

She was coming for him.

Hardy wrestled an MP5 submachine gun into place and opened fire on her from the cockpit. He doubted that it would do anything more than slow her down, if that, but he'd be damned if he didn't go down fighting. He emptied his clip, then reached for his sidearm.

The M9 semiautomatic was even less effective than the MP5, but he kept blasting away, even as she grabbed him by the neck and yanked him violently from the trashed 'copter. She lifted him above the ground with one hand.

"Do your worst!" Hardy spat at her.

Her fingers tightened around his throat.

"Be quiet, soldier," she responded. "A good death is its own reward—"

A serrated black blade was sheathed at her hip. She drew it out with clear intent to gut him. Just snapping his neck was not good enough, it seemed—she wanted to spill human blood. Or maybe she was hoping Hardy would beg for his life.

Like hell, he thought defiantly. *Get it over with, you alien bitch.*

She drew back the knife and he braced himself for the death blow. Then a blue-red blur slammed into her, loosing her grip and propelling her across the parking lot.

Hardy fell to the ground. Gasping in surprise, he saw Superman take the fight to Faora. He grabbed her flickering helmet with his bare hands and ripped it off her.

The effect came quickly. Faora shrieked and dropped to her knees on the pulverized blacktop, clutching her ears and squeezing her eyes shut. The icy beauty of her face was contorted by agony. It was as it she was being barraged with flash-bang grenades. Sensory overload incapacitated her.

"You *feel* that, Faora?" Superman said. "We're not on your ship anymore. We're on *my* world."

Forcing her eyes open, she tried to focus them on her assailant. Tears streamed down her face as she struggled to rise. Her hands flailed blindly before her, as though she could barely see.

"Savor it while you can," she hissed. "You won't win. For every human life you save, we'll kill a million more." She raised her voice until it was loud enough for Hardy and all his men to hear. "In a few days' time, they will *all* be dead."

A chill ran down Hardy's spine. There was no question as to the Kryptonians' intentions now. He knew a declaration of war when he heard one. Faora was talking genocide.

Before Superman could reply, a railway boxcar hurtled through the air like an immense steel javelin. The flying car slammed into him, knocking him through the front of Sears. The back of the boxcar jutted from the shattered wall, looking surreally out of place.

Hardy blinked in surprise.

What the—? Where did that come from?

Then the big, mute Kryptonian landed on the parking lot—and he knew who had thrown the boxcar.

All the way from the rail yard!

Hardy scrambled over to the 'copter and fumbled for his walkie-talkie. He hastily keyed the radio, even as he watched Faora get back on her feet.

"Thunder One-Two!" he said desperately. "This is Guardian. For the record, this is my call… my responsibility! Put everything you've got just north of me! This will be *danger-close*. My initials are November-Hotel-Hotel!"

The wingman's voice crackled over the radio:
"Copy danger-close. Good luck, Guardian."

The surviving Warthog zoomed down from the heavens. Per Hardy's orders, the jet fired its last four Mavericks at the Kryptonians, engulfing them in a storm of fire. The missiles devastated the parking lot, instantly reducing it to rubble. He could feel the scorching heat from yards away. Vance and the other soldiers scrambled to escape the blast.

But the ferocious air strike didn't even singe Faora's short hair. She staggered away from the flames, assisted by her hulking partner. Hardy cursed under his breath.

Could nothing hurt these bastards?

To make matters worse, one of the Kryptonian dropships joined the conflict. Sweeping in over the town, it blew the A-10 to pieces with a white-hot pulse from its cannons. The blast didn't leave enough of the Warthog to crash—all that remained was flaming debris, falling from the sky.

Great, Hardy thought bitterly. *They've got air superiority, too.*

The alien ship landed in what remained of the street. Hardy and the other soldiers prepared themselves, ready to sell their lives dearly, if necessary. But the ship had just come to retrieve Faora and the giant. The faceless brute helped the disoriented female into the ship, which then screamed off into the sky, leaving Smallville behind.

The soldiers cautiously lowered their weapons.

Hardy grimly surveyed the destruction. Smoke and flames rose into the sky. Downtown Smallville was a disaster area, entire buildings badly damaged or destroyed. Torched vehicles smoldered atop broken pavement. The remains of a crashed fighter jet and helicopter littered the battleground. The unarmed Kryptonians had nearly wiped out the town without even trying.

And the scary part was, Hardy figured they had all had gotten off easy.

The misplaced boxcar dislodged from the Sears building, and Superman emerged. Like Hardy, he paused to contemplate the wreckage that surrounded them. Vance's men, reacting to the caped alien's presence, fanned out to surround him, their guns at the ready. Fear showed on their faces.

Less than an hour ago, Hardy would have done the same.

But not any more.

"This man is not our enemy," he said firmly. "Stand down."

He looked Superman squarely in the eye. As far as he was concerned, the flying alien had proved himself more than once during the battle, and not just by saving him from Faora's thirsty blade. He accepted Superman as a brother in arms.

The soldiers lowered their weapons.

"Thank you, Colonel," Superman said. "I couldn't have stopped them without your help."

Hardy thought that might be overly generous, but accepted the compliment with a curt nod. At least Vance's team had managed to evacuate plenty of civilians from the combat zone. That counted for something.

Superman didn't stick around to exchange war stories. He took off like a rocket, flying off into the sky. Vance and his soldiers watched him go with awestruck expressions on their faces.

Hardy knew how they felt.

* * *

The farmhouse looked to be beyond repair. A tractor occupied the living room, beyond the gaping hole in the wall. Daylight was fading as Martha cautiously sifted through the rubble, attempting to rescue her most precious mementos, including a faded Polaroid taken in happier days, when Clark was only eight years old.

The photo showed the boy and Jonathan, posing with a paper-mache volcano at a school science fair. The boy beamed happily beside his father.

A breeze stirred the debris littering the floor.

"Hello, Mom."

Superman touched down behind her. Her eyes briefly registered surprise at his unorthodox attire, but then she rushed forward to embrace him. He held her tightly, just as relieved as she was that they were both still in one piece. He scanned her discreetly with his X-ray vision, but found no broken bones or internal injuries. Zod's goons must have left her alone to chase after him.

"Thank God," she murmured. Reluctantly letting go, she glanced around at the wreckage. "I was thinking I might take you up on that offer to remodel now."

He wished he had half her spirit.

"I'm so sorry," he said.

"It's only stuff, Clark," she replied. "It can always be replaced."

"But you *can't* be," he said, horrified at how close he had come to losing her. Zod and his confederates had proven that they had no respect for human life, and would stop at nothing to get what they wanted. "This Codex they're looking for. Zod says it can bring my people back."

She examined him closely, not quite understanding.

"Isn't that a good thing?"

"I don't think they're interested in sharing this world,

Mom. And I'm not sure I know how to stop them from taking it."

"I do," a voice intruded on their conversation. Superman turned to see Lois approaching from the road, where a police car with a flashing light had just dropped her off. Caught up in the emotional reunion with his mother, Superman hadn't even noticed her arrival.

Now he wondered what she had in mind.

CHAPTER TWENTY-SEVEN

The dropships docked with the *Black Zero,* where Zod and the landing party hurriedly returned to the bridge. The ship's Kryptonian environment was a relief after their ordeal on Earth.

A visible hull breach outside the science ward had explained Kal-El's escape from the ship. Clearly, Jor-El's heir was more resourceful than anticipated.

Zod resolved not to underestimate him again.

Jax-Ur was waiting for him on the bridge.

"What happened down there?" the scientist asked.

Zod chose not to rebuke him for allowing Kal-El to escape.

"He exposed a temporary weakness," Zod admitted, now fully recovered from the sensory onslaught that had undone him on Earth. Although the memory of that galling defeat still gnawed at him.

Jax-Ur shrugged. "It's of little consequence."

"How can you say that?" Faora responded furiously, her eyes still rimmed with red. "He humiliated us!" Zod had never seen her so angry—not even when they'd been taken into custody by the Sapphire Guard, back on Krypton.

The scientist smirked.

"Because I've located the Codex."

His words sent a surge of excitement through Zod. Recovering the Codex was their primary objective, more important than recapturing Kal-El.

Jax-Ur waved them over to the holographic orb that hovered above a command cylinder, where he called up his findings. Kryptonian blood cells, magnified by many orders of magnitude, were displayed in three dimensions. Red and white corpuscles drifted within a drop of briny serum.

What does this have to do with the missing Codex? Zod wondered.

"It was *never* in the capsule," Jax-Ur explained.

Faora gave him a puzzled look.

"I don't understand."

"Jor-El took the Codex—the DNA of a billion people— then he bonded it within his son's individual cells." Jax-Ur was clearly impressed by this accomplishment, and the ingenuity that lay behind it. "It was a *brilliant* solution. All of Krypton's heirs living, hidden, in one refugee's body."

He increased the magnification. Digitized information danced through the individual blood cells. The genotypes of future generations—crafted to populate a meticulously designed social order—all waited to be harvested.

Zod instantly grasped the notion.

"And you found this in the blood sample you took from him?"

Jax-Ur nodded, looking quite pleased with himself. Zod decided this discovery easily outweighed Kal-El's escape from the science ward. He stepped over to a viewport, and gazed at the planet below. Yellow sunlight shone upon his face.

"Tell me," Zod asked. "Does Kal-El need to be alive for us to extract the Codex from his cells?"

Jax-Ur grinned as though he had anticipated the question.

"No."

So be it, Zod thought. He turned his attention back to Earth, where the sun was just cresting over its western hemisphere. Now that he knew where the Codex was to be found, he could proceed with the next phase of the operation.

"Our new home awaits us," he announced. Then he turned toward Commander Gor, who was manning the *Black Zero's* controls. "On my word, Commander, release the World Engine."

The soldier inputted the go-code.

"Now."

The bridge shuddered as explosive bolts burst, disengaging the World Engine from the *Black Zero*. A three-dimensional schematic, projected above the command console, showed the bottom one-thirds of the composite vessel's bulk detaching from the original prison barge. No longer mated to the ship, the massive device ignited its independent thrusters and took off on a trajectory bound for the planet's southern hemisphere.

At last, Zod thought. *It has begun.*

A new icon appeared on the big board at NORTHCOM, vectoring away from the Kryptonian mothership. General Swanwick jumped to his feet.

"What just happened?" he demanded.

"Their ship's splitting in two!" an analyst reported. "Track 1 is heading east. Track 2 is deploying toward the southern hemisphere."

The analyst rolled back the satellite footage to show the events of a few seconds earlier. A hush fell over the ops center as the assembled personnel watched a huge black tripod detach itself from the upper tier of the mothership. The liberated module rocketed away from a significantly smaller version of the original UFO.

"Get me orbital data!" Swanwick ordered. "How fast is that bogey going?"

"Approaching Mach 24 and accelerating. Inclination TBD." He hastily called up more stats. "Looks like it's going to impact somewhere in the South Indian Ocean."

Swanwick's brow furrowed. What on Earth was Zod after on the other side of the world?

The volcanic island was little more than a clump of jagged rocks, sparsely dotted with vegetation, jutting up from the sea. It was one of hundreds of islands dotting this corner of the Indian Ocean. Remote and uninhabited, it slept quietly in the predawn hours.

Until the World Engine slammed into it like a gigantic meteor, throwing up a mile-high plume of dirt, dust, and pulverized bedrock. Seismometers across the planet registered the earth-shaking impact, even as the colossal mechanism rose up from a newly formed crater.

Supported by legs over a thousand feet high, the Engine towered above the devastated surface of the island. The tropical climate was very different from the ice planet upon which the World Engine once had languished, prior to Zod's arrival.

It paused briefly, waiting.

NORTHCOM analysts scrambled to stay on top of the rapidly changing situation. Swanwick and the others kept their eyes on the big board, where the icon representing the original dreadnought began dropping vertically toward the Earth.

"Sir!" an analyst cried out. "The rest of their ship is descending!"

I can see that, the general thought. He didn't know what it meant, but knew it couldn't be good. "Put it on the board now!"

Clouds boiled away above Metropolis as the ship descended toward the city. Its massive weight pressed down on the air, creating violent turbulence in the concrete canyons below. Skyscraper windows imploded. Sirens and car alarms went off all across the city. A shadow fell over downtown.

"My God," Perry whispered.

Along with Lombard and the others, he stared out the windows at the alien spacecraft. No longer just a distant shape in the sky, the ship now hovered directly overhead, resembling a monstrous artificial squid. It filled the sky, blotting out the bright afternoon sun.

Down in the street, thirty stories below the *Planet*'s bullpen, traffic came to a standstill. Panicked citizens and tourists alike abandoned buses, taxis, trucks, and automobiles to run for their lives. People stampeded the subway entrances or sought shelter in the nearest building. Shopping bags and briefcases were left discarded on the sidewalks. Perry had never seen anything like it.

A veteran newsman, he had covered blackouts, blizzards, hurricanes, terrorist attacks, and riots, but he had never witnessed an entire city driven into hiding by the onset of what appeared it to be an honest-to-God alien invasion.

It was the story of the century—if anyone would be around to read it.

* * *

Zod remained upon the bridge, gazing down on the humans' sprawling metropolis. It was impressive enough, in its own primitive fashion, but it in no way rivaled the grandeur of Kandor.

The city would have to be leveled to make room for a new seat of power, but perhaps there would be some artifacts left over for Kryptonian archaeologists to study. The humans deserved to have some record of their existence preserved, if only for posterity.

He turned toward Jax-Ur, who was viewing remote schematics of the World Engine. It had successfully made planet fall, and was awaiting further instructions.

"Bring the Phantom Drives online," Zod ordered, "and activate the carrier beam."

Jax-Ur relayed the commands to his subordinates.

On the distant island, the World Engine powered up. Flocks of birds took fight in a roar of flapping wings, as if they sensed what was to come.

Indicator lights pulsed along the device's head.

"Carrier beam is synchronized," Jax-Ur confirmed. He double-checked the readings, simply to be sure. "The World Engine is now slaved to our drives."

Then all was in readiness. Zod saw no need to delay any longer. They had travelled too far, sacrificed too much, to wait a moment more.

"Fire."

CHAPTER TWENTY-EIGHT

An eerie glow lit up the base of the *Black Zero*. Gravitational fluxes attracted loose particulates and other debris from the streets below. A halo of levitating dirt, glass, and litter formed around the ship, like the rings of a gas giant.

An incandescent column of shimmering azure energy, at least three hundred feet in diameter, shot down from the underside of the ship. The block-wide beam pressed down on everything that lay beneath the alien vessel. Structures began to crumble, then collapse. Abandoned vehicles were crushed like tin cans.

Gaining strength, the pulsating column expanded outward, creating an ever-widening circle of destruction. Multistory office buildings pancaked, compressing innocent men and women between the floors. Fragile human flesh was vaporized instantly.

On the opposite side of the planet, a reciprocal column was generated by the World Engine. A beam of focused gravity, it flattened all the remaining trees and other foliage on the ravaged island. The surrounding seas parted as if shoved aside by a god-like hand.

Here, too, rings of loose matter orbited the head of the gargantuan device, its gravity beam penetrated deep into the Earth until it met the beam from the *Black Zero*.

Thus linked, the machines fed each other, creating an axis of energy that traded waves of crushing gravity in a devastating feedback loop.

Huge vents opened along the top of the Engine. Noxious fumes gushed from the vents, spilling out into the atmosphere like the pyroclastic surge of a volcano. Seething clouds of alien vapor jetted forth as the device breathed upon the Earth.

General Swanwick watched in dismay as the two-part assault played out upon the big board's video screens. Satellite footage offered him—and the rest of the NORTHCOM staff—a front-row seat for the twin cataclysms.

Swanwick tried to fathom what he was seeing.

"Nuclear, chemical, kinetic—no known weapon can cause that type of damage," he said. Then he turned. "What've they hit us with?"

"Looks like some kind of gravity weapon," Dr. Hamilton theorized. He called up what he referred to as a "gravity map" of Metropolis. Most of the city and outlying boroughs were rendered in orange, indicating regions of normal gravity, while a circle centered on the Kryptonian ship edged into blues and greens.

They watched grimly as the circle steadily expanded.

Hamilton toggled to another screen. A similar graphic depicted the same destructive phenomenon at a location in the Indian Ocean, where the other segment of the ship had come to rest on an insignificant island.

A cross-section of the Earth, extrapolated from seismic readings, showed pulsing "gravity waves" ping-ponging back and forth through the planet's interior, from the island to Metropolis and back again, growing in intensity with each volley.

"It's working in tandem with their ship," Hamilton explained, indicating the anomaly on the island. "Somehow they're increasing the planet's mass. Clouding the atmosphere with particulates." A look of realization dawned on his face. "My God, they're terraforming."

"What?" Captain Farris didn't recognize the term.

"Planetary engineering," Swanwick translated. He'd read enough science fiction to be familiar with the concept. "Modifying a world's atmosphere and topography.

"They're turning Earth into Krypton," he added.

"But what happens to us?" Farris asked.

"Based on these readings," Hamilton said, "there won't be an 'us.' If this keeps up, the increased gravity alone will crush our internal organs."

Swanwick had no reason to doubt the scientist. This was more than just an enemy attack. The human race was facing extinction.

'How long do we have?" he asked.

"In Metropolis?" Hamilton performed some quick calculations. "A few hours. Maybe a few weeks for the rest of the planet. After that, Earth won't be able to support human life."

A hush fell over the trio, until a nearby analyst waved for Swanwick's attention. The man held a land-line receiver to his ear.

"Sir, I'm with the control tower. Colonel Hardy's on his way in. And he's got Superman in tow."

"Superman?" Swanwick remembered the name from

earlier, back when Lane had coined it in the interrogation room. "You mean the alien?"

"Yes, sir," the analyst said. "That's what they're calling him now. Superman."

Swanwick experienced a moment of *déjà vu* as he, Farris, and Hamilton piled out of the ops center and took a jeep to the airfield. A squadron of Sikorsky Super Stallion choppers came thundering in from west. Flying ahead of the massive aircraft was the caped alien, "Superman."

A heavy-lift skycrane helicopter was with them, towing what appeared to be a tank-sized Kryptonian space capsule. The alien starcraft was suspended in a sling beneath the skycrane.

Unlike last time, Superman's arrival wasn't greeted with an aggressive display of arms. Touching down on the tarmac, he immediately began issuing directions to the crew of the skycrane, as though this was a perfectly natural turn of events. Despite the threat of imminent annihilation, Swanwick was more than a little amused by the speed with which the illegal alien had somehow gone from inhuman threat to commanding ally.

Hardy clambered out of the lead Sikorsky, accompanied by Lois Lane. They hurried over to join the general and his entourage. Swanwick was glad to see that the reporter was both alive and free from her alien captors.

Dr. Hamilton stared with open wonder at the skycrane's extraterrestrial cargo.

"Is that what I think it is?" he said.

Lois nodded.

"It's the ship he arrived in." She shoved past the rapt scientist to address Swanwick. "We have a plan, General. We can stop the Kryptonians, but we need your men to deliver this to Metropolis."

He viewed the capsule skeptically.

"What good will *that* do?"

Superman approached the group.

"My ship is powered by something called a Phantom Drive. It bends space. Zod's ship uses the same technology. If the two drives collide with each other—"

Hamilton caught on at once.

"A singularity will be created."

"Like a black hole," Swanwick said.

"Yes," Superman acknowledged. "Zod's people spent years in the Phantom Zone. They're still tethered to the energies they were exposed to there. If we can open a gateway, they'll be pulled back."

Hamilton peered at the Kryptonian space capsule.

"You want to *bomb* them with this?"

"Sir," Colonel Hardy said. "This craft maxes out at around 17,000 pounds. We can drop it from one of the C-17s." He'd evidently worked out the necessary logistics. "It's a viable plan."

"It's our *only* plan," Superman insisted. "Every second we stand here debating, more people are dying in Metropolis. If I don't shut down that World Engine, those gravity fields will keep expanding."

Swanwick assumed the "World Engine" was the mega-machine currently wreaking havoc in the southern hemisphere. He weighed Superman's words carefully. Pure instinct told him to resist the idea of relying on an untested technology, brought to them by an alien being who had kept his very existence hidden from the world for decades. Yet he didn't see any other option—except for extinction.

Plus, Colonel Hardy seemed to vouch for Superman.

Might as well roll the dice, Swanwick decided. *And take a leap of faith.*

He grudgingly nodded his assent.

Lois Lane looked worried, though, and not just for herself. Swanwick wasn't sure, but he thought he picked up on a definite vibe between Superman and the reporter. Every now and then, they exchanged glances that carried some unknown subtext.

"If this machine is making Earth like Krypton," she asked, "won't you be *weaker* around it?"

"Maybe," he admitted. "But I'm not going to let that stop me from trying. I already lost one world. I won't let Zod take another one from me."

He looked west, to the horizon. He took a deep breath, as though steeling himself for the challenge ahead.

"You might want to back up a little," he advised.

Swanwick and the others gave him some space, not quite sure what the issue was. They stepped back a few yards.

"Maybe a little more," Superman said.

They retreated further, giving him a wide berth on the open tarmac.

He bent his knees, like an athlete preparing for a high jump, and touched his bare hand to the ground, as though drawing strength from the very Earth. The ground rumbled around him. Loose pebbles lifted from the pavement, caught up in some sort of localized gravitational effect.

The rumbling increased in volume as seismic waves radiated from his body.

He cast one last look at Lane…

Then, without a word, he rocketed into the air, punching through clouds until his was only a shrinking blue-and-red blur in the sky. A sonic boom thundered high above the airfield as he disappeared into the heavens. A long white contrail marked his passage.

Down below, Swanwick and others gaped speechlessly.

Godspeed, the general thought.

CHAPTER TWENTY-NINE

Zod watched from the bridge as the expanding gravity field pounded Metropolis. Now nearly two city blocks in the diameter, the sky-high column sheared away the unlucky buildings along its growing perimeter. Crude structures of steel, glass, and concrete lost cohesion and collapsed to the ground, before being ground to powder by the pulsing super-gravity.

Panicked humans evacuated the endangered districts en masse, unaware that there would soon be no safety for them anywhere on the Earth. Their days as the planet's dominant species were rapidly coming to a close. A better, stronger race had laid claim to their domain.

His race.

But there were still a few loose ends to be addressed.

"Faora," he called out. "I'm handing you the command."

"Yes, sir," she acknowledged. "But where are you going?"

He turned away from his birds-eye view of the city's destruction to contemplate a holographic display. A pulsing icon marked a location near the planet's northern pole. He smiled in anticipation.

"To secure the Genesis Chamber," he said, "and pay my respects to an old friend."

Superman raced over the western half of North America, flying faster than he ever had before. Fierce winds and turbulence buffeted him, threatening to throw him off course, but he held to his heading.

He hated leaving Metropolis under assault by the *Black Zero*, but the World Engine was the greater threat. He had to bring down that machine before it rendered the entire planet uninhabitable for anyone except the Kryptonians.

Earth doesn't belong to them, he thought fiercely. *It belongs to humanity. Zod doesn't have the right to steal their future from them.*

Leaving America behind, he streaked above the North Atlantic, passing over the waves like a low-flying jet. Hundred foot-high walls of water, of the sort that would have capsized the *Debbie Sue,* were churned up in his wake. He heard whales crying out in the depths. They seemed to sense what the World Engine was doing to the planet.

The whales were in danger of extinction, too, along with every other Earthly lifeform. He wasn't just fighting for humanity, Superman knew. He was fighting for the Earth.

Along with Lois and the others...

The Boeing C-17 Globemaster was a massive transport plane, nearly 175 feet long. Its generous cargo compartment was big enough to carry tanks, trucks, trailers, and even a secondhand Kryptonian space capsule.

Lois watched as Colonel Hardy oversaw the crew using a K-loader to install the capsule into the aircraft via the aft ramp. She started toward the C-17, not wanting to be left behind.

"Where do you think you're going?" General Swanwick asked.

"You need me on that plane," she insisted.

"Absolutely not," Swanwick said. "This is a military operation."

"And *that's* an alien spaceship." She glanced over at Dr. Hamilton, who was still sticking close to the general. "Do you or Mr. Wizard have any idea how to actually activate the Phantom Drive he was talking about?"

The men exchanged uncertain looks. Hamilton shook his head.

"Well, lucky for you, I do." She held up the Kryptonian command key. "Superman showed me how."

She chose not to mention that Superman's dead father had originally briefed her for this mission. That was probably more weirdness than the military could handle right now.

Better I keep to that to myself, she thought. *Along with Clark's secret identity.*

Swanwick sighed in resignation. He gestured toward Carrie Farris.

"Get her a flight suit, Captain."

"Tower, this is Guardian. Approaching the hold short, ready for takeoff."

Laden with its unearthly cargo, the C-17 taxied down the runway. Hardy manned the cockpit beside the co-pilot, anxiously awaiting clearance.

"Guardian," the tower responded. *"After takeoff, turn right, heading 090 then as filed. You are cleared for takeoff."*

Four powerful turbofan engines lifted the heavy cargo plane off the runway. It took off into the sky, escorted by a flight of four F-35 fighter jets. The fifth-generation fighters were sleeker and more high-tech than the Warthogs the Kryptonians had brought down over Smallville. Capable of breaking the sound barrier, the supersonic Lightnings could fly faster and climb higher than anything Zod's forces had faced before.

Hardy wondered if that would make a difference.

Back in the cargo hold, the Kryptonian starcraft had been jury-rigged onto a railed delivery system built to convey more earthly bundles out of the back of the plane. The C-17's designated loadmaster, a beefy grunt named Gomez, inspected the cargo to make certain it was secure, while Lois mentally took notes for the front-page story she hoped to write someday.

Like Gomez, she wore a helmet and flight suit. A radio headset—built into the helmet—kept her in contact with Hardy and the pilot. A pair of armed soldiers was there to provide security, although Lois wasn't quite sure how they expected to fend off any attacking Kryptonians. The men probably didn't know either, but they checked their weapons regardless.

She was grateful for their courage, at least.

Meanwhile, Dr. Hamilton had set up a makeshift workstation, from which he was busily monitoring the gravitational anomalies in Metropolis and the South Indian Ocean. He adjusted the settings as he established a link with General Swanwick, who had remained back at the command center.

"And we're online," he pronounced. "Are you seeing this, NORTHCOM?"

"*Roger, Hamilton,*" Swanwick replied over the radio. "*We are.*"

"General," the scientist said, "the gravity fields are expanding faster than I anticipated. At this rate, I'd say Metropolis has less than an hour left."

A display at Hamilton's station showed the C-17 inching across the map toward the city, along with its lethal escorts. On the gravity map, the growing circle was consuming a larger and larger swath.

"*Then we're throwing everything we have at them,*" the general replied.

Lois wished she could believe that it would be enough. She anxiously examined the gravity map. As nearly as she could tell, the destructive beam hadn't yet reached the *Daily Planet* building, but it was getting closer by the second.

She couldn't help worrying about Perry and her other friends and colleagues.

Even Lombard.

Confident that Hamilton and the soldiers could babysit the starcraft without her, she made her way up to the cockpit, where she joined Hardy and the co-pilot, Captain Brubaker. She arrived just in time to glimpse a flight of F-35s as they zipped past the cargo plane on their way to engage the *Black Zero*. With any luck, the fighters would distract Zod long enough for her to carry out Jor-El's plan—and send the invaders back to the Phantom Zone.

Faora tracked the approaching aircraft on a holographic display. She presided over the bridge in General Zod's absence, assisted by Jax-Ur and the senior officers. The scientist observed the display with interest.

"It would appear the humans are mounting a final defense," he observed.

Excellent, Faora thought, eager for battle. "Then they will die with honor."

The contours of the ancient scout ship were immediately recognizable, despite the heavy layer of snow that hid it. The ship had anchored itself to an icy mountain peak, much as the Citadel had been rooted to that steep basalt cliff back on Krypton.

It seemed as if the House of El had claimed a new fortress.

Zod brought his own craft down to the Arctic landscape. Exiting the ship, he set foot on the Earth once more. A force-helmet protected him, even as the memory of his debilitating weakness chafed at his pride. His slowness to adapt to Earth's alien environment had left him at Kal-El's mercy.

That could not be allowed to happen again.

He paused upon the wintry slope. Girding himself for the trial ahead, he deactivated the helmet and cast it aside. His senses once more came under assault as a riot of unfiltered sounds and color descended upon him. Prismatic hues, blindingly bright and intrusive, made his eyes blink and water. The wind whipping through the mountains sounded like a hurricane. He saw through rocky ridges and thick sheets of ice.

The world around him dissolved into a kaleidoscopic storm of shapes and colors and vibrations, not unlike the seething chaos at the heart of the Phantom Zone. He was tempted to lunge again for his helmet, to find relief from the disorientating barrage.

No, he resolved. *I must master this. I shall master this.*

He raised a hand before him, seeing past the glove. His skin, his flesh, were transparent to the bones and ligaments beneath. Skeletal fingers tightened in a fist, as he focused upon that hand, inhaling deeply to control his breathing.

The thin Terran air irritated his throat and lungs, but he stoically ignored the discomfort. He would not let this planet's wretched atmosphere defeat him again. If Kal-El, a freakish product of random genetics, could adapt to this world, then so could he. There was nothing a true Kryptonian could not do—if his will was strong enough.

Zod closed his eyes and concentrated.

When he opened them again, his fist was solid once more. He slowly unfolded his fingers, watching with satisfaction as the raucous colors subsided until his gloved hand appeared perfectly normal to his eyes.

The deafening cacophony died down as well, making it easier to hear himself think—and maintain control of his heightened senses.

That's better, he thought.

Leaving his discarded helmet behind in the snow, he confidently approached the fortress. He laid his hand on the ship's outer hull, which responded to his touch. A doorway slid open and he entered the grounded vessel.

He easily navigated the fortress's winding arteries until he reached the platform overlooking the Genesis Chamber. There he took a moment to savor the sight, knowing that he was gazing upon the very future of his race. After so many years of bitter exile, now at last he had the means to restore his people to life, and give birth to a glorious new chapter of Kryptonian history.

And this time, he vowed, *we will not allow our sacred bloodlines to become weak. Only the strongest and purest genotypes will populate our new world, which will not fall victim to the weak-willed decadence and complacency that doomed us before.*

Our new Krypton shall be bold and fearless, run with military discipline and precision.

He plucked a command key from the pocket of his uniform. The head of the key was blank, indicating that it fit all ports. A control cylinder faced the Genesis Chamber. He inserted the key halfway into a waiting port. A lambent radiance lit up the Genesis Chamber as the ancient incubator began to awaken. Budding branches waited to be fertilized with the data hidden in Kal-El's blood. Bubbles oxygenated the swirling amniotic fluid.

Zod started to press the key all the way in, to fully activate the Chamber.

"Stop this, Zod," a familiar voice said. "While there's still time."

He turned to find Jor-El—or, to be more precise, a holographic simulacra of his dead friend—standing behind him. Zod smiled wryly.

"I knew I'd find you here." He circled the hologram, finding the illusion quite convincing. Lieutenant Car-Vex had reported seeing a similar apparition aboard the *Black Zero,* assisting in the human female's escape. "Haven't given up lecturing me, have you? Even in death."

"Listen to me, please," Jor-El said. "What you're contemplating—"

"Is an act of creation. And if Earth has to die for Krypton to live, so be it."

He should have known that Jor-El—or his proxy— would balk at what needed to be done. For all his unquestionable intellect, Jor-El had always been too squeamish when it came to the judicious application of force. That was what had driven them apart so long ago.

As a soldier, Zod knew that mercy was weakness. Jor-El had never accepted that simple fact.

Which is why I'm still alive, Zod thought, *and he is long dead.*

"I won't let you use the Codex like this," the hologram insisted.

"You don't have the power to stop me. The command key I entered is revoking your authority." Zod allowed himself the luxury of gloating. "This ship is now under my control."

Jor-El was beaten—again.

Now all I need is your son's blood.

CHAPTER THIRTY

The F-35s bore down on the *Black Zero*, which hovered above Metropolis atop a pulsating energy beam. Captain Douglas Pavlinko, the pilot of the lead fighter, radioed command. Despite the urgency of the situation, he still required authorization before firing his missiles in a civilian area.

"NORTHCOM, Lightning-1 is tally the target. Requesting permission to unleash the hounds."

"*NORTHCOM, Lightning-1,*" General Swanwick replied. "*You are cleared to engage. Call complete and send battle damage assessment when able.*"

"Lightning-1 copies."

There it was, Pavlinko thought. A city boy who had grown up in the outer boroughs, the pilot was anxious to defend his hometown from the alien invader who was pounding Metropolis into dust. He led the way.

Sidewinder missiles rocketed at the *Black Zero*. Each of the heat-seeking projectiles carried a high-explosive warhead with enough punch to bring down an enemy plane or chopper. Pavlinko hoped they would put a dent in the Kryptonian mothership.

But he never got a chance to find out. As the missiles approached the rings of debris orbiting the *Black Zero*, a gravitational field captured them, dragging them down to the flattened city blocks below. The pilot cursed inwardly as the Sidewinders detonated far beneath their intended target.

Smoking fragments were sucked up into the *Black Zero*'s dusty halo.

A second salvo of missile fire met a similar fate.

"Inertial guidance and ATR on our missiles is going haywire," the pilot reported. "We're losing them! They're dropping like stones!"

Damn it, Perry thought.

Transfixed by the battle unfolding outside of the *Planet*'s windows, he had dared to hope that the F-35s and their missiles would bring the Kryptonian ship down before its destructive beam reached the *Daily Planet* building, but as he watched the Sidewinders going haywire, spinning off in errant trajectories instead of striking their target, he realized that time was running out.

The deflected missiles spent themselves uselessly across the city, adding to the devastation rather than halting it. Fiery explosions blossomed in the streets, outside the perimeter of the alien ship. Perry's heart sank. If the US Armed Forces couldn't stop Zod, who could?

Only a few blocks away, a shimmering curtain of energy—resembling a slow-motion tsunami—was grinding its way outward. Stretching higher than the tallest skyscraper, the wall of destruction chewed up everything in its path. Before his eyes, the Hotel Metropolis was pancaked to its foundations, followed by several other venerable office and apartment buildings. Perry hoped to God that the buildings' residents had escaped the doomed edifices in time.

"We need to get out of here now."

He raised his voice to be heard over the nervous chatter in the bullpen, not to mention the sounds of collapsing buildings and runaway missiles outside.

"Everyone, we need to head for the street! Take the stairs. Don't take the elevators." Hanging back to make sure no one was left behind, he hustled Steve and Jenny and the rest of the staff toward the stairwell. Conspicuously missing was Lois Lane, who had been AWOL since going on the run from the Feds. Perry hadn't heard from her since, but almost hoped that she was securely tucked away in a detention cell somewhere, far away from Metropolis.

She'd be safer there, assuming that anyone on Earth was actually safe at the moment. And that was looking more and more dubious with each passing second.

Maybe he should have run that crazy story of hers, after all.

Dawn was just a glimmer on the horizon as the World Engine hammered the island with its gravity beam. An expanding haze of alien particulates blackened the sky, changing the very composition of the atmosphere at an accelerating rate. Already the air around the island was more Kryptonian than Earthly.

Superman took a deep breath before diving into the toxic cloud.

Another sonic boom heralded his arrival. Hoping to take out the World Engine quickly, before it could irreparably cripple the planet, he streaked down from the sky with his fists out in front of him. He targeted the venting head of the huge machine, aiming to plough right through the Engine, decapitating it once and for all.

Then he could get back to Metropolis and deal with Zod directly.

One solid blow, he thought, *and Earth is safe.*

But the Engine detected the threat before he made impact. Reacting in self defense, it unfurled tendrils of magnetized geological fragments that lashed out at him, entwining themselves around him like the stinging tentacles of a Portuguese man-o'-war.

Superman's face contorted with pain as the molten tendrils squeezed his ribs. They were hundreds of time more powerful than the plasma whips that had attacked him when he first discovered the frozen scout ship.

Too bad he couldn't turn these off with a command key!

The C-17 cargo plane trailed behind the jet fighters. It made a wide loop around the *Black Zero,* with the goal of letting the F-35s soften up the Kryptonians first.

Up in the cockpit, Lois shared a worried look with Colonel Hardy as the diverted missiles dropped onto Metropolis, and not Zod's ship. The sight of the Sidewinders, blowing up her city in advance of the gravity column, made her sick to her stomach. Metropolis was taking a beating, with worse to come.

Giving up on the missiles, the fighters closed in on the *Black Zero* and opened fire with their 25mm GAU rotary cannons. They fought the effects of the gravity vortex every inch of the way. A hail of armor-piercing rounds targeted the Kryptonian ship, only be deflected by the same forces that had sent the Sidewinders astray.

Thousands of rounds of ammo went flying away from

the *Black Zero*, much of it captured by the halo of debris spinning around the vessel. Lois imagined Faora and Car-Vex and the other Kryptonians sneering at the humans' pitiful efforts.

"Lightning-1 is Winchester!" the lead fighter pilot reported. A former army brat, Lois knew that "Winchester" was military slang for out of ammo. *"Our guns are ineffective."*

Worse yet, the F-35s themselves were being caught in the gravity field. Unable to get clear of the *Black Zero*, the fighters began to spiral out of control. An edge of panic rattled the pilot's voice.

"My whole bird's being pulled off course!" His plane plummeted toward the city. *"Mayday! Mayday! Lightning-1 has lost control! Bailing out! Bulls-eye three-six-zero, for twenty!"*

Lois held her breath as the pilot ejected from the fighter only seconds before it crashed into downtown Metropolis. She couldn't see what happened to him, but had a feeling that he, too, had been caught in the inescapable destructive forces. She didn't like to think of what they did to an unprotected human body.

A second jet slammed into the city streets a few blocks away. That pilot didn't even make it out in time.

A fireball mushroomed up from the wreckage.

So much for our escort, Lois thought.

But the C-17 did not turn back. Instead the cargo plane edged closer to the *Black Zero* and the voracious gravity field. The cockpit vibrated violently, as though they were flying into a hurricane. Hardy gripped the controls, fighting to keep the plane on course. Lois held on tightly to the armrests of her jump seat. The plane's entire airframe was shaking.

"Gravity field is pulling down our planes!" Hardy

notified NORTHCOM. "If we don't fall back, we're going to get sucked in with them. Request permission to hold south-east of enemy's position."

"*Roger that, Guardian,*" Swanwick replied. "*Widen your perimeter. Alpha hold-point until further notice!*"

The violent shaking subsided as the plane pulled away from the *Black Zero* and began circling the Kryptonian ship at a safer distance. Lois appreciated not crashing, but wondered how on Earth they were going to complete their mission.

"If Superman doesn't bring down that 'World Engine,'" Hardy said, spelling it out for her, "we'll never get close enough to their ship to deliver the package."

Lois put her faith in Superman.

"If he said he *can* do it," she said, "he'll do it."

"And what happens then?" Hardy asked. "Wasn't he exposed to the same energies as the rest of them on their way to Earth? We open up this Phantom Zone thing... won't he be pulled back with them?"

That ghastly possibility had already crossed her mind.

"I don't know, Colonel. But it wouldn't be the first time he's risked his life for us."

CHAPTER THIRTY-ONE

Empty creches budded as the Genesis Chamber came online. Zod's patriotic heart filled with pride as he envisioned a new generation of Kryptonians spreading forth from this Arctic fortress to claim a virgin world.

"You should thank me, Jor-El," he gloated. "You dreamt of rebuilding Krypton. I'm making that dream a reality."

The hologram disagreed.

"You're perverting the dream," it said. "Our people can coexist with them."

"Why should we?" Zod countered. "So we can suffer through years of pain, trying to adapt like your son has?" He scoffed at so dismal a future. "That's not existing. I want to breathe the air of *Krypton* again. I want to feel the solid weight of *our* world beneath my feet."

Jor-El's hologram reacted with predictable self-righteousness.

"You're talking about genocide!"

"Yes," Zod answered without regret or apology. He started to justify his agenda, but realized how pointless that would be. "And I'm arguing its merits with a ghost."

"We're both ghosts, Zod. Don't you see that? The

Krypton you keep clinging to is gone. It *failed*... just as your desperate actions will."

Despite himself, Zod was shaken by the hologram's dire prophecy. He wanted to concentrate on the future, not dwell on the events of the past. Things *would* be different this time, on this world. No matter what this annoying simulacrum said.

"Ship," he said, raising his voice. "Have you managed to quarantine this invasive intelligence?"

The scout ship's computer, now slaved to his control, responded promptly.

"Yes, sir."

He made a mental note to reprogram the computer to address him by his proper rank of general.

"Prepare to terminate it." He cast a contemptuous look at all that was left of Jor-El. "I'm tired of this debate."

The hologram seemed undaunted by the threat of deletion. He shook his head reproachfully.

"Silencing me won't change anything," it responded. "My son is twice the man you were. And he will finish what we started. I promise you that."

Zod's temper flared. How dare this bodiless apparition compare a true Kryptonian patriot—genetically crafted to defend and preserve their people—to a misbegotten traitor who should have never been conceived?

"Tell me," he said with deliberate malice. "You have Jor-El's memories, his emotions. Can you experience his pain?"

The hologram's silence spoke volumes.

"I will harvest the Codex from your son's corpse," Zod promised, wielding his words as a weapon. He twisted the knife as he had back on Krypton, when he had killed Jor-El the first time. "And I will rebuild Krypton atop his bones."

Then he slammed his command key all the way into the central control port, asserting his authority over the scout ship and its systems. The computer purged the rogue A.I. from its memory banks, causing the image to abruptly dematerialize. Zod savored the sight of "Jor-El" dissolving into random photons before blinking out entirely.

This time around, he experienced no regret at executing his old friend.

Perhaps killing Jor-El gets easier with practice.

Turning away from the Genesis Chamber, he strode onto the bridge. Ice melted away from a frosted viewport, allowing him a clear look at the frigid wastes outside. A pilot's seat descended from the ceiling and he took his place before the navigational controls. He had found what he sought, and exorcised Jor-El's hectoring spirit once and for all, so he saw no further reason to tarry in this desolate wilderness.

Unlike Kal-El, he did not intend to hide from humanity.

He fired up the dormant engines. Thrusters on the underside of the scout ship flared brightly as it tore itself loose from the mountaintop. An avalanche thundered down the rugged slopes as he took to the air.

Zod set a course for Metropolis.

Exerting all his strength, Superman broke free from the World Engine's crushing grip. He zoomed in a corkscrew pattern around the massive machine, taking evasive action to avoid the flailing tentacles. He mentally kicked himself for not anticipating the Engine's attack.

I should have known this thing would put up a fight.

Despite its size, the Engine was faster than it looked. A tendril whipped out, snaring Superman in its punishing coils. Energized matter jolted him as the machine flung him beneath its belly, directly into the gravity column.

The overpowering force slammed him down onto the exposed bedrock of the island, pinning him to the Earth with wave after wave of g-force. The weight and pressure were so intense that he could barely lift his head, let alone fly. Was this what the gravity on Krypton had been like? Small wonder he felt light as air on Earth.

Until now.

The C-17 circled the *Black Zero*, unable to get close enough to deliver its unearthly payload. Indeed, as the energy fluctuations intensified, they were forced to widen their circle, taking them further and further from their objective.

The remaining F-35s stubbornly engaged the levitating spaceship, but to no effect. Their guns and missiles couldn't get past the distortions that were surrounding Zod's ship.

Hardy barked into the radio urgently.

"NORTHCOM, this is Guardian. Any word on that gravity field being taken out?"

"Negative, Guardian," Swanwick reported. "Return to Alpha hold-point. Keep circling."

But for how long? Lois wondered. Buckled into her jump-seat, she toyed anxiously with the Kryptonian command key. The symbol on its head caught her eye and she clung to its true meaning with all her heart.

"Come on, Kal," she whispered. "You said it wasn't an 'S'."

There had to be hope, as long as Superman was still alive.

* * *

Perry was breathing heavily by the time he and the others reached the ground floor of the *Daily Planet* building. He ushered the staff out of the lobby and onto the street, where the shimmering column could be seen advancing like a tidal wave.

Parked vehicles, streetlamps, fire hydrants, and news kiosks were flattened beneath the oncoming wall of gravity. Debris was everywhere. Neighboring buildings and parking garages were leveled. A vacant city bus was compacted to a paper-thin sheet of metal.

"Keep moving!" he shouted. "RUN!"

Up in the sky, a daring jet fighter banked too closely to the alien ship's protective halo. Snared by a pulsing wave of gravity, it spun out of control and crashed into a nearby office building. Shattered masonry and flaming wreckage rained down on the streets and sidewalk, hitting the pavement like missiles.

The impact knocked Perry to the curb, but he scrambled to his feet and sprinted away from the crumbling building. Powdered stone and ash dusted his face and clothing. Lombard pulled out ahead of him as Perry tried to take a quick mental inventory of his people, who were scattering in disarray.

"Everyone okay?"

The widening column was hot on their heels. He heard steel and concrete being crushed to bits behind them. Looming high above their heads, the coruscating wall of gravity was bulldozing its way across Metropolis, razing the entire city to the ground.

Suddenly collapsing buildings and densely packed vehicles hemmed them in, cutting off their retreat. Glancing about desperately for the nearest escape route, Lombard spied a narrow alley that ran between two endangered skyscrapers.

"I see a way out!" he hollered.

Perry stopped to look around. Where was Jenny? In the clamor and confusion, he'd lost track of the young intern. He called out for her.

"Jenny!"

A weak, muffled voice responded.

"...here..."

Her battered hand reached out from beneath a pile of rubble. Part of the building's façade had apparently broken loose and buried the girl. Perry dashed to her side and frantically began clearing away the heavy slabs of masonry. Adrenaline gave him the strength to uncover her face, which was bruised and bleeding. Sheer terror contorted her features. Tears streaked the dust coating her cheeks.

"I'm stuck!" she exclaimed. "I can't get free!"

Perry tried to excavate her, but some of the slabs were too big for just one man to lift. His desperate eyes searched for Lombard, whom he spotted several feet away, seemingly paralyzed with fear. The reporter's petrified gaze darted back and forth between the trapped intern and the towering gravity column advancing implacably toward them.

The crushing beam was less than twenty yards away now, and roaring loudly enough to rattle Perry's teeth. Unless they moved quickly, Jenny would be pulped in a matter of moments. They all would be.

"Lombard!" Perry shouted over the din. "Help me!"

The jock wavered, unable to tear his gaze away from the oncoming column. He looked like he was on the verge of abandoning them.

"LOMBARD! Get your ass over here!"

Perry's sharp tone jolted the man into action. Finding a core of bravery that probably surprised even him, the reporter raced over to assist Perry. Together, they started heaving massive chunks of stonework aside, slowly uncovering her. She struggled weakly to liberate herself.

"Don't leave me," she pleaded. "Please."

But Perry wasn't going anywhere. He glanced briefly over his shoulder, to see the looming column creeping relentlessly toward them. He lifted another heavy slab, but while they were making progress, it wasn't fast enough. There was no way they could dig her out before the gravity column turned them into greasy smears on the pavement.

Lombard knew the score as well. He glanced sheepishly at Perry, clearly wanting to run, but Perry's stoic gaze shamed him into staying. The jock nodded and took hold of Jenny's hand, comforting her in the face of annihilation.

At that moment Perry was proud of the man, who had proved that nobody had braver reporters than the *Daily Planet*.

We're in this together, he thought. *To the last deadline.*

"Oh, God," Jenny murmured, and she seemed to be going into shock. "Oh God..."

"It's okay!" he assured her. "We're going to get you out of here." Reporting the truth was Perry's business, but he figured he could be forgiven one little white lie at the end.

Foot by foot, inch by inch, the gravity column crept toward them. It passed over an abandoned food cart, crushing it like a hydraulic press. Lombard cringed, but stayed by Jenny's side. He closed his eyes, though, probably not wanting to be an eyewitness to his own demise.

Perry kept his eyes wide open.

* * *

The gravity beam pressed Superman to the Earth. Blinding light and a deafening rumble accompanied the extreme pressure weighing him down. Solid bedrock cracked beneath his prone body. Compressed matter swirled around him.

It felt as if a giant was stepping on him, grinding him beneath its heel, even as the World Engine continued to spew its toxic gases into the air. Gravity waves penetrated the Earth, increasing the planet's mass. Soon the entire world would be fit only for people who didn't belong there.

No, Superman thought, *I can't let this machine win.*

He remembered all the people who were depending on him, all the souls he'd touched and been touched by in his travels—his mom, Lois, Pete, Lana, Captain Heraldson and the crew of the *Debbie Sue,* the roughnecks on that oil rig, Chrissy the waitress, Colonel Hardy, Father Leone...

And he remembered those who had sacrificed everything to give him the chance to make a difference: Jor-El, Lara Lor-Van, and Jonathan Kent. He couldn't let them down, not with seven billion human lives depending on him.

Billions of years of terrestrial evolution, millennia of human civilization and progress, generations of men and women fighting to make a better life for themselves and their prosperity, stood to be wiped way unless he came through now—and became the hero his fathers and mothers had dreamed he could be.

"You just have to decide what kind of man you want to grow up to be, Clark. Because whoever that man is... he's going to change the world."

Or save it.

He raised his face from the gravel. Incredibly,

impossibly, he staggered to his feet. The crushing force of the column made just standing upright a Herculean feat, but that wasn't good enough. He lifted off from the flattened island, rising slowly against the pressure, then gaining speed.

The gravity deformed his face, making his skin ripple, as he stared up into the infernal heart of the World Engine. His pupils glowed red.

Crimson energy shot from his eyes, meeting the gravity beam head on. For a moment the two forces appeared evenly matched. Then, screaming from the strain, Superman broke the stalemate and drove himself upward into the belly of the World Engine. Turning his own indestructible body into a weapon, the Man of Steel burst through the crown of machine and shot into the churning alien clouds.

Suddenly brain-dead, the World Engine tottered upon its monstrous legs. Its magnetic tendrils went limp. Flames erupted from its perforated head. Unsteady legs gave out as the entire structure collapsed in on itself, crashing down onto what was left of the volcanic island, which suddenly resembled Krakotoa.

The blast from the Engine's demise knocked Superman from the sky.

CHAPTER THIRTY-TWO

After a few minutes Lombard opened his eyes, and the expression on his face showed that he hadn't expected to be alive.

Perry knew how he felt. Cradling Jenny's head, he watched in surprise as the encroaching column ground to a halt. Gravity waves rebounded back toward the hovering starship. The gigantic column, which was looming like Niagara Falls over their heads, evaporated into the ether. The debris ring orbiting Zod's spaceship fell apart. Perry ducked his head, shielding Jenny with his body, as powdered stone and glass fell like rain.

He shared a baffled look with Lombard. What on earth had just happened?

Not that he was complaining.

Sirens keened aboard the *Black Zero*. Faora stumbled as the bridge shook beneath her feet. Her fierce eyes demanded an explanation from Jax-Ur, who was viewing a holographic display with open alarm.

"The World Engine's stopped transmitting!" he cried out.

Faora knew what that meant. With its link to the Engine broken, the gravity column came apart, creating an energy discharge that rocked the ship. The bridge crew scrambled to stabilize them, even as she tried to make sense of the failure.

"How?" she asked urgently.

Jax-Ur knew better than to keep her waiting.

"It was Kal-El!" he reported. "He's destroyed it!"

The son of Jor-El? she raged. *That womanborn turncoat?*

A murderous fury ignited inside her, hotter than Earth's gaudy yellow sun. The World Engine was essential to their plans to reshape this wretched planet. Kal-El had destroyed more than just a machine—he had murdered the dream of a new world that had sustained Krypton's only true survivors through all their years of bitter exile.

She shook as her fists clenched at her sides.

The Phantom Zone was too good for such a traitor. Kal-El must pay for his perfidy, along with the miserable human beings he chose above his own kind.

"He did it!" Dr. Hamilton shouted via the comms. *"The gravity fields are out!"*

Lois grinned, trading excited looks with Hardy. The view from the cargo plane's windshield confirmed the scientist's pronouncement. The punishing gravity column had been sucked back into the *Black Zero,* while the ship's halo of levitating debris was being dispersed by the wind. At long last, they had a clear shot at their Kryptonian target.

Thank you, Superman, she said silently. *I knew you could do it!*

The C-17 banked around for its final run. Two remaining F-35s provided escort.

"NORTHCOM, this is Guardian," Hardy reported. "We are passing through phase line red. We are good to go."

"Godspeed, Guardian," Swanwick replied. *"You are cleared hot."*

Hardy glanced at Lois.

"We're lining up our final run." he said. "It's up to you and Hamilton now."

Finally, she thought. Unbuckling her seatbelt, she scrambled toward the cockpit stairs, clutching the Kryptonian command key. Hardy barked into his headset as she headed for the cargo hold.

"Loadmaster, power panel switch and open doors!"

The rear cargo ramp was just opening up as Lois rushed into the hold, joining Dr. Hamilton, Gomez, and the two armed guards. Strong winds invaded the hold, blowing against her. The Kryptonian space capsule rested securely on the rails, waiting to be deployed.

A quick glance at Hamilton's gravity map confirmed that the dangerous fields had evaporated entirely.

"Doors are open!" the loadmaster reported.

The World Engine's cataclysmic demise knocked Superman for a loop. Crashing back down onto the island, he landed in the shadow of a rocky spire outside the flattened disaster area. Displaced seawater, which had been caught up in the gravitational vortex of the machine, flowed back into the ocean, leaving behind a series of tide pools. The toxic clouds emitted by the Engine began to disperse, letting the dawn through. The morning sun shone down on the island.

Thank heaven, Superman thought.

He stirred upon the barren shore, barely able to move. His hard-fought battle against the World Engine had left him drained of energy. A shaft of sunlight, slicing toward him, might have restored his strength, but the spire's long shadow cut him off from the tantalizing yellow radiance so that it might as well have been miles away. Straining, he groped for the light, but his desperate fingers fell short by mere inches.

Salvation was just out of reach.

"Please—" he croaked, his voice barely a whisper. *"Please."*

He stretched his arm as far he could.

Hardy's voice rang out over the plane's PA system:

"We are LZ inbound and two minutes out! Lining up the drop!"

Lois joined Dr. Hamilton next to the space capsule. She shouted over the rushing wind.

"Time to activate the drive!"

He nodded enthusiastically, looking as excited as a kid on Christmas morning. Never mind saving humanity from extinction, the scientist clearly saw this as the experiment of a lifetime.

Lois took the command key and tried to insert it into the matching control port, just as Jor-El had instructed. She wished Clark's birth father was around to supervise the procedure, but apparently Boeing hadn't equipped the Globemaster with holographic projectors.

She fitted the key to the port and pushed gently, as she had in that detention cell aboard the *Black Zero.*

But the key refused to go in the whole way.

"Are you kidding me?"

Hamilton observed her difficulty. He tugged on his goatee worriedly, as though recalling that the fate of mankind depended on everything proceeding as advertised.

Frustrated, Lois whacked the key with her fist.

No dice. It still wouldn't budge.

"Let me try," Hamilton volunteered. Squeezing past her, he wrestled with the recalcitrant object, trying to force it into the port, but with an equal lack of success. "The mechanism is jammed! It must have been damaged." Stepping back, he examined the Kryptonian capsule. "Help me check the fittings, the cables… *anything!*"

Lois wondered when the capsule had been damaged. During Zod's attack on the Kent farm, or when the ship had first crashed to Earth, thirty-plus years ago? Or had it been struck by an asteroid or comet during its long voyage from Krypton?

Not that it mattered. Fixing the port took top priority now.

Working together, she and Hamilton pored over the alien capsule, examining every inch of the craft's extraterrestrial carapace and inner cavities. She took off her flight helmet to get a better look, even though she had no idea what she was actually searching for.

What did she know about the workings of a Kryptonian Phantom Drive?

She could barely change the toner in her printer!

In the cockpit, Hardy wondered what the holdup was. He hit the comms.

"This is Guardian," he asked, wanting an update. "What's our load status? Are we ready to jettison?"

"That's a negative, Guardian," the loadmaster replied.

Hardy didn't like the sound of that. Deciding he needed to see just what was going on in the hold, he turned the flight controls over to Brubaker.

"Co-pilot's airplane!"

He unstrapped and hurried for the flight deck stairs.

Faora watched from the bridge as the bulky aircraft approached the *Black Zero,* escorted by two sleek airborne fighters. She gave the human pilots credit for persistence, but was in no mood to tolerate their feeble attacks. She felt like killing something, preferably with her bare hands.

Handing the bridge off to Commander Gor, she raced to the nearest escape pod. She climbed inside the pod and sent it hurling down the launch tube. Unlike the dropships, the unit lacked weaponry and long-range flight capabilities, but that didn't matter to Faora. The enemy was right outside, and she didn't need plasma cannons to destroy them.

Maybe she couldn't bring back the World Engine, but, by Rao, she could make the humans pay.

Hardy dashed down the stairs and into the cargo hold.

"We're inbound for the drop!" he said urgently. "What the hell is going on here?"

Lois and Dr. Hamilton looked up from the balky space capsule.

"We've had a setback!" the scientist reported unhelpfully. With no time to offer a fuller explanation, he dropped to his knees and peered beneath the tethered starcraft. His eyes lit up as he spotted something.

"Ms. Lane!"

Crouching down on the opposite side of the capsule, Lois saw what he was pointing at. Two dangling filaments appeared to have uncoupled on the underbelly of the craft, just out of easy reach. Marginally closer to them, Hamilton tried to squirm beneath the ship. His trembling fingers groped for the strands.

Lois crossed her fingers, wishing him luck, only to be distracted by a sudden explosion outside the plane. Her head pivoted toward the open ramp at the end of the hold. Through the gap, she saw one of their F-35 escorts blown apart by white-hot blasts of plasma.

The crippled fighter came apart before her eyes. A fireball erupted in the sky where the plane had been.

What—?

Her eyes widened in shock and recognition as the Kryptonian scout ship from the Arctic descended from above, its cannons blazing. Another volley of blasts tore apart the last remaining F-35, leaving the C-17 on its own.

Lois gulped as the ancient UFO swept in toward the defenseless cargo plane.

This doesn't make any sense, she thought. *I thought Clark had inherited that ship!* What was it doing here— and why was it attacking them?

CHAPTER THIRTY-THREE

Zod piloted the captured scout ship. Despite its age, the venerable craft handled well, and its weapons proved more than sufficient to dispose of the primitive human aircraft that were harassing the *Black Zero*.

Having eliminated the jet fighters first, he turned his attention to the lumbering aircraft they had been guarding. He eyed the freighter suspiciously, wondering what the human pilots had died to protect. It was hard to imagine that any Terran weapon could pose a significant threat to the *Black Zero*, but it was best not to take chances—especially now that the gravity field had been disabled.

That had to be Kal-El's doing, he thought darkly. *If only he was in my sights instead.*

"Target that aircraft," he ordered the ship.

"Targeting, sir."

A tactical overlay appeared upon the viewport as the weapon systems acquired the plane. Whatever the humans hoped to accomplish, they would soon be reduced to atoms.

Along with their future.

* * *

From the aft of the cargo bay, Lois saw the Kryptonian scout ship coming in for the kill. Having already watched the alien ship wipe out two of the jet fighters, she held little hope for the defenseless cargo plane.

Unless...

Her prayers were answered as an unmistakable blue-and-red figure came streaking down from the sky. Hope restored Lois's spirits.

It's about time, she thought. *This looks like a job for Superman.*

Superman slammed into the scout ship only seconds before it could fire on the C-17. He breached the hull, invading the bridge even as Zod rose from the pilot's seat in surprise.

But he didn't give the genocidal general a moment to recover from the attack. Out for blood, and determined not to let Zod hurt anyone else, he lunged at his father's murderer, driving him back through a bulkhead and onto the floor. His fingers closed around Zod's throat as he pinned him to the tiles. After what he had just seen of the damage inflicted on Metropolis, he figured the kid gloves were off.

"It's over, Zod," he said grimly. "I'm sending you back where you belong!"

Holding onto his enemy with one hand, he began tearing apart the craft's lustrous interior panels and neural networks. Part of him regretted trashing his Kryptonian legacy like this, but he couldn't risk Zod turning the scout ship and its technology against Earth again. Without the Genesis Chamber, Zod couldn't use the missing Codex to spawn hordes of Kryptonian conquerors.

As he understood it, the exiled fanatics would sooner

die off than breed the old-fashioned way.

Caught in Superman's grasp, Zod fought to halt the destruction.

"You fool!" he ranted. "The Codex is *inside* you!"

Superman froze, caught off-guard by the revelation.

Is this some sort of trick? he wondered.

"All you need is the Genesis Chamber!" Zod insisted, half-pleading, half-threatening. He railed at Superman, frantic to get through to him. "If you destroy this ship, *you destroy Krypton*!"

"That's what I'm banking on!" Superman said.

Heat rays shot from his eyes, incinerating a molded control module that was rooted to the ceiling. The bridge pitched beneath them as the ship went into a tailspin.

Zod's face went pale as he felt the ship—and the Genesis Chamber—plummeting toward doom. An agonized cry tore itself from his throat.

"NO!!!"

The scout ship whirled past the C-17, barely missing the plane, before crashing into a skyscraper. Lois watched in horror from the back of the cargo hold as the Kryptonian ship ploughed through the building and kept on going, scraping against nearby high-rises and sending avalanches of glass and steel and stone into the streets below.

Peering out the open loading ramp, she saw that the *Daily Planet* building, with its trademark globe, was still standing, but for how much longer?

She was starting to wonder if there was going to be anything left of Metropolis before Zod and his troops were stopped.

* * *

Down on the street, Perry and his colleagues gaped at the aerial combat being waged overhead. They ducked for cover as a spiraling Kryptonian ship, which looked suspiciously like the one Lois had described in her article, took out two blocks of buildings before slamming into the streets far too close for comfort.

Lombard and Jenny both looked to Perry for leadership, but he figured all they could now was hunker down and hope for a miracle.

A lone C-17 had survived the alien ship's attack. Perry tracked the cargo plane as it angled toward Zod's mothership for reasons unknown. He offered a silent prayer for whatever brave souls were aboard that plane, taking the fight to the enemy.

Give 'em hell, Perry thought.

Explosions ripped through the bridge and Genesis Chamber, throwing Superman and Zod apart. Dormant creches crumbled to ash. Amniotic fluid boiled over, bursting the reservoir. Ripped umbilici bled into the chamber. Gouts of plasma sprayed from severed conduits.

Thunderous impacts battered the hull as the ship crashed to Earth. Flames roared through the Fortress, engulfing the two men in a fiery hell.

The escape pod arced away from the *Black Zero*, on an intercept course with the worrisome human aircraft. Inside the pod, Faora waited until she was within range of the plane, counting down the last few yards impatiently.

Almost… almost…

Now!

She tore open the pod's entry hatch and cast it outside,

then climbed out of the interior cavity, gripping the ragged doorframe. A foul Earthly wind blew past her as she leapt from pod toward the human's aircraft.

Beware, humans, she thought. *Your end is upon you.*

Dr. Hamilton wedged himself beneath the space capsule, still trying to reach the broken coupling. Lois anxiously observed his progress, torn between the technical difficulties in the cargo hold and the apocalyptic battles outside the plane. The scientist muttered as his outstretched fingers brushed against the dangling fibers.

"Almost got it—"

Faora burst through the roof of the hold, tearing a gap in the C-17's fuselage. Lois gasped as she recognized Zod's pitiless lieutenant, whose explosive entrance caused the plane to rock wildly. The flight crew fought to keep them level, but the jolt sent Lois tumbling backward out the aft landing ramp.

Panicked, she snagged the nylon cargo netting and held onto it for dear life, dangling out of the rear of plane, thousands of feet above Metropolis.

She screamed over the roaring wind.

Hamilton moaned beneath the mounted space capsule. A flying metal fragment had sliced into his side, causing him to bleed over the deck. Cold air rushed in through the torn fuselage. Biting down on his lip to keep from crying out, he watched helplessly as the woman surveyed the hold.

Her eyes widened at the sight of the Kryptonian space capsule. She stalked forward to investigate, even as the loadmaster scrambled to keep her from getting her hands on it. He hastily unlocked the cargo rails and elevated the deck beneath the capsule, trying to dump it out the back of the plane.

The starcraft rolled away from Hamilton toward the open ramp, but she caught it with one hand and shoved the nearly eight-ton capsule back up into the hold. It bounced off the rollers, lodging near the front.

Faora nodded, apparently satisfied that the capsule was secure, before spotting Lois hanging out the back of the plane. Her expression darkened, suggesting that there was no love lost between the two women. It seemed as if she still held a grudge over Lois's escape from the *Black Zero*.

But Hardy and his men had their own scores to settle. They opened fire on Faora in a determined effort that was more impressive than effective. The Kryptonian female marched unscathed through the hail of gunfire, batting the soldiers aside without a second glance as she made her way toward the cockpit.

She stalked past Hamilton, dismissing the wounded scientist with a scornful glance. He guessed that she intended to seize control of the plane and hijack Superman's starcraft.

Which meant that he needed to activate the Phantom Drive *now*, before the capsule fell into the hands of Zod.

Despite his injuries, Hamilton dragged himself across the floor of the cargo bay, over to the capsule. In a lucky break, the craft had shifted in position, exposing more of the severed coupling. His torn flesh hurt like blazes, but he ignored the pain and forced himself to concentrate on the vital task at hand.

He stretched his arm out. Trembling fingers reached for the coupling. Grimacing, he reconnected the fibers.

The effect was immediate. With the key in place, the craft's dormant engines began booting up. A prismatic distortion field enveloped the capsule as Hamilton sagged against it. He gasped his relief, clutching his wounded side. Blood seeped through his fingers.

He had done his part. The rest was up to the same Kryptonian technology that Zod had deployed against them.

When in doubt, he thought, *fight fire with fire.*

Even if it means getting burned.

Hardy saw the craft come alive. The fuse had been lit, he realized. Now they just needed to deliver the bomb before Faora destroyed mankind's last hope of stopping Zod. Abandoning the cargo bay, he raced back up the stairs to the cockpit, only a few steps ahead of the unstoppable Kryptonian invader.

He sealed the hatch behind him, but Faora tore through it as though it was made of tissue paper. She knocked Brubaker out of the copilot's seat with a backhanded swipe. He smashed into the wall, then slid unconscious onto the floor. His protective flight helmet cracked.

Hardy realized they only had seconds left. He dived for the controls and forced the crippled plane into a power dive—straight at the *Black Zero*. The ugly Kryptonian prison ship seemed to rush toward the C-17's windshield. Faora shrieked in rage, unable to prevent the inevitable collision.

Hardy shot her a triumphant grin, knowing he wasn't going to survive this crash.

"A good death is its own reward," he said.

The plane's fatal dive was bad news for Lois. She lost her grip on the cargo netting and went tumbling into the air. For the second time in as many days, she found herself falling to her death, even as she saw the C-17 smash into the bulbous mantle of the *Black Zero* with catastrophic force.

Explosions rocked the Kryptonian vessel, blowing open its armored plating. Space-time rippled around the injured ship, bleeding unnatural lights and colors into the dusky sky.

A doorway to the Phantom Zone began to open.

Stress fractures spread throughout the *Black Zero*, beginning at the impact site and branching out from there. Prismatic colors, shining through from the Zone, cast an eldritch glow over the ship's sprawling interior.

Dark, claustrophobic corridors contracted like shrinking veins. Structural ribs cracked and bled. Catwalks tore away from cellblocks. Viewports splintered, venting atmosphere into the void.

Faora, at ground zero, was the first casualty. She stared aghast as her hand dissolved before her eyes, unraveling at the quantum level. A spectral glow emanated from every cell of her body, lighting her up from the inside out. The lifeless bodies of the human soldiers lay crumpled at her feet as they took their vengeance on her from beyond the grave.

No! she thought furiously. *This world was ours!*

In a heartbeat, she vanished from the universe, sucked back into the Zone for an eternity.

The Phantom effect raced through the ship, claiming ever more victims. On the bridge, Jax-Ur, Tor-An, Nam-Ek, and Commander Gor exchanged terrified looks as the Zone began to reclaim them. Only Jax-Ur truly understood what was undoing them.

Of course, he reasoned. *Kal-El's original starcraft. They're using it as a weapon against us.* He smiled thinly. *How ingenious.*

The *Black Zero* had been designed to make the transition to the Zone in one piece, but only under strictly controlled conditions. The ship was meant to pass *through* the Projector, not have a Phantom Drive rip open the continuum right in the middle of the ship. Violent dimensional fluxes were already taking it apart before his fading eyes.

Solid bulkheads and supports sublimed away, causing the ship's myriad chambers and corridors to cave in on themselves. Matter phased into energy, sliding between dimensions. The entire ship was collapsing into a singularity, or so he theorized.

His calculations did not spare him—or any of the others.

CHAPTER THIRTY-FOUR

The *Black Zero* imploded above Metropolis.

Its mantle crumbled, while its hanging tendrils were sucked back into the roiling mass of compacted matter the ship had become. Disturbing colors from an alien spectrum strobed the atmosphere, spilling over to distort reality. Actinic flashes hurt the eyes of anyone who dared to gaze upon the hellish spectacle.

Lois glimpsed the ship's destruction as she plunged through the air, accelerating toward the ravaged cityscape hundreds of feet below. Broken buildings and shattered streets seemed to barrel toward her. Within seconds, she'd just be another piece of wreckage among the many.

But we did it! she thought. *We blew up that damn spaceship!*

Too bad she wouldn't live to write the story.

The wind howled past her face, blowing her hair back. Resigned to her fate, she took comfort in the fact that it hadn't been in vain—and that the end would be quick and painless.

Good-bye, Clark, she thought. *I wish we—*

A blur of blue and red came streaking in from the east, catching her before she hit the ground. She felt a familiar pair of arms wrap around her, holding her close. A bright red cape streamed behind her rescuer.

She clung to him with all her strength, her heart pounding wildly. An overwhelming sense of gratitude washed over her, along with a few other emotions, but Superman's intense expression told her at once that the danger wasn't over.

The singularity was approaching critical mass, pulsating above the city like a voracious black sun. The Kryptonian prison ship had been crushed into subatomic particles, leaving behind a sucking wound in the fabric of reality.

A deafening roar, like an extra-dimensional tornado, bellowed from the depths of the aperture. Blinding flashes of phantasmal light offered glimpses of a weird, purgatorial realm that was never meant to intersect with ordinary space. It made Lois queasy just looking at it.

Superman flew away from the vortex, pulling against the relentless forces that were trying to suck him back into the Phantom Zone with the other Kryptonians. Spectral colors glowed beneath his skin. His face rippled and distorted alarmingly; Lois could tell he was fighting with all his might to get them both clear of the singularity's event horizon, before he was lost forever.

She buried her face against the "S" on his chest, squeezing him tightly.

Don't give up, she urged him silently. *The world needs you.*

He strained against the pull of the black hole, barely making any headway. Lois feared the Zone would never them go, but then, just as she was on the verge of losing hope, the vortex began to collapse in on itself.

The eldritch glare faded, retreating back into the rift, while the thundering clamor quieted.

Superman gasped in relief as the Zone's ravenous pull slackened enough for him to break free at last.

No longer tethered, he coasted to a stop high above the city. He rotated in the air so that he and Lois could watch the singularity's death throes from a position of safety. Cradled in his arms, she watched it diminish to a pinpoint, and then blink out of existence.

Not with a bang, but a whimper, she thought, already composing the story in her head. *Or is that too cliché?*

The wounded sky rushed back to repair itself.

Smoke and flames wafted up from the war-torn city, as the sun sank toward the horizon.

Was it finally over?

Descending to street level, he gently set her down at the center of a battered intersection, strewn with rubble and trashed vehicles. Relatively few casualties littered the pavement, although she shuddered to imagine what the final body count would be once all those demolished buildings were excavated. She thought of Hardy and Dr. Hamilton and all the heroes who had sacrificed themselves to halt the *Black Zero*'s attack on Metropolis.

Their stories would not go untold, not if she had anything to say about it.

"Lois—" Superman said, and his voice was hoarse.

She looked up at him. To her dismay, she saw that his face was still suffused with an unearthly radiance, as though the Zone maintained a hold on him. Spectral colors leaked from his skin, the last lingering vestiges of the exotic energies he been exposed to as a child, during his long journey from Krypton. His alien past bled into the present, threatening the future.

For a moment, she feared that she was going to lose

him to the Zone after all, but he came through for her once again. With a determined expression, he kept himself rooted to the Earth—and reality.

A warm smile promised that he wasn't going anywhere.

They kissed amidst the ruins, seizing the moment after all they had been through together. The phantom glow subsided, and a much more earthly warmth enveloped them. Lois savored the kiss, grateful that they had finally made it this far. Thank God he kept saving her life—she would have hated to have missed it.

The sun was still setting when their lips finally came apart.

"You know," she quipped, "they say it's all downhill after the first kiss."

Superman smiled.

"I'm pretty sure that only counts if you're kissing a human."

Here's hoping, she thought.

Nervous survivors began to creep from the ruins, cautiously checking to see if it was safe. Bedraggled civilians, along with police officers and National Guardsmen, eyed the couple curiously. Superman's colorful attire attracted plenty of attention. One soldier's eyes bulged.

"Whoa," he whispered. "It's Superman."

Searching the growing crowd for familiar faces, Lois was relieved to spot Perry, Steve, Jenny, and a few other scattered *Planet* staffers among the survivors. Perry and Lombard helped Jenny clamber over a heap of rubble. The plucky intern was limping, but managed to make her way toward Lois and Superman. She glanced up at the twilight sky, where the *Black Zero* no longer hung above the city.

"Are they gone?" she asked.

Perry peered at the empty sky, as well.

"I think so," he said.

Jenny turned her gaze toward Superman and Lois. Blushing slightly, Lois wondered if Perry and the others had seen the kiss, and whether she could keep that part out of the papers.

"He saved us," Jenny said.

Superman heard what the girl said. He smiled at her, pleased to get such a warm reception. He scanned her discreetly, making certain that her injuries didn't require immediate attention. To his relief, she appeared to have come through the attack with only a few minor sprains and abrasions.

More survivors emerged from hiding. They milled about, gazing in amazement at the colorful hero and taking pictures with their cell phones. After keeping a low profile for his entire life, his first instinct was to flee all the attention, but instead he lingered among the people like a man with nothing to hide anymore.

He smiled warmly at the bystanders, seeking to put them at ease. It felt odd, but great, as well. Maybe he didn't have to lurk in the shadows from now on.

Maybe the world was finally ready for Superman.

A tremendous boom wiped the smile from his face and threw the crowd into a panic. The noise came from the demolished building where the Kryptonian scout had crashed.

An armored figure burst from the wreckage.

Zod!

Apparently Zod had been too far away from the *Black Zero* to be captured by the Phantom Drive, which meant that the war was far from over.

"Everyone get back!" Superman shouted. He spotted injured people in danger of being trampled by the frightened crowd. "Move the others to safety!"

His urgent instructions had the desired effect. Courageous soldiers and civilians scrambled to assist the wounded as the crowd fled in terror. Lois tried to linger, but was dragged away by her friends.

Confident that no one would be left behind, Superman launched himself into the air.

It seemed that he and Zod still had business to settle.

CHAPTER THIRTY-FIVE

Zod landed in an empty wasteland that had been flattened by the gravity beam. A circle of desolation surrounded him, bordered by the standing ruins of buildings partially sheared away by the column. The carved-up skyscrapers formed a sort of bowl around a blasted region several blocks across. Compressed matter, ground to a fine powder, blew across what had once been a thriving business district.

Superman could only imagine how many lives had been lost while he had been fighting the World Engine on the other side of the world.

Now it was Zod's turn to be stopped.

The exiled Kryptonian looked up as Superman approached. Wet eyes betrayed his sorrow. He knelt and picked up a handful of dust. He let the gritty powder run through his fingers.

"Look at this," he said. "We could have built a new Krypton in this squalor." He flicked the last of the dust from his fingers. "But you chose the humans over us."

Any doubts Superman might have had concerning that decision were dispelled by the widespread death and devastation that surrounded them. Zod and his people had brought nothing but pain and fear to the planet.

"Krypton had its chance," Superman replied, and he gestured toward the humans. "This is their world. And we have no right to take it from them."

Zod shook his head ruefully.

"On Krypton, I committed unspeakable acts of violence," he said. "I waged war. I tortured people. I performed countless executions. But there was never any malice behind my actions," he insisted. "I did them because my people asked me to. But now I have no people. And for the first time in my life, I find myself contemplating violence simply because I *want* to."

He rose to his feet and leveled his gaze at Superman.

"I'm going to make them suffer, Kal. These humans you've adopted. I'm going to take every one of them away from you. One by one."

This was no idle threat, Superman knew. Zod was serious.

But so was he.

"I'll stop you," he promised.

"HOW?" Zod bellowed. He lunged at Superman, sending him flying backward across the dusty wastes. He marched toward his enemy, continuing a blood feud that stretched across light-years of space. "Your father couldn't imprison me. You think *you* can? There's not a cell on this planet that can hold me."

One blow wasn't enough to knock the fight out of Superman. Spurred by the memory of his martyred birth father, he shot up from the ground like a torpedo, slamming into Zod and carrying them both into one of the looming ruins. The butchered edifice collapsed around them in an avalanche of sundered steel girders, rebar, drywall, stair rails, elevators, cables, furniture, pipes, and plumbing fixtures, all of which continued to crash down upon their heads and shoulders.

Tons of debris bounced off their invulnerable frames.

Zod snatched hefty chunks of concrete from the rubble and flung them at Superman, who batted them away with his arms and fists. But the barrage was just a diversionary tactic, distracting him long enough for Zod to deliver a flying kick that sent Superman hurling back out into the open, where he needed only a split-second to recover.

He shook his head to clear it.

You're going to have to do better than that, Zod.

He launched himself again, hitting his target like a battering ram. Zod smashed into a thick support column that broke apart to expose more rebar. He rebounded from the column and whipped Superman's cape over his head. Momentarily tangled in it, the Man of Steel was unable to stop his opponent from tossing him all the way into a neighboring building.

His indestructible body smashed through layers of brick and mortar before sliding to a stop in the lobby of a ruined office building. A security desk sat empty, wisely abandoned by whomever had once guarded the entrance. Plate glass windows had been blown out onto the sidewalk. A bank of elevators was blocked by fallen rubble. Superman wondered if the building's occupants had been wise enough to take the stairs.

Too many innocent people had died.

Before he could catch his breath, dozens of broken lengths of rebar flew at him like javelins, hurled at lightning speed. The improvised spears failed to penetrate Superman's suit or skin, but hurt like blazes as they jabbed him again and again. Zod's arms turned into a blur of motion even as a berserker rage caused his eyes to ignite like twin supernovae.

Crimson beams leaked from his eyes indiscriminately, setting on fire everything around them. Within seconds, a raging blaze rushed through the crumbling structures. Twenty stories of burning floors and ceilings threatened to bury them.

Zod leapt instinctively from the inferno, seeking the open air. Wincing in pain, Superman attempted to follow his lead by taking to the sky, but he wasn't quite fast enough. A toppling skyscraper clipped him on its way down, swatting him to Earth. He crashed into a deserted street a few blocks beyond the circle of destruction.

This can't go on, he thought. *The whole city is coming down on top of us.*

He staggered to his feet, reeling. He had been going nonstop for hours now, first against the World Machine, then the singularity, and now Zod. He needed a moment to recharge.

But Zod gave him no respite. He hoisted a stretch limousine above his head and heaved it at Superman, who dodged the car with only nanoseconds to spare. It smashed into the foundations of a looming multi-level carport, and exploded on impact.

A forty-ton propane truck was Zod's next weapon of choice. He hurled the truck at Superman, but hit the carport instead. The fiery explosion undermined the parking garage, causing it to collapse, level by level. Dislodged vehicles tumbled from the crumbling decks like an automotive landslide. A falling SUV struck Superman in the back, jolting him face-forward onto the pavement.

Zod rushed forward to kick his foe while he was down, but the crazed general came too close to the disintegrating parking garage. The entire structure slid down on top of him, burying him beneath a mountain of concrete and crushed metal. A seismic rumble drowned out his cries.

A billowing cloud of dust obscured the entire scene.

Rising to his feet, Superman cautiously approached the hill-sized heap of rubble, wondering if the avalanche of steel and concrete had been enough to put Zod down for the count.

Not likely, he thought.

Sure enough, Zod burst from the rubble, delivering an ultra-powerful uppercut that sent Superman somersaulting into the sky, far out of reach. Rising higher, Superman took advantage of his ability to defy gravity by hovering in the air. He soaked in what strength he could from the setting sun, hoping that would be enough.

The golden rays fed him their energy, as they had back on the island.

"There's only one way this ends, Kal!" his enemy shouted from the ground. "You die—or I do. And you don't have the will to make that happen."

Zod sprang to the side of a nearby skyscraper. Digging his fingers into the building's stone cladding, he scaled the façade at super-speed and flung himself outward. They collided in mid-air and fell to Earth together, crashing down onto a construction site.

A partially built skyscraper, its gigantic steel skeleton exposed, shuddered as the dueling supermen cratered the site. Zod seized a heavy steel I-beam from a stack of construction materials and swung it like a club. Heat-vision shot from Superman's eyes, melting the beam to slag in mid-swing. Molten steel sprayed across the site as the weapon dissolved in Zod's grip.

Furious, he flung the dripping red object away, and advanced on Superman with murder in his eyes. His face was flushed with anger.

"I was *bred* to be a warrior, Kal," he said. "Trained

since the moment of my birth, to master my senses." He sneered at his opponent, contempt dripping from his voice. "Where did you train, Kal? On a farm?"

He dropped into crouch, placing his hand against the ground, much as Superman had done back at the NORTHCOM airfield. Veins bulged on his neck and brow as he fought to bend Earth's gravity to his will. His armored body trembled with exertion.

Gravity waves distorted the air around him. Concentrating intensely, he absorbed and shaped the waves through sheer force of will.

"Whatever advantage you gained by growing up on this world—"

The ground rumbled beneath him. Dirt and rock and pools of cooling slag lifted off from the Earth, floating around him. His voice rose to a crescendo of hate.

"—it can't compare to my experience!"

A concussive burst of energy blew his Kryptonian battle armor away from him, leaving him clad only in a matte-black skinsuit. Screaming in fury, his face a mask of vengeance, he took flight for the first time.

This isn't good, Superman realized. *Zod just leveled the playing field.*

Mocking Earth's meager gravity, Zod soared above Metropolis. His flight wasn't as smooth as Superman's, but what it lacked in grace and finesse it made up for in speed and power. He looped around in a wide circle, heedless of any obstacles in his path. He smashed headfirst through the upper stories of several unlucky skyscrapers, raining steel and glass onto the streets below, where terrified men and women again ran for cover.

Penthouse apartments and sky-level restaurants were

razed by the his aerial rampage. Roofs were torn from buildings. Water towers toppled from their elevated perches. Neon signs exploded in showers of sparks. Billboards plunged like guillotine blades.

Superman launched himself, knowing fully that he had just lost his greatest advantage. The sky now belonged to Zod, as well.

Then it's time to take it away from him, Superman thought.

If I can.

They met head on—like opposing storms—in the dusky sky above Metropolis. The resulting thunderclap could be heard all the way across the city. The superhuman fracas literally rose to new heights as they traded blows in the heavens before tumbling to Earth like fallen angels.

Downtown streets cracked and cratered beneath the impact. Deserted cars and buses bounced into the air. A two-hundred-foot tall construction crane was uprooted by the tremors. Tons of metal groaned as the crane crashed down around them. A swinging boom came loose, smashing into the side of a luxury high-rise, before impaling a bus stop below. A wrecking ball bowled through the entrance of a popular nightclub.

Caught up in their never-ending battle, the combatants barely noticed.

Zod grabbed Superman's cape and swung him around, flinging him into the air as though throwing a hammer. The Man of Steel barreled through the base of a landmark office building, bringing the entire structure down. The wanton destruction tore at his soul. At this rate, it would be a miracle if Metropolis had any skyline left when the fighting was over, one way or another.

This city doesn't deserve this, he though angrily. *Earth doesn't deserve this.*

Shaking off the blow, he zoomed back to the battle, determined to get them away from the city, if possible. A powerhouse punch sent Zod tumbling out over the river, where the Weisinger Bridge connected Metropolis to the mainland. He crashed beneath it, splashing into the river. Superman flew out over the bridge and scanned the turbulent water, peering beneath the surface.

He knew better than to think Zod might have drowned.

As if in response to his thoughts, Zod blasted up through the bridge's multilane span and past its granite towers and steel suspension cables to ram his fists into Superman's chest. They shot upward through the atmosphere into space, where they were both unaffected by the freezing vacuum. A communications satellite in a low Earth orbit came into view, and Superman flung Zod into the object, which didn't survive the encounter.

Snarling, Zod hurled the sparking remains back at Superman, before flinging himself forward and dragging them both back down toward Earth.

A fiery glow enveloped both men as they reentered the atmosphere like falling stars.

CHAPTER THIRTY-SIX

Lois craned her neck back, searching the sky. Along with Perry and the others, she gazed upward in fear and awe as Superman and Zod waged war among the clouds.

Most of the city's denizens had taken shelter in basements, bunkers, and subway tunnels, but Lois had never been one to run away from danger. If the final battle for humanity's future was being fought, she damn well intended to provide an eyewitness report. And, to be honest, she was worried about Superman, too. She *had* to know what was happening to him, even if it meant putting herself at risk.

You can beat him, Clark. I know you can.

For a few moments, she lost track of the airborne titans, but then she spotted two fiery forms plummeting back toward the ground. Tracing their trajectory with her eyes, she judged that they were heading straight for the Metropolis Central Station at 45th and Swan. The station was the hub of the city's transportation system, serving tens of thousands of commuters a day. She guessed that it was packed with evacuees trying to flee the city.

Could Superman protect them all? And in the process, could he save himself from Zod?

Lois wasn't going to stand around and wait for the evening news.

Breaking into a run, she sprinted for the train station.

Superman crashed through the roof of the station and onto the grand stairway that led to the main concourse. He rolled down and into a cavernous space roomy enough to accommodate all the commuters and tourists who passed through the station daily.

Even now, with Metropolis under siege, frightened bystanders had taken shelter in the station. Startled by his tumultuous arrival in their midst, they ran madly for the cover. Dozens of feet raced toward the exits. Other evacuees fled through arched gateways and onto the railway tracks and platforms. Transit workers abandoned their posts.

Damn, Superman thought. He could hardly imagine a worse place to face off against Zod. The station was filled with defenseless innocents who stood a good chance of becoming collateral damage. How was he going to protect them and stop Zod, too?

The vengeful Kryptonian war criminal didn't give Superman time to figure out a solution. He dived through the ragged gap in the ceiling, landing on the concourse floor across from his foe. They circled each other warily, even as Superman prayed that Zod wouldn't take notice of the many innocent men, women, and children he was placing at risk.

He hadn't forgotten Zod's vow to exterminate humanity, one by one.

For now, however, Zod seemed more intent on taking

direct revenge. He charged at the Man of Steel, driving them back through the station's load-bearing walls. As a result, the upper concourses caved in, blocking the exits and trapping the scared people inside.

Transit workers, baggage handlers, police officers, and store clerks all mixed with stranded travellers, united in their common peril. Hysterical screams caught Zod's attention. A cruel smile lifted his lips as he contemplated the vulnerable humans.

"You love these people so much?" he said bitterly. "You can *mourn* for them."

A chill ran down Superman's spine. He tried to reason with Zod, reach the valiant soldier Jor-El had once called friend.

"Don't do this—"

But Zod wasn't even listening—he cared nothing for humanity, only the world he had lost. Consumed with hate, he threw himself at Superman, who welcomed the attack if it meant keeping him away from the trapped bystanders.

They fought savagely, hand-to-hand, upon the floor of the station. Their superhuman blows inflicted damage no human weapon could match. Indestructible Kryptonian fabric ripped in the struggle. Vicious kicks and jabs, delivered with Herculean force, left their faces bruised and bloodied. A fist of steel split Zod's lip, and he retaliated by driving his knee up into Superman's chin. The blow, which would have sent a cast-iron safe into orbit, loosened Superman's teeth.

He tasted blood.

But Zod's unreasoning rage made him sloppy. He charged like an animal, lowering his guard long enough for the Man of Steel to deliver an old-fashioned haymaker that sent him flying backward across the terminal. Zod hit the floor hard, only to discover that Superman had already shot across at super-speed to be there waiting for him.

Staying on the offensive, Superman got his arms around Zod's head, pinning him in a chin-lock. Zod thrashed furiously, straining to break free, but was unable to escape the grip. Pressing his advantage, Superman leveraged his knee into Zod's back. The crazed Kryptonian grunted in pain, but showed no sign of surrendering.

What would it take to stop him?

Pinning Zod's body wasn't enough, not while his eyes burned red as a distant sun. His volcanic gaze unleashed crimson rays of destruction that converged on a classical stone façade that stood across from him. Polished marble was vaporized by the beams, leaving a blackened scar across the wall.

Nearby bystanders, unable to flee, shrieked at the sight.

No! Superman thought desperately.

Straining massively, Zod slowly turned his head. The deadly beams swept their way across the terminal toward a cluster of men, women, and children trapped beneath a fallen archway. Trembling families huddled together, holding crying toddlers. Grown men and women were crying, too, or praying for mercy as Zod's heat-vision inched toward them, incinerating everything in its path.

Superman tightened his grip on Zod's head, trying desperately to hold it still, or to avert it from the endangered bystanders. But still Zod managed to push against his grip, turning his infernal gaze slowly, inexorably toward the trapped people.

"Stop!" Superman demanded. The position they were in wouldn't allow him the leverage he needed to fly—to carry them away from here. It was all he could do to restrain his opponent.

Grunting with effort, Zod twisted his head toward his intended victims. A hellish rage blazed from his eyes, seeking to avenge his vanished dream of a new homeworld. He was going to kill those people if it was the last thing he did.

"STOP!"

Spittle sprayed from Zod's lips.

"NEVER!"

Superman watched with growing horror as the crimson rays continued along their deadly path. The beams were only a few yards away from the people now. Then two. Then one.

No! Superman thought. *Don't make me do this!*

A little girl sobbed as the beam came closer, now only moments away. Superman cried out in anguish, knowing he had no other choice. It was Zod's life—or the lives of innocents. He marshaled every ounce of strength that remained within him. And then...

He snapped Zod's neck.

His form went limp, his fiery gaze extinguished instantly. Superman released the body and let it slump to the floor. Gazing down at the dead Kryptonian, he was surprised by the peaceful expression on his face.

Was this what Zod truly wanted? Superman wondered. *A glorious death in combat?*

His foe had gone the way of Krypton, but Superman wasn't sure he would ever forgive the Zod for making the hero the instrument of his death. Anguish tore at Superman's heart; he had always sought to save lives, not take them. Killing Zod took a terrible toll on him. His shoulders slumped as he stood above the body, feeling both emotionally and physically drained.

He really was the Last Son of Krypton now, he realized. Apart and alone.

* * *

Lois appeared atop the stairway, having somehow made her way through the wreckage. She stared down at him, taking in the grisly scene and reading the torment on his face. Looking up, he could tell that she understood what this bitter victory had cost him. Compassionate green eyes met his.

She raced down the steps to embrace him. Hugging her tightly, in the center of the ravaged terminal, he realized that he had been wrong.

He wasn't alone at all.

CHAPTER THIRTY-SEVEN

An array of king-sized satellite dishes searched the sky, eavesdropping on the cosmos. General Swanwick surveyed the array as Captain Farris drove their jeep past the secure NORTHCOM installation. It was an impressive setup, to be sure, but was it enough?

Now that the crisis was over, he was of a mind to beef up NORTHCOM's deep space surveillance operations. Zod and his fellow Kryptonians may have been defeated, but who knew what other threats were hiding out among the stars? The universe was a smaller and much scarier place these days.

Hell, he knew of at least one rogue alien who was still at large.

A flaming wad of crumpled metal suddenly dropped out of the sky, directly in their path. Farris swerved to avoid it, braking hard. Swanwick scrambled out of the jeep to get a closer look at the object. A few thousand pounds of mangled metal and circuitry sparked and sputtered in the middle of the road. A US flag insignia could be glimpsed on a broken wing.

"What the hell—?"

"It's one of your surveillance drones," a familiar voice stated.

The startled officers spun around to find Superman hovering in the air behind them. Swanwick's temper flared.

"That's a twelve million dollar piece of hardware!"

"*Was*," Superman corrected him, before adopting a more serious tone. "Stop harassing me, General. I know you're trying to figure out where I hang my cape. You won't."

Swanwick didn't deny the accusation. He wasn't ashamed of doing his job.

"Then I'll ask you the obvious question," he countered. "How do we know you won't one day act against America's interests?"

"I grew up in Kansas, General. For an alien, I'm about as American as you can get. But Superman has to be *more* than that. Do you understand?"

Swanwick listened, but didn't commit himself. Right now he was more interested in hearing what Superman had to say.

"I'm here to help," the Man of Steel continued. "It just has to be on my terms. You need to convince Washington of that."

Swanwick wanted to believe him. Lord knows the man had saved the entire human race from extinction, which ought to entitle him to the benefit of the doubt. But he had also shown the entire world just how unbelievably powerful he was, which was bound to make people nervous.

"Even if I was willing to try, what makes you think they'd listen?"

"I don't know, General. I guess I'll just have to trust you."

With that Superman lifted off into the sky, not like a

rocket, but leisurely and at his own pace. Swanwick tilted his head back to watch him ascend, as amazed now as he had been the first time he had seen the alien floating above the gate at NORTHCOM Command. He glanced at Farris, and was surprised to see a huge grin across the young woman's face. He scowled for form's sake.

"What are you smiling about, Captain?"

"Nothing, sir," she said with a shrug, visibly struggling to keep a straight face. "I just think he's kinda hot."

You're probably not the only one, he thought.

"He always believed you were meant for greater things," Martha said. "That when the day came, your shoulders would be able to bear the weight."

She and Clark stood before Jonathan Kent's grave. It was a clear, sunny day, free of the smoke that had blackened the sky during Zod's attack. A copy of the *Daily Planet* was folded beneath her arm. No surprise, the epic conflict in Metropolis had pushed the earlier skirmish in Smallville off the front page, which was probably just as well, Martha mused. His roots didn't need that kind of attention.

A poignant memory came back to her, of watching Jonathan watch Clark as their young son played in the grass with his dog. A red sheet, borrowed from the laundry drying on a nearby clothesline, billowed from Clark's small shoulders like a cape. Observing Jonathan's pensive expression as he contemplated the boy, she knew that—like her—he had to be thinking of the long journey ahead for their son, of the perils he would surely face, and the hope he might bring to the world...

* * *

"I just wish he could've been here to see it finally happen," Clark said.

"You weren't ready before now," she told him. "The *world* wasn't. But he had faith you'd know when it was."

He nodded, remembering the grateful people who had accepted him in Metropolis, right before his final battle with Zod, as well as the trust he had received from Lois and Colonel Hardy, and many others.

Even the talk-show hosts were no longer calling for him to reveal his true identity. Well, not most of them.

"I'm sorry you had to make a choice like that, between us and your own people." She squeezed his hand. "It must have been hard."

"I don't remember that other world," he assured her. "It's just as alien to me as it would be to you."

He lifted his eyes and gazed out over the town and farmlands below. Smallville had already started rebuilding. There was a lot of work of work to do, and fresh crops to be planted in the spring, but he had faith in the town and its people. Pete Ross and the others weren't going to let a little thing like an alien invasion keep them down for long. Smallville was stronger than that.

And so was Clark.

"Growing up here, with you and dad, that's *home*. Not Krypton." He looked up at the sky he had fallen from so long ago, and wondered if somewhere, countless light-years away, a swollen red sun still burned. "Jor-El died so I'd have a choice. But Dad taught me how to actually *make* one."

His mom unfolded her newspaper, revealing a front-page photo of a caped hero with a bright red "S" on his chest. A headline boldly christened Metropolis's mysterious savior.

"'Superman,'" Martha read aloud, bemused. "Well, I

guess the cat's out of the bag now, isn't it?"

Clark nodded, but he had no regrets.

"For as long as I can remember, I've had to hide what I can do. Now I don't have to."

It was a good feeling.

"Well, you can't be Superman all the time," his mom pointed out. "What are you going to do when you're *not* saving the world? Have you given any thought to that?"

"Actually, I have," he admitted. "I need a job where I can keep my ear to the ground. Where people won't look twice if I want to head somewhere dangerous and start asking questions."

His mom raised a quizzical eyebrow.

Lois pounded away at her keyboard, rushing to file a story. In the wake of Zod's aborted invasion, there seemed to be about a million follow-up stories that needed telling. Right now she was struggling to figure out a way to explain the Phantom Zone in layman's terms, which was no easy task, especially since she barely understood the freaky alien science herself.

"C'mon, Lois." Lombard interrupted her. He perched on the corner of her desk, nursing a cup of coffee. "When are you going to throw me a bone? I've got courtside seats to the Jacks tonight. What do you say?"

She kept on typing, not even bothering to look up.

"I say you should go back to trolling the intern pool, Lombard," she said. "You'll probably have better luck."

Out of the corner of her eye, she saw him give Jenny a speculative look. The pretty intern rolled her eyes and made a hasty escape.

Lois chuckled.

To be fair, she'd heard that Lombard had actually

conducted himself fairly well while Metropolis was under attack, but that didn't mean she had any interest in dating him. She could do better.

A lot better.

"Lane, Lombard," Perry called out. Lois noted absently that he had somebody with him. Focused on her story, she vaguely registered the presence of a tall, dark-haired guy wheeling a bike into the office. "I want to introduce you to our new stringer. I was hoping you could show him the ropes."

Lois sighed. *Like I don't have enough on my plate right now.*

Still, just to be polite, she looked up at the newcomer.

Her eyes bulged. It was all she could to keep her jaw from hitting the floor.

Clark stood before her, wearing a sports jacket, jeans, and glasses. He leaned his bike awkwardly against a cubicle, as though he wasn't quite sure where to park it. Slouching to de-emphasize his impressive height and build, he didn't look much like the hunky baggage handler she had first met up north—or the Man of Steel.

"This is Clark Kent," Perry said.

Slightly flustered, Lois did her best to act as though they had never met before. She rose awkwardly from her seat and offered her hand.

"I'm Lois," she said. "Welcome to the *Planet*."

He smiled back, sharing a private joke between them. He took her hand.

"Glad to be here, Lois."

ABOUT THE AUTHOR

Greg Cox is the *New York Times* bestselling author of numerous novels and short stories. He has written the official novelizations of such films as *The Dark Knight Rises, Daredevil, Ghost Rider*, and the first three *Underworld* movies, as well as novelizations of four popular DC Comics miniseries: *Infinite Crisis, 52, Countdown*, and *Final Crisis*.

In addition, he has written books and stories based on such popular series as *Alias, Buffy the Vampire Slayer, CSI: Crime Scene Investigation, Farscape, The 4400, The Green Hornet, Leverage, Riese: Kingdom Falling, Roswell, Star Trek, Terminator, Warehouse 13, Xena: Warrior Princess*, and *Zorro*. He has received two Scribe Awards from the International Association of Media Tie-In Writers. He lives in Oxford, Pennsylvania.

His official website is: www.gregcox-author.com.

ACKNOWLEDGMENTS

I honestly can't remember a time when I wasn't a Superman fan. I grew up on the comic books, as well as the earlier movies, TV shows, and cartoons, so it was a thrill to be able to adapt his latest big-screen adventure.

I want to thank my editor, Steve Saffel, for giving me this opportunity, and my agent, Russ Galen, for helping to make this possible. I also want to thank Nick Landau, Vivian Cheung, Cath Trechman, Natalie Laverick, Katy Wild, and the rest of the good folks at Titan Books for their valiant efforts behind the scenes.

Thanks to Josh Anderson, Wes Coller, Adam Forman, Shane Thompson, Melissa Jolley, and all the other helpful folks at Warner Bros. for allowing me access to the script and artwork and for graciously hosting me during my visit to the Warner lot and offices. Their hospitality was greatly appreciated.

In addition, I have to thank Zack Snyder, Christopher Nolan, and David S. Goyer for giving me such fantastic stuff to work with. I can't wait to see the finished movie!

Thanks also to Deborah Snyder, Charles Roven, and Emma Thomas.

Finally, and as always, I could not have written this book without the support of my girlfriend, Karen Palinko, and our various four-legged assistants: Henry, Sophie, and Lyla.